BAKING BAD

A BEAUFORT SCALES MYSTERY, BOOK 1

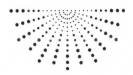

KIM M. WATT

For further information contact: www.kmwatt.com

Cover design: Monika McFarland, www.ampersandbookcovers.com

Editor: Lynda Dietz, www.easyreaderediting.com

Logo design by www.imaginarybeast.com

ISBN: 978-1-9993037-3-0

First Edition: October 2018

10 9 8 7 6 5 4 3 2 1

CONTENTS

For Dad,
who gave Beaufort not
only his name, but his predilection
for condensed milk sandwiches.

1

MIRIAM

Miriam couldn't help feeling a little sorry for the vicar. He was wedged between Alice and Gert, picking at a piece of Victoria sponge cake and nodding with the regularity and anxiety of one of those dogs you see on car dashboards. Priya kept topping his tea up every time she went past, and from the way he was shifting in his seat, Miriam thought he was probably quite desperate for a break in the conversation. Well, lecture.

"I believe we should raise the price of the stalls for this year's fete," Alice said, cutting a shortbread biscuit into precise quarters. "Don't you think so, Vicar?"

"Ah, well, now—"

"Even with the volunteers, the clean-up becomes quite costly. And it is a *very* popular fete."

"Well—"

"While we're on the fete," Gert said, placing one large hand on the vicar's shoulder and making him jump, "my nephew Pete just bought this bouncy castle gig. It'd be good to put some business his way, don't you think?"

"Well, we usually—"

"That's nepotism, Gert." Alice brushed crumbs off her fingertips with a paper napkin, her voice mild.

"It's sound business, is all. Using who you know."

"And do they have references?"

"He's my *nephew*."

The vicar took the chance to take another mouthful of cake while the two women disagreed around him, and Miriam leaned across the table with a plate of sunny yellow lemon tarts. "Gluten-free," she told him encouragingly.

"Oh, I—" He looked down at his plate, which the Victoria sponge cake was sharing with a poppyseed biscuit, half a scone, and a small, disconcertingly purple object the shape and texture of a hockey puck that Miriam thought might be Jasmine's latest attempt at a macaron.

"Never mind. I'll put some aside so you can take it home later."

"Thanks," he said, sounding less enthusiastic than one might have thought at the prospect of homemade, gluten-free lemon tart, although that might have been because Gert and Alice were turning their attention back to him.

"Now, we still have a few stalls available," Alice said. "Have you had any enquiries come through to you directly?"

The vicar swallowed a mouthful of scone hastily. "As it happens, I have," he said. "There's a gentleman from a local restaurant who wants to do some tasting plates."

"Who?" Gert demanded. "Everyone in Toot Hansell who wants to has already booked."

"He's ... he's not from *this* village," the vicar said. "He is local, though."

Alice frowned. "Not that terrible man from the gastropub, is it? The vote not to allow him back was unanimous."

The vicar picked up his poppyseed biscuit and examined it. "Everyone deserves a second chance."

Gert pointed at a plate which, unlike the others crowding the table, was still full. Small pale tarts with an unpleasant grey-green tinge were stacked in it. "He sent us caviar-custard tarts. If that's a peace offering it's a very unpalatable one, and that sort of food just doesn't deserve a platform."

"Quite," Alice said, in a tone that said the discussion was closed. "Now, Vicar, have you made a decision on the live music situation? Because we do have to get the permit application in rather soon if we want to have that option."

"Our Sue – that's my sister-in-law's niece's sister-in-law – is in the council. I can get it rushed," Gert said.

"Gert, there is a correct way to do things."

"Yes, and there's also the smart way."

"One can't just demand favours—"

The vicar sighed, and leaned over the table to take a lemon tart from Miriam, the pastry crumbling under his fingers. "It looks lovely," he told her. "Much nicer than caviar-custard."

"I should hope so," she said.

Miriam was in the village hall's slightly shabby kitchen, rinsing cups in the sink and gazing out the window into the bee-crowded flowerbeds, thinking that the day seemed a little dark. Not cloudy, or late. Just *dark*, the way some days were when they had a sad edge or a bad taste to them. She hoped it didn't mean anything unpleasant was going to happen.

Someone padded in from the hall behind her, and she turned to see the vicar come in carrying his plate and mug, his nose pink and crumbs on his front.

"Pass them here," she said, when he tried to jam the crockery into the dishwasher rack at any old angle. "That machine needs careful stacking."

"Yes. Of course. Sorry." He handed the plate and mug over and stood there in the middle of the floor, tapping his fingers on his thighs.

"Are you alright, Vicar?"

"Yes. No." He shook his head. "I thought I might be able to get Harold a stall, you know. But no one listens."

Miriam nodded. "Once the W.I. make our minds up, we do tend to stick to it."

"Which is all well and good, but he didn't *mean* to hit Teresa. He was trying to demonstrate proper pizza-making technique, and Carlotta put him off."

Miriam snorted. "I think we might have forgiven him that if he hadn't then shouted at Carlotta so much that Rosemary had to throw the ice bucket at him."

"She didn't *have* to."

Miriam smiled and went back to rinsing cups. "I rather think she did."

"One should look for the best in people."

"He never even apologised."

The vicar sighed. "You are right, of course." He looked at the hall, and rubbed his hands together. "I suppose I should go back in. Very intense, these meetings."

"This is your second summer fete, not to mention the winter ones. You should expect it by now."

"I thought maybe the first year was a test of sorts."

"Oh, no. They were easing you in gently."

The vicar looked heavenward and mumbled some small prayer under his breath, then looked back at Miriam in her voluminous pink skirt and tie-dyed blouse. "No offence."

Miriam, who liked the vicar but had no special fondness for the church, wasn't sure if he meant the prayer or the slight to the ladies of the Women's Institute, but she just shrugged and said, "None taken. Would you like me to drop some herbal tea around this afternoon? I have a homemade blend that's very good for stress."

The vicar, a small, softening man with drifting hair and old tattoos just visible under the cuffs of his shirt, scratched his head and said, "Why not? Better than taking to drink, right?"

Miriam, who had taken to drink on the odd occasion herself after a particularly intense meeting of the Toot Hansell Women's Institute, smiled and went back to the dishes.

THE W.I. MEETING wound down as they often did, slowly and with little ceremony. The debris of plates and cake crumbs was cleared away, and Tupperware containers appeared as the leftovers were shared out, complimented, and packed up. Gert produced a bottle of elderflower cordial from her cavernous knitting bag and passed it down the line of pushed-together folding tables in the hall. Miriam diluted hers generously. She didn't know how the older woman managed to ferment it, but she was fairly sure that the alcohol content in one glass was over and above the weekly allowance for any sensible person.

"Is Beaufort not coming?" Jasmine asked, leaning over to Miriam and keeping her voice low. Although how anyone could overhear, Miriam didn't know. With formalities over and the cordial flowing, the noise level was considerable.

"Not with the vicar here," she said. "No telling how he'd react."

"Oh, of course. It just seems like ages since we saw him. Is he okay?"

"He's more than okay. He's Beaufort." Which encompassed everything there was to say about the High Lord of the Cloverly dragons, well-known to the ladies of the Toot Hansell Women's Institute, if to no one else. Only a couple of years previously, Miriam had been as confident as anyone that there were no dragons left in the world, and although she usually left milk out for pixies and made kitchen witches for luck, it was more because she felt it befitted her status as the village psychic than for any real belief. But that had been before the day she had walked into her garden to find a creature that, while no larger than Pearl's Labrador, was scaled and winged and very definitely dragon-ish.

He had her barbecue gas bottle tucked under one foreleg and one of the scones that she'd left out to cool halfway to his very toothy mouth, and they'd stared at each other in mutual astonishment (as well as some embarrassment on the part of the dragon, who she later found out was called Mortimer). Then she'd said, very cautiously, "Would you like cream with that?" Which was how she had come to be the first human in a very long time indeed to have a dragon over for tea, and how the W.I. had come to embrace non-human members.

"Well, say hi from me," Jasmine said, and offered Miriam a pretty floral-patterned plate, still laden with the purple hockey pucks. "Would you like one? I know the colour's a bit iffy, but it's just because I spilt the food dye."

Miriam stared at the luminous and utterly unappetising disks. She was fairly sure macarons were meant to have a little height, and a soft dome, and definitely shouldn't smell faintly of cat food. "No thanks, love. Food dyes really play havoc with my allergies."

"Oh." Jasmine looked so crestfallen that Miriam felt bad for lying.

"Tell you what, let me have a few and I'll give them to Beaufort next time I see him. I know he loves your cooking." Which just went to show what a millennium or so of fire-breathing could do to your taste buds.

"Would you? Oh, that'd be lovely!" Jasmine jumped up to find a spare Tupperware to put the biscuits in, and Miriam decided not to tell her that she had purple food dye on her neck. It'd come off eventually, anyway.

🦢

THE CHURCH, with its small and graceful spire, heavy trees, and attendant graveyard and vicarage, nestled just across a little dead-end road from the village hall. A footpath ran behind both the church and the hall, skirting the edge of the stream that made up the village's natural boundary, gardens running up to it on one side, and trees and shrubs and farmland stretching out toward the high fells on the other. The village was entirely circled and segmented by streams and becks, but no one ever seemed to be able to agree if they were all part of the same waterway, or even what any of them should be called. Springs and wells peppered the common land, and there was a duckpond on the village green across from the hall that no one paddled in, partly because it was rumoured to be bottomless, but mostly because it was home to two permanently enraged geese. Miriam's house was on the edge of the village, with the stream running just past her back gate, and she was halfway home on the worn dirt path when she realised she'd left her cardigan at the hall.

She sighed, lifting her face to the spring sunshine filtering through the trees, and decided she may as well go back. She was still full of cake and a little wobbly from Gert's cordial, so the extra walk would do her good. She turned around, her old boots squidging in the mud left over from the last rain, and padded back up the path, humming a Stevie Nicks song to herself. It was a good day to be out. And she had a feeling that the cordial might well send her to sleep on the sofa if she got home too soon.

It didn't take her long to make her way to the hall, and she let herself in the little gate at the back of its big plot, breathing the scent of new-cut grass and admiring the flowerbeds that Teresa had rebuilt after Mortimer and his friend Amelia had done some dragonish eavesdropping in them last summer. The pansies really had recovered admirably. The hall would probably be empty by now, everyone having dispersed to sleep off the afternoon's cake, but the key would be under the usual rock in the flowerbed to the left of the back door. She was reaching for it when she realised she could hear raised voices. Well, one, anyway.

"But why won't you at least *try?*" It was a woman's voice, sharp and loud. Someone answered, too low for Miriam to make out what they were saying, and she hesitated by the door, wondering whether to knock, or wait, or just go home.

"It's not like I'm asking for much! You can manage *at least* this!"

Miriam was almost certain she didn't know the owner of the shouting voice. It was hard to tell, distorted with emotion as it was, but it didn't *sound* like anyone she knew. She left the key where it was, hesitating on the back step. It felt horribly intrusive, this, but it *was* her favourite cardie. She didn't want to risk it ending up in the charity bin – or the costume department, as her jacket had last year. She still hadn't been able to get all the glitter off it. And maybe the arguers could do with an interruption.

"No! *No!* Don't you walk away from me!"

Too late, Miriam realised the voice was coming closer. She took a step back, wondering if she could take cover behind the lavender, then the door was pulled open and the vicar hurried out so quickly that he almost collided with her.

"Oh! Miriam. Hello." His face was pale, but a flush was rising on his neck.

"Who are you – oh." Over the vicar's shoulder, Miriam saw a woman stop in the doorway that led from the kitchen to the hall. She certainly wasn't familiar, and she wore the sort of heeled boots and impractical jacket that suggested she came from Away.

"Hello," Miriam said, feeling her own cheeks pinken, as if she'd interrupted something terribly private. "I left my cardigan behind."

"That's fine, that's fine." The vicar couldn't seem to make eye contact with her. "You'll lock up when you're done, yes?"

"Yes, of course."

"Norman," the woman hissed, and Miriam was momentarily confused as to who she was talking to. The vicar hunched his shoulders and hurried around the hall, heading for the vicarage. The woman pushed past Miriam in a cloud of expensive scent, the skinny heels of her boots stabbing into the lawn and making her stagger, slowing her pursuit. The vicar threw an alarmed look over his shoulder and broke into a jog. The woman began to sprint on her tiptoes, waving her arms wildly to keep her balance. The vicar vanished around the side of the hall, picking up speed, and the woman shouted, "Dammit, Norman!" as she went over on one ankle. She recovered admirably and raced around the corner after the vicar, and a moment later Miriam heard the clatter of panicked heels on pavement and figured they'd both made it onto the road.

She shook her head, then went slowly into the hall. Each to their own. Whatever the vicar got up to with rich women from out of town was none of her business. She just needed her cardie.

SHE ALMOST DECIDED NOT to take the herbal tea to the vicar that evening. He'd been terribly embarrassed, poor man, and the last thing she wanted was him trying to explain or making excuses. She really didn't mind what he did. But he'd also be even more stressed after all that carry-on, and probably worried that she'd tell the rest of the W.I. what she'd seen. Not that she thought many of them would be bothered by it, but men could be so touchy. And more stress really did look like the last thing the vicar needed. So she decided that she'd go after all, but if he started talking about whoever the woman was, she'd have to make her excuses and leave. Or just run for it. She had plenty of experience offering support and guidance to friends, and to the people she told fortunes for, but a romantically entangled vicar wasn't something she felt particularly well equipped to handle.

Decision made, she ventured outside armed with secateurs. She was proud of her large, overgrown garden, full of pretty weeds and useful flowers, the grass long enough to brush her ankles as she walked barefoot from one plant to another. She collected a snip of vervain here, a sprig of lavender there, and some chamomile along the way, avoiding the bees and listening to the squabbling of the birds. Normally she loved being out here, in a wilderness of plants, but the day felt unsettled, and she thought it must have been the argument she'd inadvertently interrupted.

She wasn't *exactly* psychic, but she was Sensitive, as evidenced by the fact that she saw dragons very easily, even before she'd known to expect them. Her palm-reading and tarot card sessions were based more on observation and psychology, true, and she normally found what needed to be said to put people at ease more by empathy than any special powers, but she did *feel* things sometimes. Some days, like today, seemed cloudy even when the sun was out, and some nights had such bright edges that she couldn't sleep, and had to sit in the garden instead and wonder at the beauty of it. Not that she told anyone about such things. She was one cat allergy away from being the village's designated eccentric as it was.

Inside, she washed the herbs, popped them in a muslin bag, then wrote a label with instructions to steep in hot (not boiling) water for five minutes before drinking. It might not solve the vicar's woman troubles, or even do much for W.I.-induced stress, but it'd smell nice at least, and there was a lot to be said for that.

For the third time that day she set off along the stream, this time in the rapidly deepening twilight of a very nice spring evening. She had a torch with her for the way home, but for now there was enough light to see the rocky little path, and the lights that were on in the houses on the other side of the stream looked homey and inviting. She smiled to herself as she walked – who would have thought that the vicar had such secrets? Or that he was called *Norman*. She'd never actually thought about him being called anything other than the vicar, and she couldn't remember if he'd been introduced as anything other than the *new* vicar when he arrived to replace his predecessor. The previous vicar had been a nice man, too, but Miriam had a sneaking suspicion that the Women's Institute meetings had proved to be too much for him. Either that, or, as it had been around the time that Jasmine had arrived, he'd been worried that the standards of cake were going to degenerate too much.

She was still musing on what old vicars did, exactly, in their retirement, when she climbed the stile that led over the wall of the churchyard. The evening light was gentle on the old gravestones, lending them soft edges, and the trees kept heavy green watch over everything. The musty scent of stillness and silence followed her past the church to the vicarage, where she rapped on the door politely. There was a light on in the kitchen, and another in the living room, but no one answered.

She knocked again. "Vicar? It's Miriam. I brought you that tea, if you still want it?"

Still no answer. Maybe he couldn't hear her properly and thought she was the shouting woman, still chasing him down. She peered in the kitchen window to the side of the door, but it was empty, just a container of leftover cake sitting in the middle of the table. She knocked again, more loudly, then picked her way through the garden to the living room windows. She'd just see if he was inside, then she could leave the tea on the door handle if necessary. For one moment she wondered if she was better off not looking, in case she caught him with the expensive-smelling woman, but he hadn't looked like he had any intention of being caught *by* the expensive-smelling woman, let alone *with* her. So she'd just check that he was okay.

Through the open curtains of the small living room windows she could see that the TV was on, and the vicar's legs were stretched out from a chair that had its back mostly to her. She leaned over the scraggly bushes in the garden (it needed weeding) and tapped smartly on the window. The vicar didn't move. Maybe he was asleep? It wasn't even eight o'clock, though. There was a worm of unease twisting in her belly, and she was aware again of the darkness of what should have been a lovely late spring day. She extricated herself from the garden, mumbling under her breath as a particularly aggressive rose bush plucked at her skirt, and padded along the wall, to where she had a better view of the vicar.

He was sprawled in a stiff, high-backed chair that looked at least a little more comfortable than the lumpy sofa, and for one moment Miriam was sure he was asleep after all, that Gert's cordial and the excitement of the afternoon had worn him out entirely. Then she saw the mug on its side by the chair, a darker tea stain spreading across the old green carpet and the plate fallen next to it. There was a cupcake wrapper with a morsel of cake left in it sitting sadly on top of a hardcover book that had fallen to the floor with its pages all fanned out, and still Miriam tried to convince herself that he was just deeply asleep. The poor man had had a very exciting day.

But his eyes were open, and he was staring blankly at the ceiling, and try as she might, she couldn't explain that.

"Oh dear," she said softly, pressing a hand to her heart as her vision swam with unexpected tears. "Oh, you poor, poor man."

2

DI ADAMS

Detective Inspector Adams (whose mother called her Jeanette, although very few other people did) was not happy. There were several reasons for her not being happy, including but not limited to the fact that although she'd moved to Leeds from London, her mother was still trying to set her up with a nice young(ish) man who lived just down the street from her childhood home; and the fact that it was uncomfortably hot in the kitchen of the village hall but she was still wearing a suit jacket that she didn't want to take off, because that seemed terribly casual. And this particular crime scene was already far too casual, which was the main reason she was not happy at this very moment.

"James," she said sharply to the tall detective constable who had driven up from Leeds with her, "who are all these people? Why do they keep coming in?"

He shrugged, shuffling his feet without looking at her. He'd taken his jacket off and looked considerably cooler than she felt. "I'm not sure. They seem to be local."

"It's a *crime scene.*"

"Well, not technically. I mean, the actual crime scene is at the vicarage ..." He trailed off as she glared at him, palming a thin sheen of sweat off her forehead.

"Why is there *food?*"

"It's traditional," a new voice said, and DI Adams turned to find herself face to face with a slim older woman bearing a large plate of mini quiches, garnished with cherry tomatoes and sprigs of thyme. "I guess it's really to feed the family in their time of grief, but in this case, well. It's just what we do."

"And it's quite lovely of you," the dean said, accepting the quiches eagerly. As the person responsible for overseeing the various parishes in the rural deanery, he'd arrived not long after the detective inspector, and other than making tea for everyone he'd done nothing but get in the way, as far as she was concerned. The local police must have called him at the same time they'd asked Leeds for reinforcements, which had been mid-morning of the day *after* the murder, so God alone knew what evidence had gone missing already. The Skipton lead DI was on holiday in Cyprus, which apparently meant that there was no one in the area who had the experience to carry out a murder investigation. "Spring's a quiet time up here," the local sergeant had told DI Adams when she arrived. "Too much work for most folks to do for much murder or the like."

DI Adams had volunteered immediately when the detective chief inspector in Leeds had announced the case, eager to get to grips with her first murder as lead investigator. Technically she wasn't in charge, of course, not in a murder case, but the DCI had made it clear that he expected it'd be some sort of misadventure rather than homicide, and as she was a big shot cop from down south he was certain she could handle it. She'd managed not to put a fake Cockney accent on and say "awright, guv" or something equally in keeping, and had instead grimaced, nodded, and said that she was sure she'd have it tied up in no time.

She'd been here half an hour and was already wondering if she might have made a bit of a miscalculation. As well as the steady stream of women bearing baking trays and cake tins and Tupperware containers in and out of the hall kitchen, there were three dogs barrelling around the hall itself, a cat had just come in the kitchen window and stolen a piece of fish pie, setting both the dogs *and* a couple of women shouting, and the woman who'd discovered the body was being plied for details by more civilians than officers, who were mostly standing around drinking tea and eating biscuits.

"Isn't it lovely of the ladies?" the dean asked, and DI Adams dragged her attention back to him. He looked like he had enjoyed quite a lot of lovely dishes over the years.

"I'm quite sure it is, sir, but there really are far too many people in and out of here. We already know that the victim spent his last morning here, and it really shouldn't have been turned into a bloody cafe like this. Sorry," she added, not quite sure if "bloody" was the sort of thing a dean of the church might take offence to.

"*Victim*," someone said, and burst into tears.

"Oh, Jasmine," the mini-quiche lady said, relieving the crying woman of a Pyrex dish of – something. DI Adams wasn't at all sure what it was, only that it was blackened on top and appeared to be bleeding underneath. The mini-quiche lady handed the dish to the DI, whispered, "Throw that one out. She's a lovely girl, but it's not worth getting salmonella over," and led the still-sobbing Jasmine into the hall.

DI Adams stared at the plate in horror, then shoved it at one of the local constables. "Get rid of that, would you?"

He looked offended. "That's my wife's, that is."

"*Jesus Chr*— sorry, Dean. Look, just put the damn – sorry – put the bloody dish in the fridge or something out of the way, and clear this room, would you? I want everyone out of here. Now!"

❧

DI ADAMS REMEMBERED that her mother used to say that trying to get her and her two brothers organised was like herding cats. In her mind, it was a silly expression, but she was starting to see the meaning of it. For every two women who were ushered out of the kitchen, another two or three popped in, all brightly inquisitive between the condolences they offered the dean. There were an awful lot of pearls and cardigans going on, and respectable floral skirts with sensible shoes, and the mean age of the Women's Institute seemed to be well north of fifty. Which you would think would suggest reasonable behaviour, but instead seemed to make them even less manageable.

The local uniformed officers, two constables and the sergeant who'd offered the snippet of wisdom regarding murder in the spring, were milling around a little helplessly, saying things like, "That's a wonderful-looking shepherd's pie, Miss Robinson, but would you mind just waiting in the main hall? Oh, yes, of course, pop it in the fridge first if you want," and "Oh, Mrs Hart! Is that your famous spiked bread and butter pudding? Wait, let me get you a cuppa." Her DC, James, was trying to be a little more forceful, but the women kept patting his arm (and in one case his bottom) and walking right past him, and he was starting to look slightly panicked. Meanwhile, the dean was floating about, graciously accepting all these offerings of food like some hostess at a Tupperware party. The DI took a deep breath and massaged her temples with one hand. She wasn't going to start shouting. She was the DI in charge, the lead investigator, a woman who commanded respect. She did not shout. Her mum shouted. She was not her mother.

Ten minutes later she was thinking that she was just going to have to abandon her principles and start shouting anyway. The steady tide of people in and out of the kitchen had barely reduced at all, and somehow the local officers had been roped into making tea and stacking plates and organising the fridge. Then mini-quiche lady walked in, silencing James with a glare that made DI Adams straighten up quickly enough to set off a twinge in her back.

"Detective Inspector?" the woman said, and extended a slim hand, devoid of rings or decoration. "Alice Martin. Chair of the local Women's Institute."

"DI Adams," she said, trying to match the older woman's perfect posture, and feeling suddenly dishevelled in her too-hot jacket. Alice's grip was firm and calloused.

"What do you need?" Alice asked.

"I'm sorry?"

The chair of the W.I. made an impatient gesture. "Everyone out? Everyone in the hall? This softly-softly approach you have your men using will have absolutely no effect, you know."

The DI felt her cheeks heat up. It was like being addressed by her grandmother, if her grandmother had been small and white and about twenty years younger. "I can see that."

"So, tell me what you need. Always use local influence, Detective Inspector. It gets you a lot further."

DI Adams frowned. "These officers *are* local."

Alice made a sound that would have been a snort, if someone quite so elegantly turned out would do such a thing. "They're young men, all of them. What do you think they can do with women who remind them of their mothers? Or are their mothers, in some cases," she added, nodding at a woman with startling red-dyed hair, who was straightening the collar of one of the uniformed officers. He'd gone very pink.

"Well, what do *you* suggest, then?" DI Adams asked, more sharply than she'd intended. This was all she needed, some busy-body trying to tell her how to do her job. And *young men?* The local sergeant looked at least ten years older than she was.

"May I?" Alice asked, and the detective inspector sighed, then waved her on. Why not. It certainly couldn't make things worse. "Thank you." Alice clapped her hands together three times, a hard, brisk sound that cut above the babble in the kitchen, and all eyes turned to the trim woman in her teal green cardigan. "Everyone out of the kitchen," Alice said, her voice calm, and DI Adams had to stop herself following the women who had been milling around the counters as they exchanged glances then wandered out.

"Not you," the inspector called, not bothering to hide the exasperation in her voice as the two constables made to leave as well. They stopped, looking embarrassed, but she ignored them and turned to Alice instead. "Can you get them all to quiet down in there?"

"Of course," Alice said, and smiled.

DI Adams watched her go through the door to the hall, and a moment later the excited babble that had been roaring around the big room dropped to a murmur, then a hush.

"We're ready for you, Detective Inspector," Alice called, and the DI looked at the local officers and the dean, lined up against the counter as if waiting for inspection, all looking slightly nervous.

"Right," she said. "Local influence." Then she straightened her jacket and went into the hall.

TEN PAIRS of eyes followed her as she walked to stand in front of the little stage. It was at the same end of the hall as the kitchen, and there was a door marked "backstage" to one side of it, and one marked "toilets" to the other. The DI was faintly surprised to find that there weren't more people sat in the folding chairs, most of them still gripping cups of tea and all looking distinctly worried. It had sounded like a lot more.

"Is this everyone?" she asked Alice.

"Yes. Everyone who was at the meeting with the vicar yesterday, too, if that helps."

It did, actually, but that was none of Alice's business, so DI Adams just nodded and glanced at the dean, hovering nervously in the doorway to the kitchen. He had his jacket off and chocolate icing on his shirt. James stood just inside the main door, arms folded, trying to look authoritative. The local officers, huddled together behind the two neat rows of chairs, weren't even trying.

"Ladies and – ladies," the DI said, noting a distinct dearth of testosterone in the civilian audience. "Thank you for your very generous donations to the, ah, dean. I'm sure he appreciates you coming here to pay your respects. And since you are here, I'd like to impose on your time a little more. It would be very helpful to me, even if you have spoken to the officers earlier, if you would permit me to ask you a few questions and get some details from each of you before you go."

An uneasy shiver went through the room, a few whispered remarks, then it was silent again, except for a small fluffy dog whining on the lap of the bleeding lasagne woman. Jasmine, Alice had called her. The DI thought the dog might be a Pomeranian. One of those things that yap a lot and tend to get festooned with bows, anyway.

"Please let me make two things clear," she continued. "No one is under suspicion here. However, this *is* an active investigation. The cause of death is yet to be determined, but at this point we are treating it as suspicious."

Jasmine started to cry, and the dog wriggled and whined in her lap, trying to lick her face. The witness, Miriam Ellis, was sat next to her, and tried to put an arm around the younger woman. The dog snapped at her, making her jerk backward. Jasmine cried harder, squeezing the dog until it yelped. DI Adams cleared her throat, aware of Alice watching her impassively and suddenly feeling like she was in an exam room at school again.

"Ah, yes. I – I can see that this is terribly upsetting, of course, and I don't mean to make it difficult for anyone, but, ah—" Between the dog and the crying, the detective inspector was having to raise her voice, and was coming far too close to shouting for her comfort. She gave the dean a pleading look, thinking that this must fall under pastoral care, but he retreated into the kitchen. Crying was apparently not his thing. Not that it was DI Adams' thing, either. She rubbed her eyes. She seemed to be having some trouble focusing, particularly on the second row of chairs.

"Right, so I do need to talk to you all individually, if not now, then later. Let me stress again that no one is being accused of anything—"

Jasmine broke into a wail of horror, and the dog started barking hysterically. Miriam tried to intervene again, but the dog snapped at her so wildly that she jumped back, sending her chair pitching over backward. She sprawled to the floor with a yelp of alarm and a swirl of glittery, pale green skirts, catching her neighbour's arm. Her neighbour, a slight woman with long dark hair, flailed for a moment then went down as well, and the dog tore free of Jasmine and leapt on top of them as teacups and plates and fragments of cake spun across the floor. The other two dogs in the hall burst into a chorus of sympathetic barking, and a babble of cries broke out, varying from "shut up, you lot!" to "oh, the poor vicar!" One of the dogs was a Great Dane, and it dragged its alarmingly small owner down the aisle as she bellowed at it to sit, the pair of them sending empty chairs spinning to the floor in their wake. A large woman with a fading tattoo of a mermaid on one arm jumped up and scooped Jasmine's dog into her arms before dropping it again with a howl of outrage.

"It *bit* me! Little mutt—"

"*Primrose!*" Jasmine wailed, and her husband started forward from his post then stopped, looking anxiously at the DI.

"It's something that starts with P, alright," Miriam said, sitting up. "You alright, Gert?"

The tattooed woman waved a bleeding finger. "It *bit* me!"

DI Adams pinched the bridge of her nose and pointed at the PC who'd called himself Jasmine's husband, still hovering at the back of the hall as if afraid to come any closer. She didn't blame him. "Get the damn dog, would you? And someone get a first aid kit."

"May I suggest more tea?" Alice said, appearing next to DI Adams and making her jump. "You can get your men to stand by, make sure no one leaves without giving you their details. Although I can also supply addresses and phone numbers, if it comes to that."

"Tea?" the DI said. She was starting to feel like she'd stepped into some alternate universe. This should have been easy. Interview a few ladies of a certain age, collect some details, back to Leeds to follow up. Not this. Whatever *this* was. She allowed herself a moment to wonder if the DCI had known.

"Tea," Alice agreed. "It gives everyone something to do, and I find people are much less panicky with a nice cup of tea on hand."

DI Adams stared at the older woman for a moment, mystified, then nodded. The chair of the W.I. seemed to have a knack for these things, so she'd just go with it. "Dean," she called, and he peeked cautiously around the kitchen door. "Get some tea on, please. And James?" He was examining Gert's injured hand while one of the local officers pulled on the gloves from the first aid kit. Jasmine's husband had chased the dog into a corner and was brandishing a leash at it. It was growling.

"Detective Inspector?" the detective constable said, straightening up.

"Make sure you get everyone's details before they leave. I'd rather no one left before I talk to them, but let's not be too harsh about it. Everyone's a bit upset." Including her. Well, upset wasn't the right word. *Discombobulated.* That was the one. She was *discombobulated.*

"Got it." James went back to the main door, looking relieved to get away from the blood.

"God *damn* it, Primrose!" Jasmine's husband bellowed, and went sprinting out the door after the dog, waving the leash like a lasso as James jumped out of the way. The Great Dane gave an enormous woof of delight and lunged after the Pomeranian, sending his mistress to the floor and dragging her halfway across the hall before she let go. The other dog, a Labrador, ignored them entirely. It was using the distraction to hoover up the contents of any abandoned plates.

DI Adams took a deep breath, and wished she had time to count to ten. Even five. "You," she said to the officer with the first aid kit. "Leave that. And you, Sergeant. Catch those bloody dogs!"

They left the hall at a jog, and she looked at Alice again. "Is it always like this?"

"Sometimes it's worse," Alice said.

"Jesus Christ."

"Oh, I'm not sure even He can sort this lot out," Alice replied, and picked up the abandoned first aid kit. "Come here, Gert. Let's get this done properly."

The DI sat on the edge of the stage and rubbed her eyes again. They seemed to be okay now, which was good. She'd been worried she was getting a migraine. She looked at the women, all talking to each other and gesticulating rather excitedly, and wondered if transferring up here from London was going to be quite the low-stress choice she had imagined.

3
MORTIMER

M ortimer, hunkered down behind the second row of chairs with his wings folded down tightly, hissed to Beaufort, "What do we *do?*"

"It'll be fine," Beaufort whispered back. "We just have to wait for the right moment."

Which was all very well, but the right moment didn't seem to be coming. They should have left earlier, but it had seemed risky, what with the police coming in and out. So they'd waited, and now there was a rather tall police officer guarding the front door, and the detective inspector with the suit jacket and severe hair was standing at the front of the hall watching everyone, and they were stuck hiding as well as they could behind the second row of chairs. Mortimer had tried to squeeze under one, and had knocked it over instead, making Teresa jump up and fuss, pretending it had been her. Now she glared at them and put a warning finger to her lips.

Mortimer sighed. Dragons aren't invisible exactly, although they are *faint.* Some people can't see them at all, can't even hear them, while to more receptive individuals they may be a shimmer in the corner of the eye, seen and not. But they are certainly hard for anyone to spot if they aren't expecting dragons – and very few people do expect dragons, sadly. Which is helpful when trying to go unseen, but still not foolproof. All they needed was for one of the police to be sensitive enough to see them, and it'd all go wrong. There'd be shouting and panic and quite possibly tasing. Mortimer had seen tasing on Miriam's TV, and didn't like the look of it at all. At least the police here didn't carry guns.

"*Beaufort,*" he whispered again, with a sideways glance at Teresa. She was listening to whatever the detective inspector was saying, and either ignored him or didn't hear him.

"*Shh,*" Beaufort said. He was up on his hindquarters, his snout between two chairs, old gold eyes on the inspector. He looked very *interested.* Mortimer didn't like that look. That look suggested that Beaufort was about to Get Involved.

"Beaufort, we can't *stay* here!" This time both Teresa and Beaufort shushed him, as well as Pearl, who was sat next to Teresa with her old Labrador at her feet. Mortimer eyed it nervously, but the dog only had eyes for Teresa's fairy cake. Mortimer sympathised, although he wasn't sure even he could eat one right now.

They'd only come into town to see Miriam. Mortimer made beautiful, magical things from dragon scales and copper wire and gentle snippets of magic, and Miriam was his human business partner. She sold the trinkets and baubles for him, and bought human things that dragons coveted, which meant mostly barbecues these days. They were much more comfortable for sleeping on than fires, and Miriam buying them saved any more incidents with stolen gas bottles and opportunistic scone theft. She also tested out his new inventions, to make sure they worked in human hands, and always *ooh*-ed and *ahh*-ed in the best possible way. And that had been all they were doing today. Mortimer had only agreed to follow Miriam's scent to the village hall on the promise of cake.

Now here they were. Not only trapped in the hall, with sharp-eyed police everywhere (he'd already seen the inspector rubbing her eyes, suggesting she *knew* something wasn't quite right), but also cake-less and tea-less. He sighed again and wondered if Teresa was going to eat her fairy cake. He'd even share it with the dog.

§

A SUDDEN RUSH of alarmed chatter pulled Mortimer out of his contemplation of the fairy cake.

"They're going to question us!" Pearl whispered. "How can they think we had anything to do with it?"

"They can't!" Teresa said, and clutched Pearl's hand. "Can they?" They stared at each other, then looked back at the inspector, and the Labrador took advantage of the distraction to steal the cake. Mortimer glared at the dog, and caught the inspector saying something about treating the death as suspicious. A collective gasp rose over the Women's Institute, and someone started crying. Beaufort was still watching, motionless between the chairs.

"Let me stress again that no one is being accused of anything—" the detective inspector said from the front of the room, and there was a wail that sounded very much like Jasmine. This was immediately followed by an awful lot of commotion, and Mortimer saw Miriam go spilling to the floor, taking Priya with her.

"This is terrible!" Teresa exclaimed, but she was drowned out by the Labrador sitting up and joining in the chorus of barking that was really much too loud for a small hall. Mortimer flinched backward and saw a completely enormous dog rushing straight for him. He gave a shriek that was luckily lost in the commotion, and dived between the two rows of chairs as Teresa and Pearl jumped up and someone started shouting about being bitten. Rose was being dragged helplessly after the huge dog, but the other two women blocked its way and together they wrestled it to a grudging halt. Mortimer tucked his tail as close to him as he could and tried not to look at the thing's teeth. It was drooling.

"Come on, lad," Beaufort whispered. "This is our chance."

Mortimer peered around him. The door to the garden was empty, but the floor between here and it seemed terribly bare. "Are you sure?" he whispered back.

"Unless you want to wait in here."

Mortimer took a deep breath and gathered his legs under him. They couldn't stay. It was far too risky, with the dogs and all. "Alright," he said. "Let's go."

They bolted for the door shoulder to shoulder, hoping the barking of the dogs would cover the rattle of their talons on the wooden floor, and collided rather painfully at the threshold. Mortimer sprawled sideways and bumped his nose on the door-frame, then recovered himself and shot into the garden with an aching shoulder. Beaufort was old, but he was solid, and large for a Cloverly dragon. He was at least the size of a Newfoundland dog.

The barking escalated behind them, but there were no shouts of *stop, dragon*. Mortimer figured that was a good start. He threw himself into the nearest flowerbed and froze.

⁊

PRIMROSE SPRINTED stiff-legged into the pretty, flower-studded garden that surrounded the village hall and came to a halt, yapping hysterically at the top of her little doggy lungs. Jasmine's husband Ben was right behind her, swearing all kinds of bodily damage as he tried to catch her. She kept skipping out of reach, her bright eyes watching the garden.

"Beaufort," Mortimer hissed.

"Stay still, lad. It'll be fine."

Mortimer stayed where he was, feeling hideously exposed in the bright afternoon sun, and watched the fluffy dog racing toward them with his eight-chambered heart pounding far too fast and loud for comfort. The puffball seemed to have an awful lot of teeth for such a small thing.

"Primrose, you little—" Ben lunged and missed, sprawling to his knees but managing to snag her pink harness as he went down. Primrose's yapping went up an octave or two, making Mortimer wince, and she writhed desperately, snapping at her owner's wrist. "Bloody dog," Ben announced, trapping her under one hand and clipping the leash to the harness. "Should have got a cat. Cats don't do this. You hear that, Primrose? I wish you were a cat."

Beaufort gave a very quiet snort of disapproval, although Mortimer wasn't sure why. The High Lord was allergic to dogs, after all. And it was true that cats never bothered much with dragons.

Rose's enormous dog appeared around the corner of the hall, his head low and ears eager, towing a tall man in uniform behind him. The man had dropped into a crouch, clinging to the leash like a water-skier as the monster dragged him across the garden. His boots were digging neat rolls of turf out of the lawn, and Mortimer gave a very small squeak. The dog seemed even bigger out here, if that was possible.

"*Kev!*" the man being dragged by the dog bellowed. "Get over here!"

Another man, a little round and red-looking, strolled casually around the corner of the hall with an enormous grin plastered to his face. "Alright there, Ben?" he said. "Apprehended the escapee, have you?"

"Oh, ha," Ben said, standing up with the leash wrapped firmly around his hand and brushing grass off his knees. "Good to see you putting the work in there."

"You two seem to have it all under control," the officer replied, although that was a dubious statement. Primrose wasn't going anywhere, despite the fact that she was yapping and twisting breathlessly around the leash, dancing in agitation. The Great

Dane, however, was steadily dragging his captor closer and closer to the flower bed. Mortimer tried to get his trembling under control.

"Goddamn it, Kev," the tall man complained. "Give us a hand before the silly beast has me over!"

"K9 never on your list of career options, then, Sergeant?"

"So help me, Kev—"

"Okay, okay." Kev grabbed the leash, and the two men brought the enormous dog to a halt in the middle of the lawn. The beast was staring right at the dragons where they huddled in the flowerbed beneath the hall windows, and, realising he couldn't move any more, he started to bark, great shuddering *woofs* that set the birds chattering in alarm and echoed off the stone walls of the hall. Mortimer tried to become one with the dirt beneath him.

Ben looked from Primrose to the Great Dane, frowning. Both dogs were agitated, straining toward the flowerbeds and their pretty, neatly trimmed rosebushes. Mortimer resisted the urge to close his eyes, and held his breath instead. There was no wind. They mustn't move.

"You two ever thought much about that whole thing where animals see things we don't?" Ben asked.

"Nah," Kev said, tucking his fingers through the Great Dane's collar and pulling him away. "All rubbish, that stuff."

"Yeah," Ben said, starting to pet Primrose then thinking better of it when she bared her teeth at him. "You're probably right."

He gave the flowerbeds one last dubious glance and headed back inside, towing the dog behind him.

THERE WAS A PAUSE, and the birds exchanged a few pithy observations regarding dogs and men and nice sunny days, then forgot about it. The garden, heavy with spring blooms and busy with growing things, set itself back to dozing, and for a moment all was quiet. Then a bee landed on one of the rose bushes, and the bush gave a yelp of alarm, shook its head, and resolved itself into a small, rose bush-coloured dragon, wings folded tightly against his sides.

"Are you alright, Mortimer? It's only a bee," the larger rose bush said, and now it was suddenly quite clear (to someone disposed to see it) that this was also a dragon, dappled with the variegated colours of the undergrowth.

"I always worry they're going to fly into my ear. And what if I'm allergic?"

"Why on earth would you be allergic? Who's ever heard of a dragon that's allergic to bees?"

"It would be just my luck, is all," Mortimer said, and waved his paws at a bumblebee that had drifted too close. "Shoo!"

"It would be a very strong bee to sting through your scales."

"That's why I worry about them going into my ears. I don't have scales in my ears."

Beaufort nodded thoughtfully. "I have never once heard of that happening."

Mortimer thought that there were many things that had happened since he had begun spending time with Beaufort that *he* had never heard of happening before, but he kept that to himself. "That was terribly close. That dog was a monster!"

"Oh, hardly a monster, Mortimer."

The smaller dragon glared at the High Lord. "Even you aren't as big as that thing!"

"I am heavier, though. And I have wings. And a better tail."

Beaufort looked rather pleased with himself, and Mortimer sighed. "Do you think they're going to be alright in there?"

The High Lord's smile vanished. "I hope so. I wish we could have stayed, but the dogs were a bit of a problem."

"We should go," Mortimer said. "We can wait at Miriam's. She'll tell us everything that happened. We don't need to be here. It's too risky." *And there are too many bees,* he added to himself, shaking his head to scare off another one that was a little too taken with his rosebush disguise.

Beaufort gave him a grave look. "Lad, the vicar's been *murdered.* We can't just walk away without seeing if the ladies need our help."

"But how can we help, really?" It wasn't as if they had meant to come *investigating* this morning. Mortimer had no intentions of *ever* investigating, in fact. And yet here they were, hiding from the police and monstrous dogs twice as tall as he was, and Beaufort was talking about murder. He wished they'd stayed home.

"You heard it, Mortimer. That inspector is saying she wants to question everyone. She thinks they're suspects! We can't have that."

Mortimer sighed heavily. "Shouldn't we let the police handle it? They know how to do all this stuff."

"These are our friends. We don't leave our friends to the whims of law enforcement. Next you'll be telling me we should have just let the knights get on with it when they started killing us off for our scales and teeth, and calling it heroism."

"That's a bit extreme," Mortimer protested. Beaufort was still fairly sore about so-called Saint George slaughtering High Lord Catherine when she was snoozing in her favourite bramble patch. She had been a Cloverly dragon, and Beaufort's predecessor, from the days when Cloverly dragons were as large as they got. Which meant a bit smaller than a Great Dane, and put rather a different slant on Saint George's legendary courage.

"These things start small. We need to look after our friends."

Mortimer scratched his chest, noticing a loose scale, and nodded glumly. "Okay. You're right, we can't just leave them. But what can we do?"

"We need to find out more," Beaufort said. "Let's just keep our ears open, see what we can learn. In fact, you head for the kitchen window – see if there's anything going on at that end."

Mortimer swallowed another sigh and picked his way out of the flowerbed, taking on the paler green of the lawn as he scuttled around the corner of the hall. He'd better get a scone after this, he thought. Preferably several. With cream.

MORTIMER TUCKED himself into a very small shape next to the lavender bush, and concentrated on making himself very lavender-y, while watching the bees that buzzed around the actual bush suspiciously. The kitchen door was open, which left him feeling rather uncomfortable, but the good thing was that he could hear very clearly. The detective inspector was speaking, her words calm and exact.

"I'm sorry, what was your name again, constable?"

"Shaw, ma'am. Ben Shaw."

"PC Shaw, look. I'm sorry about this, but the sooner I can interview your wife, the sooner I can let her go home, okay? I realise she's upset, and I'm really not considering her as a suspect, but I can't exactly interview everyone else and not her, can I?"

"It's just – look, Jasmine isn't a great cook, okay? I know that. I don't even eat her packed lunches, to be honest. I go to a local shop. Or Gregg's, if I'm in town."

"Okay," the DI said, sounding cautious.

"But, like, if the vicar was poisoned by that cupcake—"

"PC Shaw, we're not speculating here."

Ben sighed. "I went to school with Lucas, from the morgue. We still play five a side together here and there." There was a pause, then Ben said, "Okay, not so much five a side as Dungeons and Dragons. Anyhow – he told me it looks like poison."

"PC Shaw—"

"I'm just saying, Jas would never deliberately hurt someone. But her cooking isn't – well, I mean, someone would have to eat it, which does take a brave soul, but it's been known to happen. And if it was the cooking, well, it wouldn't be deliberate, is what I mean."

"I would really rather not have to take you off this case, constable."

Mortimer didn't listen to the rest. The conversation seemed to be mostly over, just the DI giving directions, and there was a lot of shuffling going on in the kitchen. He took the opportunity to sneak out of hiding and run back around the hall, keeping close to the building and under the windows. Beaufort was sat with his back against the stone wall, eyes half-closed in the sun.

"Poison!" Mortimer hissed. "The vicar was poisoned, and the inspector seems to think it could be the W.I.!"

Beaufort opened his eyes properly and regarded the younger dragon with interest. "There, you see?" he said. "I told you we couldn't just leave them to sort it out. She's looking in entirely the wrong place if she's looking for a killer."

"Yes, but she'll realise that, won't she? She can't *really* think they did it!"

"She'll go where the evidence points. And if she spends too long thinking it was the W.I., she might miss the real killer entirely."

"But what do we do? We can't interfere. And she sounds quite, um, serious." *Scary* had been what he wanted to say, but he didn't want Beaufort turning those old eyes on him, the gold crackled with age and heat until they were like polished amber. You couldn't call a detective inspector *scary* with those eyes on you. Even though she was, in a very non-dragonish way.

"We investigate," Beaufort said, giving a toothsome grin before setting off across the lawn at a pace that had Mortimer scurrying to keep up.

"Beaufort! Beaufort, wait!" Mortimer had a not-very-good feeling about this.

☙

CLOSE UP, the vicarage looked a little sad and neglected, the white paint on the window frames stained and peeling, the flowerbeds rather less well-kept than the gardens at the hall. It smelt of dust and age and silence, and Mortimer shivered as they paused under a spindly bay tree near the front door. The vicarage had its own little yard, separated from the church by a low stone wall, but it felt as if the graveyard had crept in anyway. The grass was lush and green and a little over-long, and there was the sense of a waiting that had no need for endings. The birds were subdued in the shadows of the trees, the bees off looking for brighter gardens. It was *quiet*, and there was POLICE DO NOT ENTER tape strung across the door, but no one around.

"What are we looking for?" Mortimer asked.

"Clues." There was a sparkle in the old dragon's eyes that Mortimer didn't like any more than the interested look from earlier. The sparkle seemed very *enthusiastic*, and that tended to end in the sort of situations that caused Mortimer to stress-shed.

"But the police have already been. Surely they'll have found any clues that were here."

"They're not dragons, though, lad. They can't feel a place the way we can. They can't sniff out emotional traces."

Mortimer sighed. "There will have been so many people through there. Even if we find a scent that seems off, how do we know who it belongs to?"

"Can't tell until we try."

"It'll probably be locked, anyway," Mortimer said hopefully.

"Doesn't hurt to check," Beaufort padded across the short stretch of lawn to try the door. The handle turned under his paw, but the door didn't open, and Mortimer let out his breath softly.

"We'll try the back," the old dragon announced, and headed off around the house, Mortimer trailing after him and trying to decide whether he should be hoping the back door was locked, or hoping no one was around, or that someone *was* around, or—

"There we go," Beaufort said, sounding altogether too cheerful for Mortimer's comfort. "Someone left a window open."

Mortimer followed his gaze to the upstairs window, resting ajar on its latch. "Oh," he said. "Oh, do you think?"

"Up you go, lad. No time to waste. Never know when they'll come back."

Mortimer looked around anxiously. "But if someone sees ..."

"Nonsense. You'll be up and in before anyone catches the smallest glimpse of you. Off you go, now."

Mortimer mumbled something under his breath that suggested he was less than happy with the situation, then gathered his hindquarters under himself and leapt at the wall. He could have flown, but the closer he stayed to the wall the easier it was to take on its mottled greys and tans, and the old stone was easy to find purchase on with his talons. He scampered up the wall with his wings out for balance and investigated the window. It was old-fashioned, nothing holding it closed but a metal arm hooked over a stop on the frame, and he flicked it off, took a quick look over his shoulder to make sure the coast was still clear, then slipped over the sill and in.

He paused on the dark green carpet below the window, wings shivering as he sniffed the stale air. It was still, full of a fusty silence. No one home. The house felt long-abandoned already, as if the vicar, with all his books and his thoughts and his quiet life, hadn't been enough to fill up any of these empty rooms. It was a house that had fallen into quiet, slow decay over the years, turning in on itself even while new furniture was brought in, and TVs mounted to walls, and closets filled with the bric-a-brac of a slow succession of gentle lives. It felt sad, and he wondered if the vicar had been happy here. It seemed like a hard place to be happy, but the man's scent was layered about the house, too, and it wasn't *un*happy. It was just quiet and small and self-contained.

He put his paws on the sill and peered down at Beaufort. "Well? Are you coming?"

Beaufort shook his head. "Open the door. That window's too small for me."

Mortimer dropped back to the floor and padded quietly out of the room. He supposed that Beaufort was right, and they needed to help, but this didn't seem to be a good way to go about it. They'd barely escaped the hall unnoticed. Couldn't they just offer moral support? That seemed much more sensible, and far less likely to result in local newspapers running dragon stories on the front page. But then, *everything* Beaufort did seemed likely to result in dragon stories on the front page. Pure luck, and the fact that cameras couldn't capture dragons, were what had saved them so far. That and some rather careful manoeuvring on the part of the W.I., Alice in particular. He slipped down the stairs and into the kitchen, then unlatched the door to let the High Lord in with a sigh.

"Well done, lad," Beaufort said cheerfully, and pattered past him, nose high as he sniffed the air. "Let's see what we can find."

Mortimer followed him, scuffing the old dragon's damp footprints as he went. They'd dry soon enough, but no one needed to find dragon prints on the kitchen floor. That was just asking for trouble. More than they already were, anyway.

4
ALICE

Alice was conducting her own enquiries. It wasn't that she didn't have faith in DI Adams, who seemed like an intelligent woman with a lot of potential, but Alice did rather have the upper hand here. In this particular situation, an intimate knowledge of small village life could be as much of an advantage as formal training, if not more. And while she assumed the inspector had expected most of the women would be as shaken as poor Jasmine, and therefore not in any condition to be doing anything but wait docilely, she'd underestimated both the Women's Institute and the interest such a dramatic event would create. No one was feeling particularly docile, and the room was full of nervous energy and whispered conversations.

A large quantity of cakes and sandwiches had re-emerged from the kitchen, and Carlotta and Gert had directed the two constables to set up some of the folding tables. The women were currently playing a rather heated game of blackjack with Rose and Teresa, piles of coins stacked on the table in front of them. Rosemary had her knitting out and had set her phone up to watch something that seemed to have a lot of explosions in it, while Pearl crocheted furiously next to her. Priya was explaining to the dean that he wasn't letting the tea steep long enough, and that if he was to be the only one allowed in the kitchen then he needed to either take more time over it, or to bring it out in the big teapots from the cupboard over the fridge. The dean looked alarmed, to say the least.

Alice sat very straight in her chair, watching the dust motes drifting in the sunlight that spilled through the door. Jasmine had already gone into the kitchen to be interviewed by the DI. She'd still been crying, and cuddling Primrose so hard that Alice felt a reluctant sort of sympathy for the creature. She turned her attention back to Miriam.

"So, you see," Miriam said, her voice low, "that woman could have been *anyone!* Maybe he had a secret family!"

"You do realise that vicars are allowed to marry?"

"Yes, but, well – maybe he divorced?"

"Also allowed."

"Huh." Miriam sipped her tea and made a face. "The dean really does make awful tea. Alright. Maybe the vicar abandoned her with three small children when he was much younger, changed his name and joined the church, and she's just found him."

"And so she poisoned him why?"

"Because ... Because she was angry at him for leaving?" Miriam shook her head and put her mug on the floor. "I know, it doesn't make any sense. But it's the only thing out of the ordinary that I've seen. Ever, I mean. He was a very boring man."

Alice permitted herself a small smile. "I do guess he was, at that. But appearances can be deceiving. I heard that his past was rather colourful."

"Ooh, so you think she *was* from his past?"

Alice shrugged, a small, eloquent gesture. "Maybe. But she hardly sounds dangerous."

"I suppose." Miriam sighed, then looked up as the tall detective constable from Away stopped in front of her chair. His hair was short-cropped and dark, and his trousers were very skinny. Too skinny, Alice thought. They made him look gangly, like a teenager just getting into a growth spurt.

"Mrs Ellis?" he said to Miriam.

"Um, Ms."

"Ms Ellis, sorry. Can you come through, please?"

"Oh dear," Miriam said, getting up so suddenly that her skirts slopped into her mug. "Oh dear."

"Purely routine, ma'am," the officer said, looking even more alarmed than Miriam.

"Oh dear," she said again, and Alice gave her a reassuring pat on the arm before she padded off toward the kitchen, trailing tea droplets behind her. The Labrador followed, cleaning up enthusiastically, and Alice looked around for Jasmine. There was no sign of her. Ben must have taken her out the back door and home. That was a shame, but Alice doubted she'd have learned much from the younger woman, anyway. It had taken her a year to remember what day the weekly market was on. She wasn't the most observant person Alice had ever encountered.

WITH MIRIAM GONE, Alice moved to a spare seat next to Rose, avoiding the large puddle of drool the Great Dane was leaving on the floor. Gert and Carlotta were still playing cards, but the other two had rather wisely retreated.

"What do you think?" Rose asked, and Priya, Teresa and Pearl leaned in eagerly. Rosemary kept knitting, but she was listening.

"It's a terrible thing," Alice said.

"Of course," Rose said, somewhat impatiently, and pushed her glasses up her small nose. "But who could have done it?"

Alice spread her fingers on the table. "I don't know. We don't even know how he died yet."

"She said it was suspicious," Priya said. "And she's questioning *us*. That doesn't seem right."

"Miriam was the last to see him alive," Rose pointed out, and everyone looked at her. "I don't *mean* anything by that. Just that maybe that's why she's questioning us."

"It does seem strange to question us all," Alice said. "But she obviously has her reasons."

"I don't like it." Pearl was tracing circles in a puddle of cooled tea with one finger. "It's not *right*."

"I'm sure it'll be fine," Alice said. "After all, none of us has done anything wrong, have we?" The women exchanged doubtful glances, and she sighed. "I mean, none of us murdered the vicar."

A rush of excitable agreement greeted that statement, and she wondered just what secrets everyone was sitting on. Everyone has them, after all, those secrets that raise anxious faces to the light, whether they're worth the guilt or not.

"But who did?" Teresa asked. "And how have we been implicated?"

"Maybe it was that awful gastropub man," Rose said. "Offended by our lack of appreciation for his caviar-custard tarts."

There was a moment's silence as everyone considered it. "He was very upset when we didn't let him come to the fete last year," Pearl said, sounding doubtful.

"That seems rather slim evidence," Alice said.

"Unless it was the tarts that actually killed the poor vicar," Priya said.

"Oh, those went straight in the bin after the meeting," Teresa replied. "No one touched them."

"I imagine a posh gastropub owner has more to worry about than a village fete, anyway," Rosemary said, frowning at her knitting.

"True," Rose said. "And we're always banning people. We banned that frog collector just last winter."

Pearl shuddered. "I did *not* expect him to be wearing a frog-skin hat and dissecting things all over the place. Now he really *could* be a murderer."

The conversation drifted for a moment as Rose and Pearl argued over whether dissection could really be considered a healthy hobby, then Priya said, "What if the murderer's not finished?"

All eyes turned to Alice, and she smiled, hoping it looked genuine. "I'm sure the inspector will clear us all by the end of this meeting," she said. "And I have no doubt they'll find the murderer very swiftly."

"What if it's a serial killer?" Rosemary asked, knitting needles clicking anxiously. "They seem to be very popular at the moment."

A murmur of agreement went around the assembled women, and Alice sighed. "I'm sure it's not."

"There could be dozens of murdered vicars, a trail of bodies left across the country," Rosemary added. Teresa grabbed Pearl's hand again.

"I find it highly unlikely that a trail of murdered vicars would have escaped our attention," Alice said.

There was a pause that made her realise that she might not have been as reassuring as she'd have liked, then Rose said, "And what about the dragons? With police poking around and all?"

"We shall just have to be very, very careful," Alice replied, and wondered if that was a condition Beaufort could manage. He must be able to, to keep his clan hidden for all these centuries, but still. It didn't sound much like the High Lord of the Cloverly dragons. Not the one she knew, anyway.

BY DINT of some calculated moves around the room, and some rather severe looks at young James the detective constable, Alice made sure she would be the last one interviewed by the DI. Not only did she want to be able to ask the W.I. her own questions now, while they were fresh in her mind, she also wanted the detective inspector to be tired by the time she went in. The questions the DI asked her after talking to everyone else might just give her an idea of what the inspector was thinking. Not that she thought the police couldn't handle it, but, well. This had happened in her own backyard. It felt almost insulting.

Now she tapped the table lightly. "Hit me."

Gert looked at her narrowly, then dealt another card. Alice examined it.

"Hold."

Carlotta rubbed her chin with a heavily be-ringed hand. "Dammit," she said, then added, "Sorry, Dean."

The dean, huddled in a chair near the stage in the now almost-empty hall, jumped like she'd tickled him, and gave a weak smile.

"I fold," Carlotta announced.

Gert lifted the corner of the cards in front of her, just as if she didn't know exactly what was there, and Alice, seated so she could see the kitchen door, saw James emerge looking unhappy.

"House folds," Gert announced, and pointed at Alice. "Show your cards, woman."

Alice turned them over, allowing herself a smile. A nine, a four, and a five.

"Jesus Christ – sorry, Dean – I hate playing with you, Alice."

"I know," Alice said comfortably, and collected her winnings. "Another?"

"Does the pope – oh, God – oh, *sorry*, Dean."

"You should be ashamed of yourself," Carlotta said, getting up before James reached the table. "The mouth on you. You'll go straight to hell."

"Says the woman who takes spiked coffee to church every Sunday," Gert said, shuffling the cards with quick, practised hands.

"I get cold. Come, young man, and take me through. I don't want to sit with this blasphemer anymore."

"Ah, right. Sure." James looked distinctly uncomfortable as Carlotta linked her arm through his and patted his bicep.

"You're terribly tall, aren't you? Strong, too."

"Um," he said, and led her away more quickly than was probably entirely necessary.

Alice smiled, and picked up the cards Gert had dealt her. "Dean?" she called. "Could I trouble you for another cup of tea? I hate to be a bother, but ..."

"Of course!" he said, jumping up from the chair and dropping his phone with an expensive-sounding clatter. "Right away."

"Milk, three sugars," Gert said. "And make it strong, would you?"

"Yes, yes, of course."

"Just milk for me," Alice said, and smiled pleasantly.

The dean scuttled away, clutching his phone like a life preserver, and Gert smiled at Alice.

"So, what's on your mind, love?"

"As someone who knows everyone, Gert, do you know anything about our poor deceased vicar?"

Gert rested her heavy forearms on the table. They were deceptive, more muscle than fat, and Alice had watched her win more than one arm-wrestling contest against younger and fitter men. It was Gert's speciality at fetes. That and her strawberry jam, which was quite wonderful, and, Alice had a niggling suspicion, slightly alcoholic. "Not much that isn't common knowledge. Ran with a bad crowd as a youngster. Spent a bit of time at Her Majesty's pleasure for robbery, although I think there was more that didn't stick. Found God and spent his time after that trying to put young kids straight. Came here for a quiet life, I believe."

"No reason to think anyone from his old life would be looking for him?"

"Not so's I know. He seemed like a real bad-apple-gone-good sort. And judging by the state of his shoes and his car, he wasn't exactly getting any extra income from anywhere."

Alice nodded. "I thought that, too."

"I can ask around. Our Benny's in Liverpool these days."

"Benny your nephew?"

"No, Benny my cousin's daughter's new hubby."

"Of course."

"So shall I ask?"

"If you could. I thought the vicar was from Manchester, though?"

"Nah, that funny no-accent he's got – had – isn't his. You hear the other one come through when he gets – got – really stressed sometimes. I mean, it did. Poor man."

"*Hmm.*"

"I imagine he really wanted to leave the old stuff behind."

"I suppose so," Alice said. "He came here from Manchester, though."

"Oh, sure. I think he got out of Liverpool soon as he got out of jail."

"*Hmm,*" Alice said again, then didn't say any more, because the dean came back in with their tea, apologising profusely for it still being rather on the milky side.

THE HALL WAS quiet and still, the light grown golden on the wooden floorboards and against the walls as the afternoon edged on toward evening. The flowers the W.I. had brought in the day before for their meeting bowed their heads softly in the vases on the windowsills, and Alice could hear bird song drifting in from outside. She didn't feel cross about being cooped up on such a beautiful day, exactly, but it did seem like a shame. She could have gone for a walk. Weeded the garden. Even just sat out with a book, although it wasn't a Sunday, so that would have been terribly indulgent.

"Ma'am?" James said, and Alice smiled at him.

"Just me left, is it?"

"If you don't mind." He offered her his hand, but she was already standing, brushing her trousers off.

"You'll be happy to get home after all this," she said.

He sighed. "I won't disagree."

Alice smiled again, but it was more to herself than to him. If he was tired, the DI was probably exhausted. With any luck, she might even get some of her own questions answered.

The back door to the kitchen was open, letting cooling air in, and the room smelt of baked goods and cut grass. The detective inspector was stretching in the doorway as if she were about to go for a 10k run, and otherwise the kitchen was empty. James pulled a seat out at the table for Alice, then selected a piece of fruit cake and leaned back against the sink with an appreciative sigh.

"Have you sent everyone else home?" Alice asked.

"Everyone I've questioned, yes. And as I didn't think I really needed the manpower here, I've sent someone to keep an eye on the vicarage. Just in case anyone gets any ideas about poking around." The DI sat down and eyed Alice as if she harboured suspicions that the chair of the W.I. might be the one doing the poking.

"How very sensible," Alice said. "People can be very disrespectful. Although one would hope not in this village."

"Can't be too careful."

"Quite." They examined each other across the table, and Alice was disappointed to note that the inspector didn't look all that tired. The younger woman straightened her back, as if trying to emulate Alice's posture, and tapped a pencil on a yellow legal pad. "I thought you all used tablets now," Alice said.

"Call me old-fashioned. I like having a hard copy. In case anyone spills something on my phone."

"That was *once*," James protested.

DI Adams made a little gesture of dismissal and indicated the tablet that lay next to the pad. "I do find this very handy for research, though."

"I can see how it would be." Alice kept her hands folded neatly on the table in front of her, waiting. She had an idea where this was going to go.

"How would you characterise your relationship with the vicar?"

"We were friendly."

"Did you have disagreements?"

"Yes. Less now than at first. He sometimes had differing ideas of the W.I.'s role in the village."

"Did you ever argue?"

"I wouldn't describe it as such, no. We disagreed. Rather quickly he realised that the W.I. gets things done, and it's best to let us get on with it."

"*Hmm.*" The DI made some scratches on the pad. It could have been some form of shorthand, but it looked to Alice more like the start of a noughts and crosses grid. "Mrs Shaw was quite upset."

"Jasmine? Yes. She can be quite emotional. She fainted when her flower arrangement won 'Most Improved' last year."

"How unfortunate."

"Especially considering she landed on the flower arrangement in question."

The inspector snorted, and they shared amused grins for a moment before the DI frowned down at her pad again. "Any reason she'd be so terribly upset over the vicar, though?"

"As I say, she's emotional. She cries if one of her houseplants dies, so it's a weekly occurrence. At least."

"How was her relationship with the vicar?"

"Friendly. I don't think they had much to do with each other outside the W.I. meetings, although Jasmine always made sure to bring extra cakes for him whenever we had one. Poor man."

"I hear her cooking isn't great."

"Her cooking is disastrous. But she's lovely, and tries terribly hard, so we all pretend she's getting better all the time."

"She's not?"

"You saw the lasagne."

"Jesus, that was a lasagne?" James said. "Her poor hubby." Alice and the DI both looked at him. "I mean – obviously *he* could cook, too. And no one marries anyone for cooking skills these days. Obviously. Um." He suddenly busied himself with the sink. "I'll wash up, shall I?"

The women looked back at each other. "Mrs Alice Deirdre Martin, correct?"

"I favour Ms."

"I see here Mr Martin is missing."

"Yes."

"For about twelve years."

"Yes."

"And yet you've never declared him dead. Or annulled the marriage."

"No."

"So you still hope he might come back?"

"Not at all. It just seemed to put a lot of importance on something that I found very unimportant."

"His disappearance was unimportant?"

"The marriage, Inspector."

The inspector scrolled down on the tablet, although Alice had no doubt she knew exactly what was on there. DI Adams did not seem to be the sort of woman to forget things. "You were questioned following his disappearance."

"And never charged."

"No. Odd circumstances, though. You come home from ..." She

scrolled again, and again Alice was sure it was for effect. "... the RAF, and within a week he's gone."

"Yes."

"You were a wing commander."

"Yes."

"Fifty-five is quite young to retire."

"It was the right time for me. The only direction from there was promotion to a desk job, which held no particular appeal."

They examined each other. "He was just gone," the DI said again. "Not even his clothes touched."

"None of his belongings were taken from my house, true. That is not to say he didn't have some elsewhere. He was not a very ... *satisfactory* husband, Detective Inspector."

"I see. A curious situation, though."

"Indeed. But tell me, Inspector, do you think I'd have created such a questionable situation if I *had* disposed of him?"

DI Adams watched Alice with dark, thoughtful eyes, tapping her pen on the table, and Alice returned her gaze calmly. She'd been through all this before. She had hoped she wouldn't have to again, but it was just like Harvey to keep dragging himself through her life, making things messy.

"Apparently the vicar was afraid of you," the inspector said finally.

Alice raised one meticulously shaped eyebrow. "I am a woman of a certain age, with a certain history of authority. Many people have been afraid of me. I'm sure you have had – and will continue to have – a similar experience, Detective Inspector."

By the sink, James snorted, and tried to cover it with a cough. DI Adams took another sip of tea, and Alice could see her lips twitching. "So is that a yes?"

"It is a yes."

They watched each other for a moment, and the DI was the first to look away, much to Alice's satisfaction. The inspector cleared her throat, and said, "Well. I think that's all for now, Ms Martin. Please understand that we may need to ask you further questions, however."

"Of course." Alice rose to her feet, extending a cool hand for the inspector to shake. "Good luck, Detective Inspector. I will help wherever I can."

"One last thing. You seem to have a certain influence around here. The respect of the locals, shall we say."

"I guess you could say that," Alice said cautiously.

"So people might come to you if they needed help, or advice."

"It depends. I'm not the most sympathetic ear, but if they needed something done, then yes."

The inspector held her gaze for a moment longer, then said, "I don't have to worry about you digging around in this investigation, do I, Ms Martin?"

"It is a police affair, Detective Inspector."

"So the fact that you talked to every person in the room, and actively avoided being brought in here until you had done so, shouldn't worry me at all."

Alice bit down on a smile. "I *am* the chair of the W.I., and, as you say, people do have a certain regard for me. I thought it best to be able to offer support to everyone individually. We have just lost our vicar."

The inspector didn't look particularly impressed. "This is likely a very straightforward case, Ms Martin. You are ex-military. You must understand that civilians getting in the middle of things only ever serves to complicate matters and slow things down."

"Quite right, Inspector."

The DI shook her head and sighed, and Alice saw just the slightest dip of weariness in her shoulders before she straightened up again. "Okay. Thank you for your cooperation."

"Always a pleasure to help," Alice said, and picked her bag up off the table.

"Ms Martin?" DI Adams called, just as she was stepping out into the warm afternoon light, crisp and fresh-smelling after the long day indoors. "You will, of course, contact me immediately if you happen to be told anything that has any bearing whatsoever on this investigation."

Alice turned back to her and smiled. "Of course," she lied, with perfect innocence.

5

MIRIAM

There was a sharp and instantly recognisable knock on the kitchen door, and Miriam rushed to open it. She wasn't even sure why she had it shut, really. It was a perfectly wonderful afternoon, the heat baking her garden and filling it with the scents of flowers and sweetly ripening vegetation, and the bees ambling sleepy and slow around the hanging baskets under the eaves. But then, there had been a murder, so she supposed it was only reasonable that she felt a bit uncomfortable having the open door at her back. Anyone who could kill a vicar ... Well, there was no telling what they were capable of.

She opened the door wide to let the two dragons in, Mortimer looking even more anxious than usual.

"Hello, you two," she said, trying for bright and breezy but hearing a squeaky edge to the words. "Come on in. I've just put the kettle on."

"Afternoon, Miriam," Beaufort said. "Tea would be wonderful. We've had a very exciting time of it."

"Have you?" Miriam asked distractedly, already busying herself with the biggest teapot. "Well, yes, I imagine getting out of the hall with the dogs and everything must have been quite exciting."

"We've been breaking and entering," Mortimer said, examining the corners of the room as if expecting someone to jump out and arrest him at any moment. "We're criminals!"

"You *what?*" Miriam dropped the kettle in the sink, splashing water all over herself and the counter. "What are you *talking* about?" She grabbed the dish cloth, patting at the front of her top and only making it more damp.

"Mortimer, do calm down. There was no breaking involved," Beaufort said, as if that made anything better.

"There was entering. We entered a crime scene. I'm sure that's illegal."

"No one *saw* us."

"It was so close, though!"

"It was a little close," Beaufort admitted.

"And we didn't even find anything out!"

"Mortimer, would you like some banana cake?" Miriam asked. The smaller dragon had collapsed on the floor of the kitchen, barely inside the door, and taken on the grey of the stone floor. He didn't look well.

"No, I don't want banana cake! I want to not have broken into a vicar's house!"

"We didn't *break in,*" Beaufort repeated. "That window was basically an invitation."

"You broke into *the vicar's house?*"

"Yes!" Mortimer wailed.

"No," Beaufort said, very firmly. "And I would love some banana cake, Miriam. That's very nice of you."

"But why did you break into the vicar's house?"

"Because he was murdered," Beaufort said, as if that should make perfect sense. Mortimer muttered something that Miriam couldn't quite hear, but it sounded a lot like *silly old dragons*, and she saw the High Lord's ears twitch slightly.

"Tea," she said. "Tea, and banana cake, and then I'm sure this shall all make sense."

"But it *already* makes sense," Beaufort protested.

She ignored him and got the cake from the pantry.

MORTIMER HAD PEELED himself off the floor and shuffled further inside, and was now sitting up in the sunshine washing through the small panes of the deep-silled windows. He was working on his second cup of tea and third slice of cake, and was looking slightly less grey.

With the immediate concern of a fainting dragon set aside, Miriam took a relieved sip of her own tea, and said, "But why on earth did you go to the vicarage? I was worried enough that you weren't going to get out of the hall without being seen!"

"It was the only sensible thing to do," Beaufort said. He was crouched in the doorway with his paws tucked under him, like some enormous green cat, and Miriam wondered just what he based his estimation of sensible on. "We figured we couldn't do anything at the hall, so we'd go have a little look at the vicarage while everyone was otherwise occupied."

"Only they came back," Mortimer said around a mouthful of cake. "The police."

"Yes, most unfortunate, that. We were having a little look around downstairs, just to see if there were any scents or anything we could pick up—"

"The whole place smells sad," Mortimer said. "Terribly sad."

"Lad, someone just died there. It's not going to smell of roses and kittens."

Mortimer looked at his empty plate wistfully. "Yes, but it was awful."

"Scents?" Miriam said. "Like tracker dogs?"

"We're not *dogs*," Mortimer said indignantly, and licked the crumbs off his plate.

"Emotional traces," Beaufort explained. "We can't smell physical traces like dogs can—"

"Dogs are horrible," Mortimer announced, looking hopefully at the cake on the table.

"Dogs are very nice creatures," Beaufort corrected him. "And very good at tracking physical scents. Every creature's very good at something. That's what makes them all so wonderful."

Mortimer muttered something dubious, but didn't contradict him.

"And *did* you find anything?" Miriam asked. "We were all questioned, you know. Like we were suspects!"

"You *are* suspects," Beaufort said. "We overheard that it was probably poison, and that there was cake involved."

"*Poison?* They really think he was poisoned? *Deliberately?*"

"It sounded like it," Beaufort said.

"But surely they can't think any of us would do it! Not really!"

"Well, if it was cake, and it happened right after a W.I. meeting ..." Beaufort trailed off as Miriam gave a horrified gasp and pressed her hands to her mouth. The kitchen was still, only the ticking of the clock above the mantel and the terribly distant happiness of bird song outside to be heard. Miriam couldn't seem to breathe, the thick-beamed ceiling that was usually so cosy pressing down heavy and claustrophobic above her, the thick old walls less protection and more prison.

All those questions in the hall that she'd so willingly given answers to, thinking she was just *helping*, that it was all just what the police did after a murder. To think that all that time the detective inspector was *suspecting* her, was imagining her a murderer! Suddenly everything the inspector had asked, every repeated query, every one of her own straightforward answers, seemed desperately suspicious. What if she'd said something wrong? What if she'd incriminated herself? Or, worse, one of the others?

She jumped up, sending her chair slamming into the wall behind her. "I need some air." She scrambled past Beaufort and out into the garden, almost running down the overgrown path to the rickety garden table nestled in its surrounds of trellis and vines. She leaned against it, cold in spite of the sun, while black spots swam in her vision and the sky reverberated with every breath, far too dark and low. They thought it was one of the W.I.! A murderer in their midst! How could this happen? How could *any* of this happen?

SHE WASN'T sure how long she'd been out there when Mortimer shuffled outside with a cushion in one fore paw, and her cup of tea (slopping slightly, as although dragons *can* walk on their hind legs, it's awkward) in the other. He placed the cushion on a chair and the tea on the table, then went back inside. A moment later he returned, this time with a large bag of cheese puffs from Miriam's secret stash.

"How did you know about those?" she asked him.

"They smell really strong, even when they're not open," he replied, and handed the packet to her.

She sighed, and opened the bag, watching Beaufort pad across the backyard toward them, a trail of thoughtful blue smoke drifting behind him.

"So, what *did* you find out at the vicarage?"

"Not much," Beaufort admitted, sitting next to the table and folding his front paws over his belly. "There are so many emotional traces there, so many people over the years coming and going. It makes things complicated."

"Could you tell anything at all from it?" Miriam asked, licking cheesy orange dust off her fingertips and offering the bag to Mortimer, who wrinkled his nose and shook his head.

"We were looking for someone *angry*. Passionately angry. Someone who wished the vicar harm. But emotions don't fade the same way scents do, so it's hard to tell if we're smelling a person who was there and angry yesterday, or just a generally angry person who was there last year."

Miriam took another handful of cheese puffs. If this wasn't a non-organic, artificially-flavoured cheese puff day, she didn't know what was. "So we don't know anything else, then."

"There was something," Beaufort said. "It wasn't entirely clear, but there was something. The only thing I can say definitely, though, is that the person who did this wasn't inside. Not recently, anyway. If they'd been there, the whole house would have reeked."

"Outside?" Miriam asked, thinking of the angry, expensive-smelling woman who had chased the vicar from the village hall the day before.

"We didn't have much time to look around," Mortimer said. "We were kind of running from the police."

"Don't be over-dramatic, Mortimer. They didn't even see us."

"They would have, if we hadn't run."

"You really do need to relax, Mortimer. You wouldn't have survived a day back in the Middle Ages with that attitude."

Mortimer plucked at his tail and mumbled, "They sound horrendous anyway."

Beaufort ignored him. "But we do need to go back."

"Go *back*?" Miriam exclaimed, at the same time Mortimer said, "Why?"

He gave them both an amused look. "Because there was something in the room with the internet thingy. You said as much, Mortimer."

"I *know*, but I didn't have time to look properly. Not really. There was just a whiff. It might be nothing, just an angry email or something. One of those chain thingies, even."

Beaufort looked puzzled, then said, "Well, at the moment we have precisely nothing to go on, so any sort of something is an improvement. The worst that could happen is we go for a look, and still have nothing."

"The worst that could happen is we get arrested," Miriam pointed out.

"Or tasered. I don't like the look of that." Mortimer was twisting his tail anxiously, the scales scraping under his paws.

"Do put your tail down, Mortimer. No one's getting tasered." Beaufort frowned. "What is that, anyway?"

"Um," Mortimer said. "It's this thing the police have. It electrocutes you."

"*Electrocutes* you?" Beaufort asked, one paw on his chest.

"What's this about getting tasered?" a new voice asked, saving Mortimer from trying to explain further, and they turned to see Alice coming down the path. Miriam stashed the cheese puffs hurriedly behind her seat and wiped the crumbs from her mouth. Finally, a voice of reason. Alice would talk sense into Beaufort, if anyone could.

"I THINK we definitely need to get into the vicarage," Alice said, and Miriam and Mortimer looked at her in horror.

"*Really?*" Mortimer wailed.

"But it's a *crime scene*," Miriam said, and pulled the cheese puffs out again. If she got arrested she'd have years without cheese puffs, so there was no point hiding them now. Mortimer held his paw out, and she passed him the packet.

"It's our best lead," Alice said. "We don't know who this woman was that you saw, Miriam, so we have no way of tracking her down. But if we can get onto the vicar's computer, we might find some emails from her. Or someone else, if it wasn't her."

"But I told the inspector about her. Surely she'll look into it?"

"Miriam's right," Mortimer said. "We shouldn't get involved. The police know what they're doing."

"Not all the time," Alice said. "At the moment, we're their main suspects. They'll be concentrating on us, not looking at other options."

"But how can they look at *us?*" Miriam demanded. "Why would *we* kill the vicar?"

"It's the cake," Beaufort said. "Where else would the cake have come from?"

"But *no one—*" Miriam began, and Alice patted her hand.

"Of course not," the older woman said. "But poison is traditionally a women's weapon. Method, opportunity. Now all she's looking for is motive."

"But none of us *has* a motive!"

"Don't we?" Alice smiled, but there was a tightness to it that made Miriam's stomach twist. "The vicar was scared of me. He banned Gert from having poker nights in the village hall because it was gambling. Carlotta thought he wasn't as devout as the last vicar, even though she likes the trappings more than the substance. Rose argued with him over his 'no dogs in church' policy. Jasmine could have done it purely by accident. Knowing her, she might have picked up the rat poison thinking it was sugar. Even you, Miriam. You argued with him over decorations more than once."

"Never seriously! He just didn't accept that religious holidays have pagan roots that should be celebrated!"

"*I* know that. *You* know that. But you see? The detective

inspector has a whole pool of suspects to choose from. Any one of us could have done it. And sometimes, all anyone's looking for is an answer. It doesn't have to be the right answer."

There was silence then. The sun still shone, the light long and low and hopeful as only spring days can be, and it should have been filled with warmth and easy conversation and the delight of the oncoming summer. Instead Miriam just felt sick, and wished she hadn't eaten so many cheese puffs. Her gloriously overgrown garden seemed messy and threatening, and the day felt full of unfriendly eyes, all waiting to see how she might incriminate herself.

"So what do we do?" she asked eventually.

"We investigate," Beaufort said, and Mortimer sighed.

WHICH WAS how Miriam found herself, an hour later, standing on the edge of the shadowy graveyard and twisting her skirt through her fingers.

"I don't like it," she said, for what seemed to be the hundredth time.

"Do calm down, Miriam," Alice said. "It's very simple. I will go and talk to the policeman on duty. If it's the same one as when I left, I think it's that nice Sergeant Graham. I'll take him a sandwich, have a chat, and meanwhile Mortimer will go in the window, let you in, and you can see what you can find on the computer."

"You make it sound so simple," Mortimer said. He was still on the other side of the churchyard wall, peering over the top at the others.

"It *is* simple. Now come along."

Alice had the sort of voice that made disagreement difficult, to say the least, so Mortimer climbed over the wall with a reluctant sigh, and they set off among the cool shadows of the trees that sheltered the flower-scattered graves. Miriam concentrated on pretending she was just out for an evening stroll and not doing anything that could remotely be construed as breaking (or even bending) any laws. She tripped over the edge of a half-buried marker, fell onto another, and knocked a vase of plastic flowers into the long grass.

"Sorry," she mumbled, and righted them before hurrying on.

Before they reached the vicarage itself, Alice made Miriam wait in the whispering shelter of a heavy-limbed oak tree, and she circled the garden's low stone wall with Beaufort following her. The big dragon was light-footed and silent, barely disturbing the grass, and he slipped into the garden itself to hover at the corner of the house as Alice went on ahead. It wasn't long before voices drifted back to them, a man's low laughter and the quieter murmur of a woman's voice. Beaufort turned and came trotting back, pausing here and there to gesticulate at Mortimer.

"I think he wants you to go in," Miriam said.

"I can see that. But I don't want to," Mortimer replied. He seemed to be struggling to stay grass green, and kept fading to a sad grey colour.

"Neither do I," Miriam admitted. "But do you want to say no to them?"

Mortimer groaned. Beaufort had stopped under the open window and was sitting on his hindquarters, waving both paws at them wildly. "Dammit," the young dragon said, then scampered across the grass and went scratching rapidly up the wall, his scales flashing from grey to pink in alarm.

"Oh dear," Miriam whispered, clutching her skirt in both hands. "Oh, do be careful, Mortimer!"

He paused at the window, unlatched it, then scrambled over the ledge, and for a moment Miriam thought it was going to be just fine. Well, as fine as breaking into an active crime scene could be. Then, just as the dragon vanished from sight, his tail hooked the window and it slammed behind him with a crash that echoed across the graveyard and bounced off the walls of the church.

Miriam squeaked and darted behind the tree. Beaufort froze where he was, taking on the colours of the bushes that circled the house, and a moment later the sergeant came jogging around the corner, a half-eaten sandwich still clutched in one hand. Alice was close behind him, and she stopped between him and Beaufort and pointed at the window, which had bounced open again and was still swinging lazily above them.

"Look. It must have been the wind."

"There isn't any," the sergeant said.

"What else could it have been?"

"I don't know." He gave her a slightly suspicious look. "Anyone else here with you?"

"Just me," she said.

He tried the door, found it locked, and turned back to Alice. "I'll have to check it out. You better go, Ms Martin. Thanks for the sandwich."

"My pleasure. I hope you have a nice evening, Graham." She put her hands in the pockets of her light jacket and strolled across the grass to the back gate of the vicarage garden, letting herself out and taking the path than ran between the grave markers to the church. She didn't even glance around to see Miriam hiding behind her tree. Miriam stayed where she was and tried not to feel offended when Graham looked at his sandwich somewhat apprehensively. He sniffed it, shrugged, then took another bite and headed back to the front of the house.

Beaufort ran to her as soon as they heard the front door open, and they crouched behind the tree together, peering around the trunk to watch the windows anxiously.

"Where *is* he?" Miriam hissed.

"He'll be fine," Beaufort said. "He's a clever lad." But he sounded worried. Lights were coming on in the downstairs rooms as the officer inspected the interior, and there was still no sign of Mortimer. Miriam kept expecting a scaly head to appear at the window, but there was nothing. Lights on upstairs now, probably on the landing. The officer was moving fast without rushing, and Miriam wondered if she should run to the front door, knock on it or something, give Mortimer a chance to escape. But she was frozen where she crouched, her heart pounding so hard against her ribs that she thought she might pass out. She didn't know how criminals did it. This was awful!

The lights came on in the room with the open window, and she ducked behind the tree as Graham leaned out and peered into the lengthening shadows. She heard the window shut, the latch lock into place, and when she peeked back around the tree the room was dark again.

"He's still in there!" she whispered to Beaufort.

"I know." The High Lord's eyebrow ridges were drawn down anxiously.

6
MORTIMER

There had been a moment there, when Mortimer had knocked the window with his tail, when he'd frozen so completely that he'd thought he wasn't going to be able to move at all, that the sergeant was going to come into the room and find a living statue of a dragon crouched in the middle of the old green carpet, cycling sadly from frightened pink to grass green to stone grey to a strange, mottled purple-blue that wasn't even his normal colour, but a very stressed semblance of it.

Then he'd heard Alice's crisp voice from below the window, blaming the wind, and he'd bolted out of the room and straight into the one next door, which turned out to be a bathroom. He scrambled into the bath, turned around twice, realised that it not only offered him no protection at all, but that the tap was dripping on his tail, and fled, leaving a sparkle of water drops behind him. The next room was full of stacks of old parish newspapers and church magazines, dusty taped-up boxes and a sickly-looking fake Christmas tree, plus a mannequin by the window that scared Mortimer so much he almost tripped over his own paws turning around again.

He heard the front door open as he dived across the hall and pushed himself under the vicar's bed. The space was only just high enough for him to squeeze into, and his wings were jammed uncomfortably against the base. But he *was* in, and unless that officer, Graham, came right into the room and peered under the bed, he should be alright. He held his breath as he heard feet on the stairs.

"Anyone here?" Graham called. He sounded like he was trying for authoritative, but the words were a little shaky around the edges. Mortimer thought that maybe humans weren't entirely immune to the sense of houses, after all. This was a sad, tired house, and something quietly tragic had just occurred here. The whole place felt unhappy and restless, and when the sergeant walked carefully along the landing, his baton in one hand, the floorboards cried plaintively.

"Damn old houses," the sergeant grumbled, and edged into the spare room, where Mortimer had entered the house so ungracefully. The dragon took his chance and started to wriggle out from under the bed, hearing Graham pulling the window shut. He had time, if he was quick. His nose and shoulders were out, then he was pulled to a halt by a sharp, biting pain in his left wing. He gave a little whimper of alarm, swallowing it quickly, and heard the sergeant say uncertainly, "Hello?"

Mortimer thought of about a dozen highly inventive curse words he'd like to use, and backed up as rapidly as the cramped quarters would let him. Only just in time, too. Graham appeared in the doorway and flicked the unshaded overhead light on, flooding the room with over-bright light.

"Anyone here?"

There was something tickling Mortimer's nose. The place was alive with spiderwebs and dust bunnies, and his eyes were starting to water. He wriggled his snout desperately.

The sergeant crossed to check the windows, and Mortimer

heard him open the closet. *Don't look under the bed,* he thought. *Please, please, please. Just go out.* He was concentrating on being as *faint* as he could, but his heart was beating so hard he was surprised the bed wasn't shaking with it, and his wing hurt, and he wanted to scratch his nose, and this had been a really, really *spectacularly* bad idea. A millennium of being nothing more than myth, and it was all going to go to pot because they'd got caught up with the Toot Hansell Women's Institute. The historians were just going to *love* that. He squeezed his watering eyes closed, trying to ignore the persistent tickle in his nose, and hoped ostriches were actually onto something. There was nothing else he could do.

The man's footsteps paused at the side of the bed, and Mortimer held his breath.

"Old houses," Graham muttered again, then walked out of the room, switching the light off as he went.

☙

Mortimer let his breath out in a slow, shuddering sigh, sagging onto the floor, then scratched his nose wildly. Okay, so he was safe for now. But he still needed to get out without being seen. There was no question of letting Miriam in, even if the sergeant went back to his car, and he certainly wasn't going to mess around himself trying to see what was on the computer. He'd tried using Miriam's before, and his claws got stuck in the keys. They weren't made for dragons.

He was distracted from his thoughts by the sight of the sergeant's boots, stopped in the middle of the landing outside the door. They seemed terribly efficient, these police. Weren't village policemen meant to be all relaxed and easily distracted? Maybe Alice should have tried with cake, rather than a sandwich.

The man sighed, loudly enough to startle Mortimer. "Attic," he said. "Of course there's an attic. Although with all the crap in that

spare room, it's either boarded up or empty. Or hoarder central."
He sighed again. "But can I not go up? No, I can't. Because bloody
Detective bloody Inspector bloody Adams ..." He was still grumbling as Mortimer heard the catch on the trapdoor click, and the
ladder ratchet down, apparently more easily than the sergeant had
expected. The man jumped back, swearing, and said, "And I bet
there'll be spiders. Or rats. Maybe both."

His boots vanished up the rungs, and Mortimer extricated
himself from under the bed, not without some difficulty. His wing
was still smarting, but he didn't think he'd hurt it too badly. And
there was no time to check, anyway, because he could hear the
boards creaking in the ceiling as Graham patrolled the corners.
There was a certain amount of swearing, mostly regarding spiders,
drifting down too.

Mortimer was halfway to the bedroom door when a thought
occurred to him, and he stopped, wriggling in anxious indecision.
He couldn't exactly grab the computer and run out with it, but
maybe, there might be ... No. No, he had to *go!* He turned toward
the door, heard Graham bump his head in the attic and curse the
house and all its occupants very thoroughly, then turned back
again, thinking up some equally inventive curses for himself. He
scampered to the bed and checked the bedside table, trying to keep
his breathing shallow in case he inadvertently scorched something.
That'd be just marvellous. Burn the vicarage down with a police
officer inside it. He scrabbled impatiently through the small debris
of the vicar's life. Books, books, some socks and medications in the
top drawer, a jumble of old bookmarks and charging cables and
foreign currency in the bottom. And now there were footsteps
creaking back along the attic floor, and he leapt onto the bed itself,
flinging the pillows out of place. Surely, surely – *there!*

He threw himself off the bed without bothering to put the
pillows back, and ran lopsidedly for the door, clutching his prize
in one paw. He heard a foot scuff on the ladder as he shot silently

past it, then he was on the stairs, hoping the man's sounds would mask his own.

The steps were trickier than he'd thought, with only three paws to navigate them, and he was rounding the turn in the stairs when he stumbled, his tail catching the wall a solid thud.

"Who's there?" Graham demanded behind him, and Mortimer heard a much louder thud that he knew was the man dropping off the ladder to the floor of the landing. He lunged downward with a squeak of panic, and his front paw slid on the edge of the step. His hindquarters got the message too late, and he teetered on the point of balance for one moment, his stomach sick, thinking, *oh, bollocks.* His wings flared to try and save him, but they were hampered by the wall on one side and the banister on the other, and there was no stopping his forward momentum. His hindquarters overtook his sliding fore paw, and he tumbled tail over head all the way to the bottom of the stairs, hearing Graham shouting behind him.

He did a full roll as he hit the floor at the bottom, fetching up against the hall table and sending a vase of flowers crashing to the carpet.

"*Stop!*" the sergeant bellowed, but he hadn't reached the turn of the stairs yet, and Mortimer bolted for the front door, claws snagging on the carpet and almost tripping him again. This was it, this was how it happened, this was how the modern world was going to discover dragons. By arresting one trespassing on a crime scene. He whimpered and tried to go faster.

A shadow loomed through the frosted glass of the front door, and Mortimer was still trying to stop when it swung open in front of him.

"Hello?" Miriam called. "Anyone – *ooh!*" She jumped back as Mortimer accelerated past her, spines flat to his back and wings long and streamlined.

"Who's there?" Graham bellowed. "Stop where I can see you!"

Mortimer stopped just before he ran snout-first into the low wall that surrounded the vicarage and looked back, panting with fright and effort. Miriam was standing in the doorway, smiling brightly up at the man who'd pushed past her into the garden.

"I just thought I'd pop by and see if you wanted some tea bringing down or anything, Graham. I didn't realise you'd be in the house. I thought it was like one of those movie stake-outs, where you sit in the car all night and eat doughnuts."

He took a few steps toward the gate, frowning as he examined the yard and the shadows beyond it with unnervingly sharp eyes. "Did you see anyone else, Ms Ellis?"

"Miriam, please. The number of times you and Colin have stopped in for tea and sandwiches!"

He looked at her finally, and sighed. "What are you doing here, Miriam?"

"I just wanted to see if I should bring you some tea."

"No, you shouldn't. And you shouldn't even be here. You must realise all the W.I. are under suspicion."

"Yes, and it's completely ridiculous." She sounded outraged, and Mortimer felt a rush of admiration for her. He didn't think he could have faced the sergeant quite so boldly.

Graham sighed again and ran both hands over his greying hair. "*Did* you see anyone else?"

"Not a person," Miriam said confidently, and Mortimer supposed that was technically correct, although he did feel that "person" was a term that could be used more broadly than humans tended to.

§♠

GRAHAM SENT Miriam away with an admonition to do herself a favour and not hang around crime scenes anymore, and to tell her friend the same thing.

"What friend?" Miriam asked brightly, but Mortimer didn't

think she lied quite so convincingly this time, and apparently the sergeant didn't either, because he shooed her away and went back inside, locking the door firmly behind him. By the time they reached the tree where Beaufort sat waiting, his tail curled neatly over his toes, every light in the vicarage was on, and they could see Graham going from room to room. Mortimer had a feeling that he wouldn't be skipping checking under the beds this time.

Miriam didn't pause or glance at either dragon, just walked straight through the grave markers, grown dark and sombre as the dusk drew in, and headed for the stile that led out of the church-yard. Mortimer followed her, still hobbling on three legs, but when Beaufort caught up to him and said, "What've you got there, lad?" he just shook his head and clutched his prize more tightly. He didn't want to look at it, even *think* about it, until they were out of sight of the house. It was taking all his concentration just to stay faint, and his wings itched as if he could feel the sergeant watching them from the vicarage windows. In the rapidly fading light it was doubtful the man would even see the way the grass stayed flat-tened for a little too long after Miriam passed, let along discern the two dragons trotting behind her, but still. It wasn't worth taking the risk.

Miriam climbed over the stile and promptly collapsed on the soft grass to the side of the path, narrowly missing a nettle. Mortimer sprawled next to her, his legs feeling too shaky to hold him up very much longer and his wing still smarting. Plus it felt like he'd grazed his nose in the tumble down the stairs.

"*There* you are," Alice said. "That took rather a long time, didn't it?"

"Mortimer was *stuck*," Miriam said, pushing her hair out of her face and huffing in relief. "Graham almost saw him! It was a terribly close thing!"

"So close," Mortimer mumbled, and rubbed his cheek on the grass, barely resisting the urge to roll. It smelt an awful lot better than under the bed had, and he felt like the sad stink of the house was clinging to every scale.

"But you weren't caught," Alice said, her voice matter-of-fact. She was picking early bramble berries and dropping them into a bag, as if the whole breaking and entering thing was rather secondary to some evening foraging.

"And you did *wonderfully*, Mortimer," Beaufort said. "Honestly, lad, you were very clever, getting out again like that."

"I'd have been stuck if it wasn't for Miriam," Mortimer said, sitting up and struggling not to flush a pleased orange. "If she hadn't opened the door right at that moment, I don't know what would have happened." He shuddered, imagining being trapped against the door as Graham ran toward him, his scaly form slowly coming into focus, and the sergeant suddenly realising he was chasing a *dragon*. Because sometimes faint isn't enough, and sometimes even humans have to believe what they see, and he had an idea that police were probably good at that. A good thing they didn't carry guns here. And Mortimer hadn't seen a taser, but that didn't mean the sergeant didn't have one. Maybe it was hidden. His stomach rolled over in alarm, and his colour drained sadly away.

"I'm glad I helped," Miriam said. She looked much paler than usual, and her hair was standing out at worried angles. "But I think I may have acted a little suspiciously. I can't help it. I get nervous."

"Nonsense! You were wonderful," Beaufort said. "And never mind about the internet machine, Mortimer. We'll come up with another plan."

"About that," Mortimer said, and finally allowed himself a small, relieved smile.

"Oh, Mortimer," Alice said, as he held up the tablet he'd found under the pillows. "You are *quite* the housebreaker."

THE WALK back to Miriam's felt horribly long to Mortimer. Alice had taken the tablet and tucked it into her bag, but either he'd hurt his shoulder in the tumble down the stairs, or he was just stiff from the fright of everything, because he was still hobbling. Worst of all, he kept hearing the thunder of the sergeant's boots on the stairs behind him, and that terrible lump of fear was still sticking in his throat. It was something physical and awful, and he couldn't seem to budge it, even when he paused to drink from the stream that ran next to the path.

The water was cool, though, and soothing when he splashed it on his scales. And his heart seemed to have finally slowed from its panicked rhythm. He crouched for a moment on the verge of the stream, feeling the rocks beneath his paws and the softness of the night air, counting the night noises as they slowly crept up to supplant the day. The stink of the vicarage and his own panic was fading, being replaced by the quiet mossy scents of the wood, and the first of the stars were surfacing in the sky. He took a deep, careful breath, and realised that he was alright. That was a much bigger and more difficult thing than people realised, he thought. To be alright.

He stayed where he was for a little longer, until the night had stolen the sharp edges from the day and the world had settled around him, then turned to follow the path toward Miriam's. She and Alice had gone on ahead, using Alice's phone as a torch, but Beaufort was sitting quietly under the trees, his nose lifted to the stars. He looked like a misplaced statue, lost in the woods. He got up and fell into step with Mortimer, and they walked in quiet companionship for a little.

"Are you alright there, lad?" Beaufort asked finally, his voice low. Something in the underbrush scampered away in alarm, and somewhere else an owl called an unanswered question into the dark.

Mortimer sighed. "It was awful, Beaufort. I'm not cut out for this sort of thing."

"You did very well."

"I don't feel like I did very well, but that's not even the point. We *know* we need to be careful, we *know* it's risky even having the W.I. aware of us. I mean, you told us all what it was like in the old days."

"It was terrible," Beaufort said quietly, a softness in his voice that made Mortimer feel suddenly guilty for complaining, as if he were acting like a child, making objections and fussing without understanding. "But what's gone before does not dictate what happens now. We were hunted, yes. Many of us were slaughtered. That doesn't mean it'll happen again."

"But we're risking everything. We're risking people we don't trust finding out about us. Not just people, authorities. *Police.* They might try to capture us, want to examine us, or, or anything."

"So you think we should just step aside? Let the police handle everything?"

"It is their *job*, Beaufort."

Beaufort sighed slightly and looked up at the pale swathe of sky visible above them. "If we don't take risks for our friends, how can we call them friends? Friendship isn't a casual thing, Mortimer. Not true friendship. True friendship is the sort of thing that can save you. But it can also hurt you. Or get you discovered."

Mortimer couldn't think of a reply. He didn't think there was one. His tail still trembled when he thought of the sergeant so close behind him, and his wing hurt, and more than anything he just wanted to find a warm spot to curl up and sleep off the whole astonishing day, but friendship was friendship. No matter what the species.

They walked in silence after that, and it wasn't until they were wandering into the fragrant wilderness of Miriam's garden that Beaufort said, "Never mind, lad. Not everyone's cut out for housebreaking. You're terribly good at what you do, you know. No one has to be good at everything."

Mortimer opened his mouth to point out that he wasn't worried about being *good* at it, just that he'd almost been caught, then closed it again with a sigh. Because he had gone back for the tablet, hadn't he? He'd taken that risk, because he hadn't wanted to let the others down. He just hoped it had been worth it.

They headed toward the door, lying open on the warm, mellow light of Miriam's kitchen, and smelling of scones and flowers and friendship.

7

DI ADAMS

DI Adams stared at the ceiling of the interview room that was currently serving as her office. There was a cup of very watery black coffee in front of her, and she was wondering (again) what the hell she'd done, volunteering for this assignment. What the hell she was doing in *Skipton*, which was actually the biggest town in the area. Biggest. Town. As far as she could tell, its claims to fame were great pork pies and the fact that you could smell sheep from pretty much anywhere. Leeds was one thing. Small, sure, but you still felt you were in a *city*. It might not be the melting pot that London was, but it was still easy to pass unnoted. Plus you could get a decent cup of coffee, and a fry-up at any hour of the night. Here, she harboured suspicions that even the 24-hour shop wasn't actually open 24 hours.

She groaned and rubbed a hand over her eyes. She wasn't even sure why she was here. They had nothing to go on, and no one had even been in when she arrived except for the desk sergeant and one startled cleaner. So here she was, drinking crappy coffee and eating a yoghurt from the aforementioned may-not-actually-be-a-24-hour shop, and rereading her notes from yesterday's interviews. Not that they amounted to much. Bunch of gossipy women who had asked as many questions as they answered, as if her sole purpose there was to tell *them* what had happened. Give her Leeds any day. Or preferably London. That was *proper* policing. Not impromptu bloody bring-a-plate lunches and local officers not able to do anything about women wandering all over the place because it was their mum, or auntie, or whatever else.

She got up, stretched, and packed her tablet and notepad into her bag. This was pointless. She'd gone over the notes half a dozen times already, and nothing was helping. Sure, that Gertrude Lawrence woman had links in Manchester to some pretty dodgy characters, but most of it was from decades ago, and nothing that suggested she'd want to off the vicar. Then there was Alice Martin and her disappearing husband. That case was still technically open, which was interesting but probably not relevant. As for the rest of them, well, she wasn't going to learn any more sitting here staring at the walls, that was for sure. She'd run up to Toot Hansell (even the name was ridiculous) and see if anything new had turned up. Maybe knock on some doors. You never knew what you could rattle loose just by being *around*.

Toot Hansell nestled in the folds of the fells, in a valley that seemed to overflow with sunlight, rendering the stone houses bright and the flower-festooned gardens friendly. The waterways that surrounded the village and meandered between the buildings caught the sun with almost painful luminescence, and birds spun across the treetops. There were patches of mist collected in dips here and there in the fields, giving the whole place a fairy-tale edge, and no car was moving on the road but her own. There were a couple of people out walking dogs as she crossed the little bridge over the stream and slipped into the village streets, and they regarded the car with surprised but friendly expressions as she passed. One of them even waved, and DI Adams waved back automatically, then scowled and planted her hand back on the steering wheel. This place was *weird*.

She was pleasantly surprised to find that the tall sergeant (Graham Harrison, if she remembered right, and she almost always did) was awake and leaning on the bonnet of his car when she pulled up to the vicarage. She'd half expected him to have gone home at nightfall, or to be having tea with some woodland creatures or something.

"Morning, Inspector," he said as she climbed out of her car. It was splattered with mud and smellier things, and she'd managed to bash the wing mirror on a stone wall while trying to squeeze past a tractor. She examined the damage and sighed.

"Morning, Sergeant. Nice morning."

"It is," he agreed, and took a sip from a large pink thermos mug. There was half a bacon butty lying on a sheet of wax paper on the roof of his car, and her stomach growled. She could never work out how people went through the day on yoghurt and weren't ravenous all the time.

"No one relieved you last night, then?" she asked him.

He nodded thoughtfully. "PC Ben Shaw did ten till four. I kipped at his place."

"Oh. Well. That's nice."

He looked amused. "Easier than me driving home then coming back. Or someone else coming out. We manage, Detective Inspector."

"I'm sure you do," she said, reminding herself that she didn't need to feel like she'd just insulted him. It wasn't as if it was a professional rota system, was it?

The sergeant didn't seem bothered, anyway. He just drank his tea and watched the morning as if it were a spectacle laid on especially for him. DI Adams started to lean against her own car, remembered all the debris splattered across it, and just shoved her hands in her pockets and regarded the church instead.

It was still early, and the mellow morning light turned the old stone luminous, lit the trees and flowers that interspersed the gravestones, and painted the edges of everything in bright fresh shades. What could have been severe on a winter's day was gilded and full of a slow, gentle peace, a haven away from a world that was rushing uncontrollably from one distraction to another. It was a place that invited stillness, and DI Adams instinctively reached for her phone, meaning to put it on silent, then realised she was being ridiculous. The world didn't stop just because you were in some dead-end little village an hour's drive from anything that even resembled civilisation.

"All quiet, then?" she asked.

"Pretty much," he said, and pointed at the sandwich. "Do you want some? It's got HP sauce on."

DI Adams gave an impatient wave. "What d'you mean, *pretty much?*"

He picked up the sandwich and took a bite, chewing carefully and swallowing before he answered. The inspector wondered if he was being deliberately slow, but she had a feeling he just didn't want to talk with his mouth full. "Well, Mrs Daniels—"

"Rosemary Daniels?" She flicked through the files in her mind, seeing women sitting across from her at the table in the village hall kitchen, over and over again. Daniels, Rosemary. Tall, blondish, bit of a horsey look to her. Loud laugh. Didn't stop knitting throughout the questioning.

"Yes, that's her. She came by with tea and a sandwich only about ten minutes ago. You just missed her."

A tragedy. Although, the sandwich was still making her stomach growl. Funny how bacon could still do that after fifteen years of vegetarianism. "You know we have reason to believe poison was involved here?"

"I know," Graham said comfortably, and took another bite. After more careful chewing and a swallow, he continued, "Considering I wrote down everything that happened while I was on watch, they'd be a bit silly to bring me a poisoned butty."

"You wrote it down?"

He patted his breast pocket. "I quite like pen and paper, Inspector. You can't delete much on pen and paper. Not without leaving some traces."

"You can if someone just steals your notepad."

"I'd be very surprised if that happened."

Looking at him, DI Adams had to admit that she'd be surprised if that happened, too. The sergeant was not a small man. "And did anything else happen, other than you being supplied with breakfast?"

He put his sandwich down, wiped his hands on a yellow spotted paper napkin, and pulled his notebook out of his pocket. "As a matter of fact, it did." He cleared his throat. "Eight-nineteen p.m., Ms Alice Martin brought me a sandwich. Ham and cheese on granary. With pickle."

DI Adams found herself wanting to roll her eyes and controlled the urge with difficulty. "You seem very popular with the sandwich-making brigade."

He grinned at her, and for a moment he looked like a cheeky schoolboy, even if he was well over six foot, and the wrong side of forty to boot. "I'll charm anyone for a bacon butty, me."

The inspector snorted. "I'm sure you would. Did Ms Martin want anything else? Ask any strange questions?"

"No." He shifted against the car as if it was suddenly no longer such a comfortable spot, and looked at his tea rather than at her when he answered. "But something, well, *weird* happened while she was here."

"Weird? Weird how?" The day sharpened around her, the tease of a case a better pick-me-up than any triple-shot coffee.

"Well, I heard something from the other side of the house. When I went around to check it, there was an upstairs window open."

"Was it open when you arrived?"

He looked uneasy. "I think so."

DI Adams took a deep breath. She'd been on scene earlier, too. She couldn't blame him. She should have noticed it herself. She nodded. "And?"

"And I sent Ms Martin away, and went through the house. I was checking the attic when I heard, or thought I heard, someone on the stairs." He hesitated, a flush creeping up under his collar. "So I identified myself, and gave chase, but when I got downstairs there was only Miriam – Ms Ellis – opening the door from the *outside*."

"Ms Ellis? She was with Ms Martin?"

"No, Ms Martin had already left."

DI Adams frowned. "That seems like quite a coincidence, them showing up one after the other."

"I suppose." He didn't sound convinced.

She supposed that half the village had been around feeding him, so maybe it wasn't that far-fetched. "And Ms Ellis couldn't have been inside?"

"No. I'd have caught her. And she wasn't even breathing hard."

Ellis, Miriam. The witness. A little below average height. Somewhat round. Lots of curly, grey-streaked hair. Smelt of incense and that wood all the hippies like. Sandalwood. No, she didn't look like she'd be able to out-run an officer, especially not one who looked as fit as the sergeant. "She was definitely coming in from outside?"

"Yes. I was in a rush. I didn't lock the door."

"And no one went past her?"

"I went straight out. There was no one there."

DI Adams sighed and rubbed her forehead, the sharpness of the day fading. "What did she say she wanted?"

"To see if I needed any tea."

"Of course." They stood in silence for a moment, watching the house, then the inspector said, "You searched the house."

"Yes. Straight away."

She sighed again. "Alright. I'll just go in and take a look anyway." She held her hand out for the keys, then let herself in the rickety little gate and walked to the front door, feeling the warmth of the sun fade as the house swallowed her in shadows.

SHE PULLED on some disposable gloves as she checked the downstairs rooms, but they were as she remembered from the day before. Old, mismatched furniture and threadbare carpet, the curtains a little sad and ragged. Either the parish didn't have much money, or the vicar had been particularly unconcerned about his living arrangements. It smelt musty, too, of old meals and mildew, and she shivered despite herself.

The outdated kitchen was untouched, the same mug and bowl in the draining board, the fridge wheezing to itself in the corner like an exhausted donkey. She checked the lock on the door, and the window latches, but they didn't seem to have been tampered with. For someone to have climbed in the upstairs window would have taken a seriously good climber or a good-sized ladder, which the sergeant could hardly have missed. She worked her way back to the hall, wondering how long he'd been away from the front door. Long enough for someone to let themselves in? She'd have to see just how accurate his note-taking was.

The morning light coming through the open front door lit the worn carpet, and the inspector stopped, frowning, then crouched down. From here it looked like – she inched her way forward, running her fingers over the carpet. There were *tears* in it, slashes so long and fine that they could have been made with a scalpel. She found a pen in her pocket and worked the tip into one, peering at the floor underneath. Yes, scratches on the old wood, like someone had run a Stanley knife over it. But *why?* She frowned at it for a while, then pulled her phone out and took some photos, making sure to indicate the length of the slashes, and where they were in relation to the stairs and door. They made her think of a cat, sliding down the trunk of a tree.

She was trying to get the angle right to take one last photo when her knee went in something wet. She gave a *gurk* sound and shuffled back on her haunches to investigate. There was a broad patch of dampness not far from the hall table, almost invisible against the dull carpet, and on closer examination she found a few flower petals stuck to the wet material. She got up and walked to the door, shaking her trouser leg out.

"Oi! Did you knock over the vase on the hall table?"

Graham, who'd been looking at his phone, jumped guiltily. "Um, yes. I think."

"You think?"

"It was over when I went back in to check on the place, after Ms Ellis left. I guess maybe I bumped it on the way down the stairs and just didn't notice."

DI Adams went back inside without answering, and looked from the hall table to the stairs. He must have been careening about like a drunken zebra, then. She jumped up and down on the floorboards a few times, and they creaked obligingly, but the hall table was old and solid, and the flowers barely shivered.

"Huh," she said, and took another picture, then made some notes on her phone. And then she went upstairs.

SHE WASN'T ENTIRELY sure what she expected to find, but none of it made any more sense than the slashes in the hall carpet. There were more scratches on the stairs, and some scuffing on the banisters that looked fresh. After shouting a question to Graham, she went into the spare bedroom and examined the window that he'd found open. Scratches on the sill, not as deep, but again as if a cat, a big one, had clawed its way into the room. She hung out the window, and although the light was still dull on this side of the house, she could see clean, light grey stone where more scratches were cut through the weathered surface of the wall.

She took more photos, although she wasn't sure what she was taking photos *of*. Someone had walked up the side of the house in, what, ice crampons? And then left them on and gone sliding about the hall in them? Even if they had, surely they would have just caught in the carpet, not sliced it so neatly. So someone walked up the wall in ice crampons, skipped down the stairs in them, then slashed the hall floor with a Stanley knife, just for the fun of it?

She put her fists on her hips, puffing air over her bottom lip. This wasn't making sense. They couldn't mean anything, those scratches. On the wall, maybe, but in the *hall?* She walked into the vicar's bedroom, tapping her pen off her teeth, and stopped short.

The bed *had* been made. She was quite sure of it. She was especially sure she'd have remembered the vicar's bright blue-and-yellow Minion print pyjamas, which were neatly folded where the pillows had been. Poor guy. Those pyjamas were about the most alive things in the whole damn house.

The thought was fleeting, and she shook it off, examining the bed carefully, taking photos as she went. The blanket was rucked up, as if a dog had been playing on it. It seemed intact, though, unlike the pillows. She poked one, and it burped feathers into the still air of the bedroom.

"Huh," she said again, and poked the other. That one had less holes, but it was definitely leaking. Feathers floated about the room in the dusty air, and she sneezed. Great, that was all she needed. Hay fever kicking in. She stood back, crossed her arms and considered the bed, then crouched down and peered under it.

There were a lot of dust bunnies under there, a sock, a couple of pound coins, and a broad swathe of carpet that was cleaner and darker than the rest of it.

DI Adams sighed, took her jacket off, and wriggled under the bed on her belly, poking into the corners and examining the carpet for more of those scratches. There were some, although not as long or deep. They were more the sort of scratches an animal might make crawling into a burrow. So now she was thinking about rabbits. Rabbits, dogs, and giant cats. Superb. Three months out of London and she was inventing mysterious beasts rather than solving crimes.

She sighed deeply enough to send a couple of spider webs drifting away from her, and wriggled out backward, her shirt tangling up under her armpits. She sat on the floor for a moment, wondering if she could still get her old job back, then lay on her back and pulled herself under the bed again, using her phone as a torch to examine the underside of the bed base. You never knew. Hair could get snagged, scraps of clothing. Scales.

She blinked, and reached out to touch it, then recovered herself and took half a dozen photos first. Then she pulled the – well, yes, the *scale* for want of a better word (although it was as big as her thumbnail, and unless the vicar was storing large game fish under his bed, she couldn't imagine what it had come from) clear of the bed base, and pushed herself back out into the room. Then she sat there in the morning light washing through the dusty windows with her hair fluffed out in uncooperative directions and a spider web festooning one ear, and examined it.

The scale was translucent, running with the sorts of blues and greens and golds that you found in opals, and it was so light in her hands she barely felt like she was holding anything at all. It was hard, though. When she ran her finger along the edge there was no give to it. She tried twisting it, gently, but it didn't flex. She tried to bend it in half, and it stayed resolutely solid. It was beautiful. And utterly, utterly impossible.

"Huh," Detective Inspector Adams said to the empty house, and tried not to think of London. Not the good bits, like proper 24-hour shops and decent coffee and food of every sort you wanted to name, but the way that things had got *weird*. Because that was done. That was gone. And this was just, well, this was just, "A scale," she said firmly, and wondered if the sergeant had any other food in his car.

8
ALICE

Alice inspected Miriam's basket of scones with what she hoped was merely a quizzical expression on her face. She knew that she sometimes tended to look a little *severe*, and Miriam was nervous enough this morning, as evidenced by the broken mug sitting by the back door and the tea-stained cushion drying in the sun.

"Wholemeal flour, Miriam?"

"Um. Spelt. And chickpea flour."

"How interesting." She couldn't quite bring herself to say *lovely*. The scones looked as if Mortimer had sat on them, and they were very well cooked. She could see where Miriam had scraped the charred bits off the edges.

"I'm sorry," Miriam said, sitting down at the garden table with a sigh, and making it rock enthusiastically. Alice rescued her tea before it could slop over. "I should have just done plain scones."

"You didn't have to do anything. This is a strategy meeting, not morning tea."

"I don't think Beaufort would have been very impressed if there weren't any scones."

Alice smiled. It was true that the High Lord was unimpressed with any gathering that didn't include baked goods. After they'd made their way back to Miriam's last night, they'd had a cup of tea while they decided what to do, and the dragons had polished off not just the remains of the banana cake but two packets of crumpets that had been in the freezer as well.

In the end they'd decided that it was late, and that they should wait to look at the tablet. In that particular part of northern England, the sun didn't set until almost nine at night in springtime, and it had been down long enough for it be almost full dark by the time they made it back to Miriam's. And while that wasn't *late* exactly, it was late enough for a day that had involved dealings with the police and some lightly criminal activity.

Alice touched the tablet where it lay on the garden table next to the jam and butter dishes. Miriam always went to such effort, she thought. Tea in a proper teapot, milk in a jug, jam and butter decanted into their own little containers. She had a sneaking suspicion that it wasn't how Miriam usually ate, especially judging by the fact that the containers in question looked distinctly like those pots you could buy desserts in at the supermarket, but still. It was nice.

"Have you looked at the tablet yet, Miriam?" she asked.

"No! Oh, no. I didn't want to look at it." Miriam wrinkled her nose and poured some more tea. "It feels like prying."

"That's investigating for you."

"I know, but still. It feels wrong," Miriam said, and wiped her mouth. There were a few crumbs still stuck to her cheek from those dreadful cheese things she ate whenever she was stressed.

Alice nodded in understanding and took a sip of her tea. Not everyone was suited to investigating.

They sat together quietly in the warm morning sun, listening to the soft chatter of the stream beyond the gate, and to the bees going about their business amid the blowsy roses and sweet-smelling honeysuckle, and they waited for dragons.

&

THE DRAGONS WEREN'T LATE, exactly. Alice always wondered how they knew what time to arrive, given that they didn't use clocks. Mortimer had been the first to start embracing modern technology, although it had so far been mostly limited to the gas barbecues, and a fascination with both Miriam's TV and Etsy. The barbecues had been a huge success among the Cloverly dragons, and made their caverns much less smoky as well as saving them spending an inordinate amount of time searching for firewood. Mortimer, however, was already calculating how many dragon-scale toys he'd have to sell in order to be able to buy the older dragons AGAs. He was very taken with Miriam's.

However they told the time, it was only a few minutes after nine when the dragons let themselves in the gate and came padding up the path, having stopped flying a safe enough distance from the village to avoid being seen. It's hard for even the most stubborn brain to argue against the existence of dragons when they're winging across the sky. Miriam patted Mortimer on the shoulder and got up to put another pot of tea on.

"Good morning, Beaufort, Mortimer," Alice said gravely. "How's everyone feeling this morning?"

"Terrible," Mortimer announced. "I had nightmares about that huge dog all night."

Beaufort inspected the table with interest. "Now, lad. I'm sure he's very nice if you get to know him." He selected a scone, and Alice dolloped jam and cream on it before he could try doing it himself. Spoons are tricky for dragons.

"He's drool-y," Miriam announced, reappearing with two oversized soup mugs and a new, catering-sized pot of tea. "Not very clever, and drool-y."

"There you go, lad," Beaufort said, and gave Mortimer the scone Alice had handed him. "He doesn't sound dangerous at all."

Mortimer sighed, and took the scone. "Maybe not, but I'd rather not meet him again."

Alice doled out more cream and jam while Miriam poured the tea, and for a moment there was just the soft rumbling sound of contented dragons, and the click of claws against porcelain. Then Alice said, "So. Shall we proceed?"

"Oh, do we have to?" Miriam asked. She'd been looking the happiest she had since discovering the vicar two days ago, but now anxious lines popped up on her forehead. "I really think this is a bad idea. We should just put it back."

Mortimer spluttered on his tea. "I'm not putting it back! That was quite enough criminal activity for my entire *life*."

"You're only a hundred and twelve, lad," Beaufort said. "Don't limit yourself like that."

Mortimer gave him a distinctly murderous look and took another scone.

"Well, we could just leave it somewhere where someone else will find it," Miriam said. "Like in the hall, or the church or something."

"And what if that someone steals it?" Alice asked. "Then no one gets to find any clues on it."

"But the vicar would have had a phone. And there was a computer in the vicarage, I know. He asked me to help him update his blog on it once." Miriam was a firm believer in both the power of essential oils and spirit guides, and the necessity of having a good web presence for the modern self-employed clairvoyant.

"Then no one will miss this one." Alice looked at the tablet, the screen flat and black and innocuous in the sunlight. "Unless you think you might not be able to get into it, or something. I imagine it's probably pretty tricky, even for someone as good with computers as you."

"No," Miriam said firmly. "No, don't do that. I'm not silly enough to fall for that." But her hand twitched toward the tablet.

"Of course, if we *did* give it back, we'd have to make up a story about where we found it," Beaufort said innocently. "And that detective inspector already sounded rather suspicious."

"She'll have been talking to that Graham at the vicarage," Mortimer added, sounding glum. "She'll know you were both there last night."

"What, *you* think we should do this, Mortimer?" Miriam demanded. "Snoop in a dead man's business?"

"We may as well," the young dragon said. "I didn't go through all that just to put it back again."

"Well." Miriam looked deflated, then pushed up her sleeves. "*Fine.* But I still think this is not a good thing to be doing. It must be terrible karma."

"Hopefully only for the murderer, when we catch them," Alice said.

THEY STARED AT THE TABLET, propped against a flowerpot full of basil in the middle of the garden table. *Hello, Vicar,* the screen said, making Alice think of one of those old and slightly dodgy TV shows. They'd been staring at it for a while now, long enough for the last of the tea to grow cold.

"Well, say hello to it," Beaufort said, for at least the third time.

"It doesn't work like that," Miriam said. "It needs a password, Beaufort."

"Try Toot Hansell," Alice suggested. It was what she used for most things, even though Miriam had told her more than once that it was too easy to guess and that she needed different ones for everything.

"I did. All one word, all lower case, changing the o's for 0's, the s for a 5. That's not it."

"Hello, small internet machine," Beaufort said, loudly and very close to Alice's ear. "We would very much like to look at some things on you." Alice leaned away and rubbed her ear briskly.

"It's not *voice-activated*," Mortimer said, sounding superior. Beaufort glared at him, and the young dragon buried his nose in his mug. "I mean, some things are. But not this. I imagine it'd have to be fancier than a tablet."

"Or just a fancier tablet," Miriam said, trying "vicarage".

"Can you not get in without the password?" Alice asked. Computers remained a mystery to her. Her phone she could just about manage, and the GPS in her car, but her laptop she only turned on when strictly necessary.

"I'm not a *hacker*."

"You fixed my laptop for me before. You're very good with them."

"Alice, you had no anti-virus software. I just ran a scan."

"They have viruses?" Beaufort asked, moving away from the table. "Are they catching?"

"Not that sort of virus," Alice said, and pointed at the screen suddenly. If the vicar was the sort of person who had trouble with computers, too ... "Try 'hello'."

"Well, it won't be *that*," Miriam said, typing it in.

The screen blinked, then the plain Windows blue slid aside to reveal icons scattered haphazardly across a Minions background. They were waving bananas.

"I said you had to say hello to the machine," Beaufort said. "You youngsters. No etiquette."

🐉

ALICE WASN'T QUITE sure what they were hoping to find. An email with the subject line, "ha-ha, I did it," perhaps? But it felt good to be doing *something*. It was the helplessness she couldn't stand. She'd known when the inspector had started asking about useless old Harvey that it was all going to come back, but she'd tried to ignore it. It hadn't been until late last night, lying in her bed and staring at the ceiling, that she'd felt that terrible constriction winding down over her chest, the sweat rising on her forehead despite the open window and the curtains moving softly in the night breeze.

She'd gone downstairs and made herself a decaf coffee with a healthy dose of whisky in it, and drank it sitting on the bench in the quiet, safe dark of her garden, listening to the little snuffling noises of the night creatures. It had been twelve years, and she could still smell the interview room at the police station, still taste the bleak coffee and anaemic toast that she'd made herself eat, just to keep her energy up. Getting too tired, getting teary or emotional, that wasn't an option for her.

She'd answered the questions they threw at her in a flat, reserved tone, denied the accusations, direct and implied, without ever raising her voice. And she knew what they said: cold, hard, emotionless. That was fine. She would not – she would *never* – have them call her irrational. The situation was ugly enough as it was without enduring that.

And eventually they had let her go, as she'd known they'd have to, because there was no evidence against her. And maybe she should have been the one to report him missing, and not his golf buddies, but it had seemed so *unimportant*. The marriage had limped along because she had been stationed away most of the time. When she came home, it had seemed inevitable that it couldn't continue. And the way it had happened had saved her having to deal with the messiness of a divorce, with all its attendant petty squabbles and emotional bubblings.

But the helplessness, not able to do anything more than affirm her innocence over and over again, to answer the same questions over and over again, and to wait for people she didn't know to decide on her freedom ...

That had been intolerable.

And now here it was again, being dug up in another village, another time, and the spectre of all those hours of questioning, all that hideous confinement, loomed over her like some stalking giant. But she would not be helpless. Not this time. She cleared her throat slightly, and took a sip of tea, pleased to see that her hand wasn't trembling. "Do we have anything, Miriam?"

"A lot of junk," Miriam said. "He must have been signed up for every rubbishy newsletter in existence."

Alice peered over her shoulder. Holiday brochures. Double-glazing companies. Clothing. Movie offers. A wine club – no, two – no, *three* of those. Things for comparing utilities, or car insurance, or life insurance. "This is why I don't like email," she said. "At least with the proper mail, you can put a note on the letterbox and you don't get all this rubbish."

"It should all just go into spam," Miriam said.

"Spam?" Beaufort asked. "Isn't that some sort of sandwich meat?"

"If you can call it that," Alice said.

"I wouldn't say no to a sandwich," Beaufort said, regarding the empty scone plate sadly.

"I'll make some in a moment," Miriam said, and Alice watched her tap over into the email folders, swiping past things like *Church Accounts,* and *Fete Bookings.* "Ah, here we go. *Personal.*"

"Ooh," Mortimer said as soon as she opened it, and Beaufort forgot about the sandwich.

"Oh dear," the High Lord said.

"What?" Alice couldn't see anything in the innocuous email headings that could have them so worried.

"Can't you feel it?" Mortimer asked.

"Feel what?"

"All the anger," Beaufort said quietly. "All the worry, the fear, the sadness. Every time the vicar opened that folder, it's all he was feeling. Those thingies there are soaked in it." He pointed at the screen, and Miriam pulled the tablet back in time to save his talon chipping it.

"You can tell what he was *feeling?*" she asked.

"Emotional traces linger. Over and over he looked at those message things, and felt terrible emotions, and now they reflect it back every time anyone looks at them."

Alice tapped her forefinger against her lips gently. "Can you tell what the people who sent them were feeling?"

"Well, no," Beaufort said, as if that should be obvious. "If it was real mail, that the person had touched, yes. But this is just thingy. Dingbats." Alice, Miriam and Mortimer stared at him. "Dinghies. Didgeridoos. Dirigibles. Mortimer, you know what I mean."

Alice and Miriam looked expectantly at the smaller dragon, and he frowned, then said, "Oh. Digital?"

"That's the one."

"Well. Life is nothing if not a learning experience," Alice said. "Can you tell if it was maybe one in particular that made him feel like that?"

Both dragons leaned over the screen, and Miriam opened the first one. It was from a parishioner who had just signed herself Kelli, with a sad face as well as a kissing emoji, and asked the vicar why he wouldn't come around for tea. Her previous invitation and his reply were below the message. His included lots of sorries and a very firm no.

"Keep going," Beaufort said, and she opened the next.

Hey Norm, it said. *It's been too long. The boys and I are still set on this deal. You in, or are we going to have to come drag you out?*

It was signed only S.B., and Miriam tapped the screen. "That's been sent to a different email address. It's not the vicar@toothansell.com one."

"Interesting," Alice said. "So the vicar had two email addresses? That seems suspicious."

Miriam wrinkled her nose. "Not really. I have one I use for important stuff, and one I use to sign up for newsletters and things, so the main one doesn't get clogged up."

Alice thought that one email address was more than enough for any sensible person, but she let it go. "What does that, um, smell like?"

"The same as the other," Beaufort said apologetically. "Angry, sad, worried, scared."

"I think the whole folder is the same," Mortimer said. "It's what he felt about any of his personal things, maybe."

"That's terribly sad," Miriam said quietly, and clicked on the next email.

Hello, Vicar! Lol, that still makes me laugh. Didn't think I'd forgotten you, did you? Get back to me. S.B.

"This S.B. may be worth looking into," Alice said. "Did the vicar reply to him?"

"Doesn't look like it," Miriam said. "The replies should be with the emails, like with the first one. I'll check the sent items after we've been through them, though. Just in case."

The next email was from someone calling herself Violet.

Norman, if you don't call me back IMMEDIATELY I'm coming up there!!!!

And another, a few days earlier:

Norman! Why are you ignoring me??? Answer your phone!!

"Violet seems very fond of exclamation marks," Alice said.

"Never a good sign," Miriam replied. "I wonder if she was the woman I saw the other night?" There were a few more emails from her and a couple more from S.B., all of which Miriam pointed out had been sent to the vicar's private email rather than the vicarage one, and then a new one. It was to the vicarage email address, and was from bestbakerboy@yahoo.com.

Why havnt u answered my msg?? Its about my entree in the fate!!!!

"The fate?" Beaufort asked. "He's having a starter with Fate?"

"I'm guessing he means an entry in the summer fete," Alice said. "But he likes exclamation marks, too."

"There's more," Miriam said.

R U listning??? Answr me!!! Ur in bed w the WI, giveing them all the prizes!!! Its corropt!!!!

"Well, that's rather inappropriate," Alice said.

"It was sent at two in the morning. All the ones from him are around that time," Miriam said.

"So he couldn't sleep?" Beaufort asked, scratching his ear. "That seems a poor excuse for being so rude."

Alice smiled. "I think Miriam means that BestBakerBoy may have been a little tipsy."

"Oh. Well, it's still no excuse." Beaufort leaned forward again as Miriam clicked on a third message.

Dont ignor me!!! I will win the fate and u kno it!!! Not thos old cows in the vilage!!

"I thought it was mostly sheep around here," Beaufort said.

"Not those sort of cows," Alice said. "The W.I. sort of cows."

The old dragon huffed yellow steam. "The horrible man! What a horrendous thing to say. I shall go visit him immediately!"

Miriam laughed. "We don't even know who it is, Beaufort."

"But he has an address!"

"It's an internet address," Mortimer said, clutching his mug to his chest in both paws. The High Lord had gone a threatening puce colour.

"Well, I, I—"

"More tea?" Alice suggested. "Maybe a sandwich."

"Well—"

"I think that's a good idea," Miriam said, moving the tablet before Beaufort's furious breath could melt the edges. "Then we can have another look."

"I suppose it couldn't hurt," Beaufort admitted. "One doesn't want to come across such an unpleasant individual on an empty stomach."

"Quite," Alice said, and Mortimer let out a little sigh, his shoulders slumping. Miriam got up to go back into the house, and at that moment a clear voice echoed across the garden.

"Hello? Ms Ellis? It's DI Adams. Are you out here?"

9

MIRIAM

M iriam squeaked, tried to get out from behind the bench, stepped on her own skirt then Mortimer's tail, and would have fallen into the hydrangeas if Alice hadn't grabbed her arm.

"Just out here, Inspector," Alice called, and Miriam gave a little hiccoughing cry of alarm. Alice lowered her voice. "Are you quite alright, Miriam?"

"*No*," Miriam hissed back. "She's *here*! That means she knows about last night! And now she'll ask about the tablet, and oh, oh—" It suddenly felt very hard to breathe, and she sat down heavily on the bench.

"Please pull yourself together," Alice said mildly, and although Miriam wanted to wail that it was entirely unfair to expect anyone to be together, considering the circumstances, she managed, after a fashion. Mortimer was clutching his tail, looking both pained and alarmed, and she whispered, "Sorry." He nodded violently.

Miriam was still taking deep breaths and concentrating on soothing her aura when the detective inspector ducked under an overhanging branch of the apple tree and stood looking at them in a way that suggested she was probably trying to appear friendly and approachable but wasn't quite sure how to go about it.

"Good morning Ms Martin, Ms Ellis," the inspector said.

"Good morning," Alice said, smiling, and nudged Miriam.

"Eep. Morn. Morning," Miriam managed, and felt herself going pink.

"Are you alright, Ms Ellis?"

Miriam nodded enthusiastically. It was the 'Ms Ellis' as much as anything else that unnerved her. If DI Adams would only call her Miriam, she would feel much better. But she'd asked the inspector to do just that during the interview at the village hall, when they had gone over and over Miriam discovering the vicar's body while the inspector pried at her answers from every direction with an inexhaustible persistence that now seemed dreadfully threatening. She'd insisted on calling her Ms Ellis all the way through. It was probably some rule about not being too friendly with suspects. Suspects! She swallowed hard and tried to focus on her aura again.

"May I offer you a cup of tea, Inspector?" Alice asked. "And are there any more scones inside, Miriam?"

Miriam shook her head, and tried to say that she'd get the tea, but she couldn't seem to make her voice work. And the tablet was there, *right there* on the table. What if the inspector was looking for it? What if she *knew* it was missing? They were all going to jail. Well, not the dragons. But she and Alice were.

"A cuppa would be lovely," the inspector said, still looking at Miriam curiously. Miriam tried to infuse her aura with innocence, but she was pretty sure that if the detective inspector *could* see auras, she'd have arrested Miriam by now.

"Do sit down," Alice said. "I'll be right back."

Don't go! Miriam wailed, but inside her head. The detective inspector sat down and smiled at her. She had a nice smile, with slightly crooked teeth. It would have put Miriam quite at ease, if her eyes hadn't been so keen and quick above it.

"This is a lovely garden, Ms Ellis."

Miriam nodded enthusiastically, spreading her fingers to show just how appreciative she was of the inspector's compliment.

"So many wonderful plants. I'm terrible with plants. I had a spider plant in London once, but it jumped to its death from the top of the fridge rather than put up with me."

Miriam made a sad face.

"Do you grow a lot of your own produce?"

Miriam nodded. This was okay. She could do this.

"And is this a herb garden here?" the inspector asked, pointing at a Miriam's crowded collection of staggered, mismatched pots and troughs, all full of medicinal herbs and plants that she steeped, or dried, or crushed into pastes. "What have you got here? I recognise the mint, but that's about it."

Answer, Miriam's brain commanded, but her tongue was stuck to the roof of her mouth. She had the momentary, panicked thought that she might never be able to talk again, then one very sharp claw tapped her bare foot, not hard enough to break the skin, but hard enough to make her jump up and run across to the herb beds.

"Lemongrass," she said, pointing wildly. "Verbena. St John's Wort. Valerian. Ginger. Um. Yes."

"Oh, are you showing Detective Inspector Adams your herb garden?" Alice asked, coming down the little path with a clean mug in one hand and the regular-sized teapot in the other. Miriam felt her shoulders slump at the sight of her. Things couldn't go too wrong with Alice here. "She does have a wonderful garden, does Miriam."

"I was just complimenting her on it," DI Adams said, looking away from Miriam finally. Her eyes slid over the garden, up rather than down, as if there was something on the ground that she didn't want to see. Miriam raised her eyebrows at Beaufort, and he grinned back, teeth yellow against his greenish skin. Mortimer didn't look at either of them. He was flat on his belly with his front paws over his eyes and his wings wrapped around him like a bat, as if that was going to make him somehow less visible. Miriam thought he needn't worry. It didn't seem to her like Detective Inspector Adams was the sort of person who saw dragons, even if she had an uneasy feeling that she saw an awful lot else.

"It's wonderful," Alice was saying. "Miriam keeps us all supplied with cold remedies, stomach ache cures – everything one could wish for, really."

"I mostly make soaps," Miriam surprised herself by saying. "And skin creams. To sell."

"They must be very popular," the inspector said, watching Alice pour out the tea. Beaufort and Mortimer's big mugs sat squatly on the end of the table, and some messy flowers had appeared in them, as if they had every right to be there. Miriam supposed that dragons must be quite adept at hiding any evidence of themselves, after all these centuries of pretending to be nothing more than stories.

"They do okay," Miriam agreed, starting to feel a little more confident.

The inspector took a sip of tea and gave an appreciative sigh. "Oh, that's very nice."

"Can't beat a good cuppa," Miriam agreed, and grimaced when Alice looked at her sharply. Oh, no. She was going to start babbling now, wasn't she? First she couldn't talk, now she was going to babble? She swallowed hard against a horrified giggle and concentrated on her mug.

There was a moment of quiet as the women sipped their tea, and the inspector looked everywhere except at the dragons. Finally she nodded almost casually at the tablet, still lying in plain view, and said, "That seems a bit out of keeping."

Miriam tried to say *isn't it* and *it isn't* at the same time, and came out with something that sounded like "Isnisn."

"Sorry?" The DI looked perplexed, and Miriam squeaked when Alice trod rather firmly on her bare toes.

"Our Miriam does very well, selling online," Alice said. "Etsy and so on."

"Is that so?"

"*Mm-hmm*." Miriam decided she was better not to speak.

"It's rather clever. Quite beyond me, all this stuff. But she was just showing me her new listing for crystal-embellished dream-catchers. They're very pretty indeed. Would you like to take a look, Inspector?"

Miriam almost spat her tea out. Alice couldn't mean that she wanted her to fire up the *vicar's tablet*, right here in front of the inspector? That was madness! Then she saw that DI Adams was shaking her head firmly and making those little hand movements people use when they're trying to be polite but really, really don't want something.

"No, no. That's fine. Wonderful that you can find such an audience for your, ah, work."

The busy garden silence descended again, and Miriam allowed herself a moment to feel both impressed by Alice's judgement of the inspector's character, and mildly insulted that she'd been able to hear air quotes around the word "work".

"So," DI Adams said, and placed her mug very neatly on the table, the handle exactly parallel with the edge. Miriam was embarrassed to see it was a cartoon donkey one that she'd brought back from Spain. "I understand you were both at the vicarage last night."

Miriam opened her mouth to deny it, and Alice spoke over her. "That's right, Inspector. We only realised when we met for tea this morning. I imagine we were both worried about Graham out there all the night with no dinner." She sounded faintly reproachful, and the DI opened her mouth, shut it again, then finally found her words.

"Well, you'll be pleased to know he wasn't there all night, and that he didn't starve, either."

"Oh, I'm glad to hear he got a break. And Rosemary did say she was going to take him breakfast, so I guess we covered all bases."

Alice and the inspector were watching each other in a strange, cautious way that made Miriam uncomfortable. Alice was terribly *good* with people. She always seemed to be able to get them to do pretty much as she wanted, and they'd think it was their own idea. But Miriam thought that the detective inspector was something beyond what Alice was used to dealing with, and she wondered if Alice herself realised that. If she realised that she couldn't deflect an investigation with a stern look and a sharp comment. She hoped very much that Alice *did* realise it. It could be the undoing of them all if she didn't.

"It appears there was some disturbance at the house while you were both there, too," Detective Inspector Adams said.

"Graham heard a noise, yes," Alice said. "And Miriam told me this morning that he came rushing out of the vicarage just as she arrived."

"So you two didn't know the other was there? You didn't cross paths?"

"There are at least three separate ways to get to the vicarage, Inspector. We live in different parts of the village. It would have been more surprising if we *had* crossed paths."

The inspector took another mouthful of tea, frowning at the garden as if realising that something wasn't quite right, but not sure just what. She put the mug down, rubbed her eyes, and looked at Miriam. "Why did you open the door on an active crime scene, Ms Ellis?"

Miriam squeaked. She couldn't help it, it just slipped out.

"Inspector," Alice said, the word an admonishment.

The inspector ignored her. "Why didn't you just knock?"

"I *did*," Miriam managed, feeling suddenly indignant. As if she'd have just walked in *anywhere* without knocking! "But I heard Graham shouting, and thought maybe he was saying to come in." She hadn't thought anything of the sort, she'd been worried he was shouting at Mortimer, but she couldn't exactly say that, especially with the inspector looking increasingly uncomfortable, frowning unhappily and rubbing her eyes every time she looked at the garden.

"Why would you think he was telling you to come in?"

"Well, why wouldn't he?"

"Because it was a *crime* sc— Oh, forget it." The detective inspector got up so hurriedly that her chair almost tipped over. She grabbed it, and said, "I'm sorry, ladies, but I'm going to have to go. I think something in your garden is triggering my allergies."

"Oh, I'm so sorry," Miriam said. "Can I get you something? Some local honey tea, maybe, or a neti pot?"

"A neti …? No. No thanks." DI Adams looked faintly revolted. "Is there a chemist in town?"

"Not here," Alice said. "You'll be best going back to Skipton for that."

"Of course I will." The inspector sighed heavily, and, still not quite looking at the dragons, said, "Why are there empty plates on the ground?"

"Pixies," Miriam said, without hesitating. "I always put food down for the pixies if we eat in the garden."

"Pixies."

"Pixies." Miriam smiled, trying to project absolute trustworthiness.

DI Adams looked from one woman to the other, as if she had more questions to ask but wasn't sure she even wanted the answers. Then she just nodded, and said, "Have a nice day, ladies. Please stay away from crime scenes."

"Of course," Alice said, and they watched her walk down the little path, still rubbing her eyes. She paused to crush a mint leaf between her fingers, breathing in the scent deeply, then reached for another plant.

"Oh, not that one, Inspector," Miriam called.

"No?"

"No. That's belladonna. *Very* poisonous. You don't want it on your fingers."

The inspector looked at the plant more closely, then back at the two women, and Miriam's heart dislodged itself from her chest, winding up somewhere in the pit of her stomach. The DI's smile was gone, and the look she gave them was cold, evaluating. "Thanks for the warning," she said, and walked away.

ॐ

"*ALICE*," Miriam hissed, and the older woman gave a single sharp shake of her head. Beaufort was already moving, low and silent and fast for a big old dragon, while Mortimer appeared to have gone into hibernation. The High Lord vanished through the overgrown garden with barely a whisper of shifting vegetation to mark his passage, and Alice covered the cream with a napkin to keep any flies off, then sipped her tea. Miriam tried to imitate her, but her hand shook and she knocked the mug against her teeth, so she put it back down with a sigh. She was going to need to break into the chocolate Hobnobs at this rate.

It wasn't long before Beaufort came trotting back down the path, his head high and his wings shaken half out, the sun sliding off his natural greens and golds and making him luminous.

"She's gone," he said cheerfully. "She's a very intense woman, isn't she? I wish we'd left some scones for her. I think she could have used a scone. They always make me feel more relaxed."

Miriam thought the inspector might have used the scones to

try and force a confession out of them somehow, but she didn't share that idea. Instead she looked at Alice and said, "Did you see how she looked at me when I said about the belladonna? You don't think ...?"

"I don't know," Alice admitted. "But Mortimer already heard that it was poison, didn't you, Mortimer?"

"That it might be," he said, muffled under his paws.

"Sit up, lad. She's gone now. And she strikes me as a very nice lady." Beaufort patted Mortimer on the back, which only made him curl up more tightly.

The detective inspector struck Miriam as a lady who wanted very much to arrest someone, which kind of negated any niceness, in her view. "Alice, what do we *do*? What if it *was* belladonna? What if she thinks it was *me*?"

"I think it's very clear to anyone who meets you that you don't have the constitution to be a murderer," Alice said.

Miriam wasn't quite sure whether she should be flattered or insulted. Alice's tone didn't make it immediately clear.

"However, I think we can be sure that she's still looking at the Women's Institute," Alice continued. "So we need to be very discreet as we continue our enquiries."

"As we *continue* them?"

"Of course." Alice tapped the tablet. "We have at least three possibilities here to look at. Violet, who may or may not be the woman you saw at the village hall the night the vicar was killed; S.B., who seems to be someone from the vicar's past; and the person who was upset about the fete. BestBakerBoy."

"But why can't we just leave it to the inspector? She'll have *seen* all these emails! It seems very silly to still be poking around when she *suspects* us!" Miriam's face had gone very hot, but she planted her hands firmly on the table and tried to look stern.

Alice smiled at her. "In my experience," she said, "when the police decide that they have the murderer, they become very fixated on them, whether there's evidence or not. So leaving things be when they may have evidence that points to us seems rather foolish to me." She finished her tea and put the cup down, while Miriam wondered what the older woman meant by *in her experience.* Alice had just arrived in the village one day, moved into her pretty little cottage, and taken over the W.I. with perfect, ruthless efficiency. She didn't talk much about what happened before that, and somehow no one asked any questions. She supposed they must have, initially, but she certainly couldn't remember Alice answering any.

"But what are we supposed to do, Alice? We're not trained investigators. Look what happened when we went to the vicarage. Mortimer was almost caught!"

"Then we shall have to be more careful."

Mortimer made a small noise and tucked his tail a little tighter around him. Miriam rather wished she had some wings to hide under, too. "But what can we actually find that the police can't?"

"We will find the things they're not looking for," Alice said simply. "We are two intelligent women, and two very talented dragons. What more could we possibly need?"

Miriam had to question just how intelligent they were, to even be discussing doing something that she was pretty sure would be classed as interfering with police business. Which probably carried a jail sentence, to add to the murder charge.

"I do rather think you're right," Beaufort said. "We can't just sit aside and hope the police decide it's not you. Not when we can do something about it."

Miriam covered her face with both hands. "I really don't want to go to jail," she said, her voice muffled. "Who would take care of my garden?"

"Neither of us are going to jail," Alice said. "We're going to make sure of it, aren't we?"

Beaufort nodded enthusiastically, and Mortimer shifted one

wing, uncovering an amber eye that glared at them. "I'm still not sure this isn't the worst idea since the ice dragons did that country swap with the Hawaiian clans, but fine. We'd only have to break you out of jail, and that would be even more complicated."

"Well done, lad," Beaufort said, and gave him another of those painful-looking pats on the back. "Now, what do we need?"

"We will need something very, very concrete to go to the police with," Alice said. "A solid suspect. So I think you'd best take a look at those emails again, Miriam. Let's see what else we can find out."

Miriam tapped her fingers on the table, looked at her friends, then picked up the tablet again with a sigh. "Alright. Yes. But can we at least have some sandwiches now? Being suspected of murder apparently makes me very hungry."

"A dragon can't fight on an empty stomach," Beaufort said, and next to him Mortimer covered his eyes again and whispered, "*Fight?*"

10

MORTIMER

There was a lot to be said for a nice egg sandwich, Mortimer thought. Scones were lovely, but they just didn't fill you up like a nice egg sandwich. And with any luck, if he ate enough of them, he wouldn't be able to fit through any more windows, either. He nibbled the crust contentedly, thinking that whatever spices Alice put in the filling were very tasty. Miriam tended to get heavy handed with the paprika, which could lead to sneezing, and dragon sneezes are rather risky to the furniture.

They'd moved inside, to the kitchen table, just in case DI Adams decided to pop back unexpectedly. Mortimer felt distinctly more secure inside. While the sun was lovely on his scales, particularly the new ones on his tail where he'd been stress-shedding, Miriam's low-ceilinged kitchen, with the heavy beams overhead and the AGA baking quiet heat in the corner, felt very *safe*. And he needed safe right now. He wasn't sure he'd quite recovered from the close calls with either the giant dog or the police officer yesterday. He wasn't sure he'd *ever* entirely recover from them.

Unlike Beaufort, who was sat back on his hindquarters, his

head level with the table, offering Miriam advice as she dug around in the vicar's tablet.

"What's that? What does that do?"

"It's a music thingy."

"Oh. And that?"

"For TV."

"I say, these are terribly clever things, aren't they? Mortimer, do you think we should get one?"

Mortimer scratched his ear. "We don't have anywhere to charge it, Beaufort."

"Ah, of course. We really need to update things around the caverns, don't we?"

Mortimer had a sudden, alarmed vision of Beaufort contracting an unsuspecting interior decorator to redesign the ancient, scale-polished caves above the lake, but before he could say anything Miriam stretched and said, "I don't think there's much else on here. Not that I can figure out, anyway."

"Well done, Miriam," Alice said, and set a fresh cup of tea in front of her. "I'd have lost patience long ago."

Miriam looked pleased with herself. "Well, it wasn't exactly hidden in secret files or anything." She gave the tablet a dubious glance. "I don't think."

"And do we have anything beyond Violet and S.B.?"

"Not if we don't count BestBakerBoy."

"Ah. Him." Alice tapped her fingers together, then said, "Can you check the vicar's work emails to see if that man from the gastropub contacted him?"

"Harold?" Miriam asked, picking up the tablet again.

"That was him."

Mortimer put his forepaws on the table to watch Miriam scrolling through the emails, eventually stopping on one from a Chef Harold.

"Here," she said. "*Any luck getting the W.I. to budge? I know it's important to keep the locals happy, but think of the prestige of having a chef of my level at your fate! Let me know. And remember, dinner and drinks on me any time you fancy it. H."*

"They seem very chummy," Beaufort said.

"Well, Harold was," Miriam said. "The vicar's just put, *Sorry, no,* in his reply. Not even a hello!"

"He's not BestBakerBoy, anyway, is he?" Alice asked. "Not unless someone else wrote this for him."

"It's from a different email address, too," Miriam said. "And he seemed to be trying to butter the vicar up, what with sending stuff to meetings and offering him meals. He wasn't threatening him."

"Well, then," Alice said, and held another half sandwich out to each of the dragons. Mortimer took his eagerly. They really were *very* tasty. "It was a stretch. And I would think it'll be more likely to be someone from the vicar's past than an unhappy baker. Did you find out if the vicar answered any of the emails from the other two?"

"He doesn't seem to have."

"Well, he always was quite the nonconfrontationalist." Alice smiled at the dragons. "Can I get you anything else, Mortimer? More tea? Beaufort?"

Mortimer nodded around a mouthful of egg mayonnaise, but Beaufort looked at Alice with amused gold eyes. "Not that I disagree with the tactic, but are you using sandwiches to soften us up?"

Mortimer froze, his mouth still full, and Alice laughed.

"Was I that obvious?"

"I'm very old, Alice. Although I admit I've never been bribed with egg sandwiches before. Once upon a time it used to be gold. Or sheep."

"I'm rather in short supply of both of those."

Mortimer swallowed with difficulty. "Why are we being bribed?"

"Not bribed, Mortimer, dear," Alice said. "We all needed a bite to eat after that little encounter with the inspector." Although, Mortimer noticed, she'd only eaten half a sandwich herself. He sighed heavily.

"Please don't tell me I need to break in anywhere. I don't feel I have enough of a criminal nature to keep breaking in places."

"You absolutely don't, lad," Beaufort said. "That's one of the things that makes you such a wonderful young dragon. There's not a bad scale on you."

Mortimer tried to maintain a suitably annoyed and anxious look, but he could feel a happy orange flush creeping up his tail. He'd never been very good at keeping his colour changes under control.

Alice put big mugs of tea in front of the dragons. "I don't intend for anyone to have to break in anywhere again. But I would like you to come with me to the church and see if you can find anything else in the churchyard, any of those emotional traces. We can't go back to the vicarage, and from what you say I rather think the village hall will be nothing but a mess of all the same smells."

"That sounds like an excellent idea," Beaufort said. "We should go immediately, before too many other people track their scents about the place."

Mortimer ate the last piece of his sandwich in one despairing gulp.

"Should we even be going to the church?" Miriam asked. "I mean, mightn't that look suspicious?"

Alice smiled at her. "The church is not part of the crime scene, Miriam. And it still needs fresh flowers, which is a perfectly reasonable explanation for us being there."

Miriam made an uncertain little noise, and Beaufort said, "Miriam may have a point, though. It might be best for just Mortimer and I to go and see what we can find."

"Nonsense," Alice said. "We agreed to investigate this together. I don't know how you propose we do that, if Miriam and I are left at home."

Mortimer sneaked a look at Miriam. She looked like she wouldn't complain about being left at home.

"Well, then." Beaufort finished half his tea in one swallow. "That's all there is to it. Shall we get going?"

"Just as soon as we have some flowers together," Alice said. "We best have our excuse for being there in evidence. Plus I need to make a couple of phone calls. I think it's time to delegate a few investigative duties."

"Delegate to who?" Miriam asked.

"Well, Gert has her sister-in-law's niece's sister in the local council offices," Alice said. "Or sister's sister-in-law. Or niece's sister-in-law. I'm not sure. I can never keep these things straight. Anyhow, she might be able to find out if the vicar was married to anyone called Violet."

"That's terribly clever," Beaufort said.

"One must use the resources one has," Alice said. "I also want Gert to find out about this S.B., since she still has contacts back in Manchester. And I'd like to see if someone can look into bakers while we're at the church, too."

"Do we even really need to go to the church, then?" Mortimer asked. It seemed uncomfortably close to returning to the scene of the crime.

"We must cover all bases, lad," Beaufort said. He looked like he was enjoying this far too much.

"But someone might see us," Miriam protested. "Can't we at least wait until tonight?"

"I rather doubt anyone would believe we were replacing the flowers in the middle of the night," Alice said, and Miriam looked crestfallen.

Mortimer took a deep breath. "Um," he said, then faded to an anxious grey when everyone looked at him. "I hate to, you know, be, well, a bit—"

"Spit it out, lad," Beaufort said, and Mortimer felt the colour come back into his tail at the affection in the old dragon's voice. "You do come up with some very good points."

"Oh. Oh, okay." Mortimer was almost fully his own purple-blue again. "But what exactly are we hoping to find? Say we think we have the scent, how does that help us? We can't follow it, unless they left on foot. If they got in a car, it'll be gone. We'll know someone was there and was angry, and if we stumble across them we'll recognise them, but that's all."

There was a pause, and Miriam was starting to look almost relaxed when Beaufort spoke. "I remember when certain dragons used to train up to track scents. Not just track them, but build a description from them. Male, female, adult or child, if they were a big human or a small one, if they were brave or cowardly, even their favourite meals. Not that the meal thing was so helpful, but the rest was very useful if there were knights sneaking around looking for a dragon to murder. Amazing what knights used to think would impress a princess. And every princess I met was really rather fond of dragons!"

"You don't say," Alice said, and Miriam snorted.

Beaufort looked puzzled, then said, "D'you know, I was never very interested in tracking, personally. It was by nature quite a solitary activity, because a brew of dragons charging around the countryside looking for a fight tended to overwhelm any emotional traces of lovesick knights. But Lord Walter—"

"*No*," Mortimer said, with more emphasis than may have been strictly necessary. He grabbed his tail as everyone looked at him, worrying at the loose scales. "No, Beaufort, he's *terribly* antisocial. He'll try to eat someone."

"Nonsense," Beaufort said. "Walter would never do such a thing."

Mortimer opened his mouth to protest that he thought that Walter might, and was in fact rumoured to be one of the last dragons who actually *had*, but the High Lord was looking stubborn. And there was no point talking to Beaufort when he was looking stubborn. All he could hope for was that Walter was in one of his periodic mini-hibernations. They came on without warning and could last a month or so.

"I'm sure we can come up with another plan," Miriam was saying, looking alarmed.

"Not at all. This is a fabulous idea!" Beaufort got up and headed for the door. "Come along, Mortimer, lad. Alice is quite right about using all the resources at our disposal. Let's go and see if we can roust old Walter. He'll be so excited. It'll be just like the old times for him."

"Wait, Beaufort—" Mortimer ran after the High Lord, who was already settling into a steady trot as he headed for the back gate. "Not Walter!"

🍂

"AMELIA! AMELIA AMELIA AMELIA!" Mortimer barely folded his wings before crashing into the entrance to his workshop. It was only a small cave, and not at all deep, with low stone benches running along the walls and forming a broad work surface in the centre of the floor. Crystal prisms caught the light from outside and focused it on the workspaces, splintering rainbows across the stone walls. There were dwarf-made tools hanging in marked places on the walls, tongs and pincers and little rounded hammers, all modified for dragon claws and resistant to dragon heat, and in the corners were deep barrels filled with shed scales and copper wire. The stone floor was perfectly clean, and baubles made of magic and dragon scales drifted gently across the low roof like a flock of sedate, multicoloured birds. It was a terribly peaceful spot, Mortimer's place of ideas and quiet craft-dragon-ship, his refuge from the stresses that life as Beaufort's unwilling escort into the modern world always seemed to bring.

"Amelia!" Mortimer shouted again, rushing into the dimmer light of the workshop and colliding with a small dragon who yelped in shock. "Amelia?"

"Nooo," the small dragon said, and waved a tangle of wire and scales at him. "Look, you made me crush it! It was going to be so good!"

"Gilbert?"

"He's helping out," Amelia said, emerging from the end of the cavern with a half-made glider in one paw. "We've got too much to do between now and the fete for just the two of us." Mortimer heard a little note of reproach in her voice, and she didn't have to add, *especially with you not being here half the time.*

"I'm sorry," he said, a general apology that took in him not being here, knocking Gilbert over, and interrupting them. "Look, you *have* to help me. Beaufort's convinced Lord Walter to try and track a human, and—"

"*What?*" Amelia asked, as Gilbert breathed, "Holy cow."

"Yes! I know! And he won't listen, and Walter's all puffed up about being asked to help, and I'm scared he might *eat* someone!"

"Well, he *probably* won't," Amelia said, a little dubiously.

"Probably isn't going to cut it, Amelia!" He swallowed as she glared at him. "Sorry."

"Things would be so much easier if everyone was just vegetarian," Gilbert said, putting his tools back on the wall. "I mean, no one's worried about me eating a carrot in a moment of wild abandon."

Mortimer covered his mouth with both paws. "*They've already left!* What do I *do?*"

"Gilbert, keep working," Amelia said, putting her tongs down on a bench.

"Aw, man."

"We're going to be flying. You want to fly?"

Gilbert gave her an unimpressed look. It was no secret that the young dragon was acrophobic, but his sister was usually a little more diplomatic with him, if with no one else. Mortimer took a deep breath. Okay, if he had Amelia, at least that was two sensible dragons against two old ... somethings.

"Amelia, I owe you for this."

"I know," she said, and led the way out of the cavern.

It was mid-afternoon in the churchyard, the light bright and the dappled shadows of the trees nowhere near as thick as Mortimer would have liked them to be. Alice and Miriam were waiting for them by the stile, carrying baskets filled with flowers from their gardens, and Mortimer banked a little to the right, planning to land on the path. They'd risked flying all the way, because there was no way Walter would walk any of the distance at all. He disdained walking as the locomotive method of animals.

"*Mortimer!*" Amelia yelled. She'd just started to bank in the opposite direction, maybe thinking they'd fly right into the churchyard.

Mortimer gave a strangled yelp as their wing tips tangled and they crashed into each other with a solid *thud* and a clatter of scales, then plummeted into the brambles.

"Mortimer! Are you alright?" Miriam asked, and Mortimer sat up to see her watching them with wide eyes, her basket crushed to her chest. At least *she* seemed to have some idea of how serious all this was.

"Yes, yes. Are they here yet?" he asked, struggling to disentangle himself from both a grumbling Amelia and the brambles.

"Are who here yet?" Alice asked. "And that was rather risky, flying all the way here."

"It's an emergency," Mortimer said.

"Well, you're certainly acting like it is," Alice said. "Hello, Amelia."

"Hello, Ms Martin." Amelia pattered out onto the path and eyed Alice's basket expectantly.

"Alice is fine, dear. Where's Beaufort?"

"They must already be here. We need to get to the church quick as we can," Mortimer said. He had a bramble caught over his shoulder and was thrashing wildly to try and get it off. "Oh, what are they going to be *doing*?"

"Do calm down, Mortimer," Alice said, lifting the bramble clear. "Apparently the DI is watching the vicarage, but Rose and Jasmine are going to keep an eye on her, and they'll distract her if she seems like she might come near the church. Everything will be just fine."

Mortimer had serious doubts that was going to be case, but he scooted out from under the bramble without commenting further and set off over the stile.

BEAUFORT AND WALTER *had* already arrived. They were sitting in the sun on the church steps like two ageing gargoyles, faces upturned and contented streams of green smoke drifting from their nostrils. No one seemed to be quite sure if Walter was actually older than Beaufort, or if he just wore his years badly. His scales were patchy and dry-looking, and he seemed small and bony inside them, as if he'd started to shed then forgotten to keep going. His eyes were milky green when he looked toward the little group coming across the grass, and his nostrils flared wide and quivering.

"Lord Walter," Mortimer said politely.

"Mm," the old dragon said, still looking at the women. A small thread of drool appeared on his lower lip. Miriam looked alarmed, and even Alice didn't seem entirely comfortable.

"Walter," Beaufort shouted. "These are our friends, Alice and Miriam."

Miriam waved nervously.

"Eh?"

"I said—"

"I know, I know." Walter waved impatiently. "Don't *shout*, Beaufort. You hurt my ears."

Alice handed the old dragon a slice of parkin. "Pleased to meet you, Lord Walter."

He took the parkin, sniffed it, then ate it in two hasty gulps. "I say. That's not bad."

"I always think the cakes are perfectly wonderful, personally," Beaufort said, and got up. "Come on, then. What can you tell us?"

Walter sighed. "What do you want to know, exactly? Plenty of human stink around here to choose from."

Mortimer shook his head, and Beaufort opened his mouth to say something, but it was Alice who answered.

"There is absolutely no need for that sort of talk. Do you hear me saying that your claws are filthy or that your scales look dreadful? No. Of course not. Because I have manners."

There was absolute silence while the old dragon stared at the chair of the W.I., then he gave a rasping chuckle, and said, "D'you know, you're right. I am sorry, young lady."

Alice nodded. "As you should be," she said, and walked into the church with a very straight back. Miriam fluttered her hands about, mumbled something Mortimer couldn't quite understand, then fled after her.

Walter looked at Beaufort. "You do find them," he said, then closed his eyes and squatted there like giant winged toad, his nostrils flaring, while Mortimer looked around anxiously. It felt very exposed out here. The road was out of sight beyond the high churchyard wall, and the vicarage was lost at the other end of the graveyard, barely glimpsed through the trees, but there was no cover on the church steps. He plucked at his tail and waited.

For a moment, it actually felt like things might go smoothly, that he might have overreacted. Amelia stole into the church after Alice and returned with a piece of parkin, which she sat nibbling on happily in the shade of a headstone. Beaufort wandered off around the outside of the church, looking up at the roof and sighing about the lack of gargoyles, and Walter crouched on the steps, breathing slow and steady.

"Lots of happiness, lots of grief," he said, almost to himself. Then, "Quite recent anger. A woman, a man."

"Can you tell anything else?" Mortimer asked.

"Maybe a little, if I can get a clearer scent," the old dragon said, and got up stiffly. Eyes still closed, he snuffled his way down the steps to the path. "It's hard. There are lots of other scents, lots of modern *stuff*. I don't do those so well." He opened his milky eyes and looked at Mortimer. "What on earth is Beaufort doing?"

"What?" Mortimer looked around, half-expecting to see the High Lord hanging off the church steeple.

"No, this. *All* of this. Everyone knows you've got his ear. What's he up to?"

"I wish I knew," Mortimer said truthfully. "I think he just likes being involved."

"He'll get us all killed," Walter grumbled, and shuffled a little further along the path. "I don't know about this. It's all a bit muddled, these smells. People are very complicated. Lots of emotions."

He didn't know the half of it, Mortimer thought, then saw the dog. *The* dog. The monstrous, long-legged thing from the village hall, just venturing into the graveyard. "Aw, *no*."

"What? What is it?" Walter looked around wildly, but Mortimer wasn't even sure what he could see through those old eyes.

The dog gave a delighted bark and shot toward them, and somewhere still out of sight a small voice yelled, "Angelus, come back!"

"Walter, run!" Mortimer bellowed, and tried to usher the old dragon off the path.

"*Run?* I don't *run!*" Walter planted his four squat legs and roared. The dog stopped so hard his nose almost hit the gravel of the path, and the faint voice shrieked for Angelus again.

"Mortimer?" Amelia scrambled to her feet. "What do we *do?*"

"Get out of here!" He tapped Walter's shoulder awkwardly, trying not to look at the dog. The great, slobbery, barking, *toothy* dog. "Lord Walter, we really—" Walter backhanded him with surprising strength, sending him sliding across the path, and the dog gave a yelp of excitement and bounced forward, legs stiff. "*Ow!*"

"Walter? Mortimer? What's going on?" Beaufort came around the church at an ungainly gallop, and Mortimer righted himself, flinging his wings wide to make himself look bigger.

"Shoo!" he said to the still-bouncing dog, and Walter gave him a withering look.

"Shoo? You should be ashamed to call yourself a dragon. Let's eat him."

"No one eat him!" Beaufort shouted, just as Alice and Miriam appeared on the church steps with a tall, unfamiliar man following them.

"Why not?" Walter demanded.

"Who's there?" the man on the steps said, and the dragons froze. "I heard voices! Have you got friends out here?" he asked the women, looking about the place uncertainly. The dog barked, and bounded toward Mortimer then away again. Mortimer gave a horrified squeak at the back of his throat.

"Angelus?" the distant voice called, coming closer.

Walter growled.

"Walter," Beaufort hissed warningly.

"Can anyone else smell that guy?" Amelia said, her voice clear and carrying. "He *stinks.*"

Two dragons and two women turned to join Amelia in staring at the man. "What?" he demanded of Alice and Miriam. "What? Did someone say something? Someone *said* something."

Walter lunged at the dog. The dog gave a yelp of real alarm and bolted across the graveyard, the old dragon scuttling after him in drooling pursuit.

"*Walter!*" Beaufort roared, and charged after them. Amelia threw herself into the chase, and Mortimer turned frantically on the spot, not sure whether he should join them, or, or what? Keep an eye on the man? He *did* stink, of old, ingrained violence, and Mortimer didn't want to just leave him with Alice and Miriam. But what could he do? It wasn't like he could singe him or anything. How could they explain *that?* Alice had hold of one of the man's arms and was talking to him severely, and he pulled away from her, starting down the stairs. Mortimer took a hesitant step after Walter, hearing the not-so-distant woman still shouting for Angelus.

Then Alice grabbed the man's arm again, and he *pushed* her, and she fell back on the steps with a little cry of astonishment. Mortimer gave one furious roar, a sound he'd never made before, never even thought he *could* make, and charged.

11

DI ADAMS

D I Adams had relieved Sergeant Graham Harrison after her interesting little meeting with the Ellis and Martin women. She wasn't really sure there was much use keeping watch on the vicarage, except to see who else might bumble past. But she wanted to think things through before she did anything else, and there was no point braving the ridiculously narrow, winding roads all the way back to Skipton, not if she was just going to have to come back here again anyway.

She'd found the tiny village shop and bought some supplies, although it was mostly Lucozade and biscuits. The packaged sandwiches were not only a brand she'd never heard of, they had the dried, shrivelled look of things that had not heard of stock rotation. The pretty little village square, with its stone well in the centre of the marketplace and happy tumbles of flowers in hanging baskets on every available post, had a couple of nice-looking village pubs, plus a greengrocer and a bakery that seemed to double as a deli, but she hadn't been in the mood for braving more locals.

An old woman clad entirely in yellow houndstooth print,

including her hat, had tapped on the inspector's car window while she was checking her phone and demanded to know if she was investigating flower thefts. DI Adams had said it wasn't really her department, and the old woman had turned around without another word and marched off, muttering about the declining standards of police work in the modern world. Then an astonishingly round and red-faced man with badly fitting false teeth had accosted her as she got out of the car and demanded to know what the police were going to do about whoever was vandalising his tractor. That had been more than enough contact with the locals for one morning, and the shop had been the closest thing to her. She grabbed some supplies and fled.

But, as it turned out, she needn't have worried about food. She looked a little guiltily at the small pile of Tupperware containers on the passenger seat of the car. First it had been morning tea, delivered by a pretty woman who looked younger than the white streaks in her hair suggested. DI Adams recognised her from the village hall (Davies, Pearl), and she brought a tartan thermos and shortbread fingers that were so buttery and indulgent that the inspector didn't think she'd be able to eat more than one.

Somehow they were all gone, although she had at least managed to make them last until after lunch. That had arrived carried by a very, very small man, who whispered that Gert had sent him, and that it was all vegetables in case she was one of those meat-haters. He handed her a white casserole dish capped with a dome of flaky pastry, all nestled into some sort of quilted pot-holdery thing and still piping hot, took a set of cutlery and a bottle of homemade lemonade out of a carrier bag, and tiptoed off again. When another W.I. member (Robinson, Teresa), a tall woman with a heavy mass of grey braids and an evident fondness for pink Lycra, came by with peanut cookies, DI Adams started writing down who had brought what so she could figure out how to get the containers back. Village life was very *odd*, but the food was good. She could give it that. No wonder Sergeant Harrison hadn't seemed too worried about being on stake-out duty.

Now she leaned against the bonnet and stretched luxuriously in the sunshine. All the sitting around and unseasonable warmth was making her feel dozy, which worried her in some undefined way. She wasn't a dozy person. Even as a child, her mother never tired of telling her, she never slept in the day. "Always up, always prying, prying, prying. Questions. Looking. No wonder you don't have a boyfriend, all those questions!" But it had always seemed to her that there was too much to know to waste time sleeping.

Of course, it could just be all the food making her sleepy. She never normally ate pie in the middle of the day. She never normally ate pie, full-stop. But then pie very rarely tasted like that one had done. Never mind the shortbread and the peanut cookies. She patted her belly absentmindedly. She must have needed it. Something was certainly a little off. She'd had a persistent headache since the visit to the Ellis house, when her eyes had started going all funny. Every time she'd looked at the ground in the garden, it had been like she just couldn't find anything to focus on, and her gaze had drifted off at strange angles. She'd only been drunk once or twice in her life, and it had been a bit like that, as if nothing was quite *right*, her senses suddenly rendered untrustworthy. Maybe a migraine? She rarely got them, and they were usually accompanied by the annoying little swimmers in her vision, but maybe this was some new variation?

"Joy," she said to the churchyard, and became aware that she could hear someone shouting for their dog. And there had been those completely empty plates that Ellis had claimed were for pixies. Wouldn't put it past her, but it was cream you left out for pixies, and at night, not in the middle of a nice sunny morning. DI Adams shook her head. And she could blame her mother for that particular piece of useless information. It was like when she'd seen that *stuff* in London. Her mother had been terribly sympathetic, had listened as her daughter described the horrible tricks her mind had played on her, and then she'd gone and said it was *real.* The shouting afterward had been real, that was for sure.

The dog walker was still calling for her dog, getting a little closer. A woman, sounding increasingly anxious. DI Adams wondered if she should go help. It was probably the kind of thing the police did around here. But she did have a house to watch. She looked at the vicarage, then fished in her pocket and pulled out the scale, running her fingers over the smoothness of it, holding it up to the light to see the way the sun shone through it, turning it into something between shot silk and stained glass. She still couldn't begin to imagine what it might be. Some sort of art thing, maybe? But what was it made of? And why had it been under the bed?

A sound caught her attention. Didn't catch it, *seized* it. It set the hairs on her arms leaping away from the skin, and a chill ran up her back, leaving her suddenly breathless. It had been, what? A howl? No. A *roar.* Something that her animal heart recognised even if she didn't. Something toothed and clawed, something to be held at bay by fires in the night, something ... Something like London? No. Not that. That had been stress. Exhaustion. This sounded *real.*

"Angelus!" the dog walker wailed, and now DI Adams could see her, a small woman trailing a leash and trotting as rapidly as she could toward that terrible sound. Howard, Rose, also from the W.I., the one with the Great Dane that was as tall as her, near enough. No wonder it had got away on her. Christ, she was almost ninety, and looked like a chihuahua could get away on her. The average age in Toot Hansell was proving to be a little concerning. There was another woman too, younger, with some fluffy thing in her arms. Shaw, Jasmine. The constable's wife and possible accidental poisoner. DI Adams focused on the women and let the rest fall away. Whatever that noise was, these civilians were not equipped to deal with it. She was. In theory, anyway.

•

She shoved the scale back into her pocket and ran toward the dog-walkers, booted feet sure on the grass. "Ladies! Ladies, stop right there!"

The women turned toward her. Shaw was pale, her eyes huge, and the fluffy dog was wriggling wildly, trying to get free.

"My Angelus is in there!" Rose wailed. "And did you hear that *sound?*"

"I'm sure it was just the wind, Mrs Howard," DI Adams said, feeling sure of nothing of the sort. "But stay here while I go take a look, alright?"

"*Angelus!*" Rose shouted again, and DI Adams winced. She had some lungs on her. Shaw's dog obviously thought so too, because she writhed so wildly that she flung herself free of the younger woman's arms and bolted through the gateway arch and into the churchyard, headed for the source of the roar.

"*Primrose!*" Jasmine screamed, and ran after her.

"*Stop!*" DI Adams bellowed, and Rose gave her an apologetic look, then ran into the churchyard, surprisingly quick for such a little old thing. "Oh, Christ," the inspector said, and gave chase.

❦

"*WALTER!*" The word that rang among the gravestones was clear, the voice *odd*. Raspy, like a lifelong smoker, but full of more power than any pair of tar-choked lungs had any right to. Commanding, too. DI Adams thought it sounded like one of those old theatre actors, with their classical accents and booming voices. A very exasperated one.

She ran harder, passing Rose and shouting, "Go *back*, dammit!" The woman gave her a little *I'm sorry* finger wave and sped up.

The inspector swore, jumped a grave, hurdled a bench, and shouted as she went, "Police! Everyone *stop what you're doing!*"

Jasmine kept running. That ridiculous little dog was still

running ahead of her, ignoring the woman's panicked calls for her to come back. And now the path curved toward the church, and DI Adams saw women on the steps (Ellis, Martin, her mind supplied without hesitating), and a man as well. He pushed Alice and she fell back onto the steps, looking more annoyed than frightened, and there was another one of those *roars*, making DI Adams stumble and catch her hip painfully on a headstone. It hadn't been as deep or full-throated as the first, but it was a *roar* nonetheless, and there was blurred movement in the corner of her eye that she couldn't quite catch. Then the man yelped and fell over, Miriam threw herself on top of him like a rugby player diving on a ball as he slid down the stairs, and Alice scrambled up and followed them, waving a bag around like she was going to gag him with it.

"*Stop!*" the DI bellowed again. "*Everybody stop right now or so help me I'll arrest every single one of you!*"

There was a last brief scuffle on the steps, then a breathless stillness, broken only by the fluffy bloody dog, which was bouncing about the place yapping hysterically.

"*Walter!*" someone shouted from beyond the vicarage, and Rose caught up to them, still huffing.

"Where's my Angelus?" she demanded, then said, "Oh, hello, Alice, Miriam."

"Hello, Rose," Alice said. She had a cotton shopping bag with *Shop Local, Live Local, Love Local* and a lot of cheery flowers printed on it pulled over the man's head, and was sitting behind him with his head rested in her lap. It might have looked like she was protecting him from the stone steps, if she hadn't also had both legs over his upper arms, and her feet hooked under his back. It looked painful, and he wasn't moving much.

Meanwhile, Miriam had belly-flopped on him, and her technique appeared to simply involve trying to cover as much of him with her own body as she could. "Hi, Rose," she said breathlessly.

"*Let me up!*" the man in the bag bellowed in a muffled voice.

"*Crazy old—*" Miriam elbowed him somewhere and he gasped, then fell silent.

"Get up," DI Adams said, ignoring another shout of "*Walter!*"

Neither woman moved.

"*Get. Up.*" She didn't shout. Shouting when running was one thing, but the situation was static, and she was back in control. Sort of. Either way, she didn't need to raise her voice. But she did put a certain amount of emphasis on the words, and she had a sneaking suspicion that an outside observer might have *thought* she was shouting.

Alice got up first, leaving the bag on the man's head, and helped Miriam to her feet. The man sat up and pulled the bag off his head, greying hair dishevelled and his shirt torn at the shoulder.

"Arrest them!" he shouted. "They're crazy! They should be locked up!"

DI Adams didn't entirely disagree, but she just frowned at him. "I believe I saw you push Ms Martin?"

"She grabbed me! And her dog bit me!"

"I don't have a dog," Alice said.

"*Something* bit me!" The women stared at him, even Jasmine distracted from trying to catch Primrose. There was blood on his jeans, and he pulled the leg up gingerly to reveal a neat and rather large semi-circle of teeth on the shin and the calf. "See?"

DI Adams looked at Rose. "Does your dog bite?"

"*No,*" she said indignantly.

"Just asking." The inspector looked back at the women on the church steps. "So what bit him?"

"I think he was bitten before he got here and is just blaming us," Miriam said. She'd gone a very odd shade of pink.

"*What?* I don't even think I can *walk* on this! It was one of your friends, one of the ones hiding in the graveyard!"

"*Walter!*" someone bellowed, a little closer. They sounded as if their patience was running out.

"Yeah, him!" the man said. "And whoever else was out there making those noises!"

DI Adams rubbed her eyes. The migraine vision was back again, making the lower edge of the steps hard to look at, and when she caught movement out of the corner of her eye she jerked toward it. There was nothing there, just a flowerpot fallen off a gravestone. She looked back at the sorry little group. Jasmine was staring at the man in round-eyed astonishment, her dog still barking, and Rose seemed too interested in what was happening to bother looking for her dear lost Angelus anymore.

DI Adams opened her mouth to say something, possibly related to what sort of friends the man thought might bite, and her phone rang. She swore, held one warning finger out at the scene in general, then checked the screen.

DCI Temple. Also known as Temper. Also known as the man that had given her this assignment with a dig about how boring it would be for a big city cop. Well. That was just perfect. "Hello, sir."

"Adams? How's it going up there? Thought maybe the murderer had got you, since it's been nothing but crickets here."

"I'm in the field, sir." Well, graveyard. She peered into the shadows under the trees curiously. Whoever was looking for Walter was getting closer.

"And?"

"And I'm currently looking at a new suspect." Sort of. The man on the steps stared at her with a disbelieving expression, and she ignored him.

"Well, that would be good. Lab results are back, which you'd know if you ever got around to checking in. We do that sort of thing up here, you know."

"I'm sorry, sir. I'll check in as soon as I'm done here. Ah, was it …?"

"Poison. Belladonna, apparently, and you don't get much more country living than that."

"I see." Walter – or Walter's owner/pursuer/whatever – sounded like he should be in sight at any moment. The inspector turned in a slow circle, looking for movement, those blurs playing across her vision again and making her eyes feel swimmy and uncomfortable.

"Don't eat anything the ladies of the Women's Institute give you, Adams. That's all I can say." The DCI laughed, and the inspector chuckled obediently, thinking of pies and cookies and homemade lemonade, and wondering if belladonna ever had migraine-like symptoms. Then a Great Dane came careening across the graveyard with no respect for graves or markers, running flat out with his gangly legs flying everywhere, slipping on the grass and sending vases of flowers spilling to the ground.

"Call you back," DI Adams said, and hung up. "Control your dog," she said to Rose. He was racing toward them, the whites of his eyes showing and drool flying in strings from his wide mouth, and showed no signs of slowing. "*Control that damn dog!*"

"Angelus!" Rose shouted. "Come to Mummy!"

The dog swerved toward her, accelerating like a greyhound on a track, and DI Adams realised that he wasn't going to slow down.

"*Sit!*" she bellowed. "*Stop, sit, stay – sh—*" She jumped out of the way of the dog as he bolted toward his tiny owner, then ran after him, lunging at the leash.

"*Sit, Angel! Sit!*" Rose yelped, looking horrified. The dog's eyes rolled, his legs bunching as he tried to obey, but his forward momentum was too much. He was sliding on the slick grass, Rose scuttling backward as the inspector made another wild grab for the leash.

"*Stop!*" Alice and Miriam shouted from behind her, and a male voice shouted, "Walter, *no!*"

DI Adams almost had the leash when her legs went out from under her, and for a moment she thought there was another dog, that there *must* be another dog, because *something* hit her legs, she was sure of it. Then she was flat on her back, wheezing, and the only dog she could see was the Great Dane as he came to a sliding halt inches from his tiny mistress, shoving his giant face into her belly as if trying to hide from something.

"Inspector!" someone shouted, and then Alice was leaning over her, looking worried. "Are you hurt?"

DI Adams shook her head, then pushed herself onto her elbows. The man was still sitting on the church step, looking bewildered. She knew how he felt. "Who's Walter?" she managed.

"Must be a friend of his," Alice said, nodding at the man. "I don't know anyone called Walter."

The inspector rubbed her eyes and sat up. "So where's the other dog?"

"What other dog?" Alice asked.

"The one that knocked me over."

Alice frowned. "There wasn't another dog."

DI Adams blinked at the green-dappled world of the church-yard. All those strange *blurred* spots in her vision. They were all over the place. She should get an MRI. But she'd had one after the incident in London, and it had been clear. Still, this couldn't be normal. Shaw's yappy dog ran over her lap, still barking, and she grabbed the noisy mutt by the collar instinctively.

"Shut *up!*" she told the dog as the thing stared at her in aston-ishment. Then bit her. She yelped, let the dog go, and scrambled to her feet, shaking her injured hand. "Nobody move. Nobody. *Move!*"

She was fairly sure she was shouting, but right now she really didn't care.

12
MIRIAM

Miriam was both astonished by how quickly things had gone downhill, and not surprised at all. She and Alice had been in the church, removing old flowers from the chipped vases and rinsing them out in the little half-kitchen, not really talking, just going about their business in quiet companionship. Miriam had just arranged a spray of snapdragons to her satisfaction and was carrying the vase back to the main room when a man emerged from the door in front of her. She squeaked, and almost dropped the flowers. He seemed just as startled, but managed to grab the bottom of the vase and help her steady it.

"Who're you?" she demanded, her heart hammering so loudly that she could barely hear her own words. Then, before he could answer, "What're you doing in the supply cupboard? That's the supply cupboard!"

"I—" the man began.

"Alice! Alice, there's a man in the supply cupboard!"

"I can see that," Alice said, from over Miriam's shoulder, making her squeak again. This time she saved the vase herself.

"Ladies," the man said, pleasantly enough. He had a friendly smile, Miriam thought, but it didn't quite reach his eyes. The eyes looked wary, and they darted about the place as if looking for a way out.

"What are you doing here?" Alice asked.

"Meter reader," he said. "Can't find the meter."

"May I see your card?" Alice asked. Miriam shifted her grip on the vase, just in case she had to use it as a weapon, then immediately felt horrified with herself for even thinking such a thing.

The man hesitated, his smile fading, then nodded. "See there's no putting anything over you two."

"You look old enough to know better," Alice replied.

The man gave a little huff of amusement, and Miriam saw his posture change. He'd assumed something almost obsequious before, the lost meter reader in the cupboard, innocent and a little confused. Now his jaw lifted and his weight shifted, and she had to stop herself taking a step back. "I'm an old friend of the vicar's, is all." She could almost hear the quotation marks around "vicar", as if it was a word he was unfamiliar with. "Heard what happened, and thought I'd come up and see if I could do anything to help the investigation."

"That's a job for the police," Alice said, and Miriam just managed not to snort.

"The police don't always know what they're looking for."

There was a moment's silence, then Miriam blurted, "S.B."

"What?" the man asked, glaring at her.

"S.B. Are you S.B.?"

The pause that followed was long enough for Miriam to see indecision flash over the man's face, then the hardening of the line of his mouth. He seemed to be preparing himself for something, but before any of them could move there was a *roar* from outside.

"Oh dear," Alice said, and the man said something spectacularly rude before mumbling an apology.

"Oh *dear*," Miriam said, and dumped her vase on the floor as she ran for the door, hearing Alice and the man who might be S.B. following her.

§⋅

THERE WAS a lot of confusion outside. Rose's Great Dane was blaring his enormous hellhound bellow at Walter and Mortimer, and Beaufort was shouting at Walter not to eat the dog, and Walter didn't seem to be too keen on listening. Mortimer was waving his wings about in alarm, and Amelia was bouncing around as if she didn't know which way to turn. Miriam started down the steps with every intention of boxing the old dragon's ears, but Alice grabbed her arm.

"The inspector," she said quietly, nodding across the graveyard, and now Miriam realised she could hear very human shouts over the dog and the dragons. She supposed that distracting detective inspectors was rather difficult when it came to roaring dragons, and said something only marginally less rude than what maybe-S.B. had said earlier. Both he and Alice looked at her in astonishment, then the man went back to peering around the graveyard with a frown on his face.

"Who's there?" he demanded. "I heard voices! Have you got friends out here?"

"No?" Miriam offered, and maybe-S.B. glared at her.

"Angelus!" someone, probably Rose, shouted in the distance.

"I heard something," the man insisted.

Walter growled, and the man spun back to look at the grave-yard. "What was *that?*"

"The dog," Alice said, as Beaufort growled, "Walter."

"Who said that?" maybe-S.B. asked.

"I did," Alice said.

"Not 'the dog', 'Walter.'"

"Who?" Alice asked, her voice mild, and the man glared at her.

"Oh dear," Miriam said, to no one in particular.

Rose was getting closer, and Miriam could hear the inspector shouting, too.

Then Amelia said, very clearly, "Can anyone else smell that guy? He *stinks*."

Miriam and Alice both stared at the man. "What?" he demanded. "What? Did someone say something? Someone *said* something."

And then everything went *really* wrong. Beaufort and Mortimer were looking at maybe-S.B. too, and Walter took the opportunity to throw himself at Angelus. The dog yelped and bolted, Walter in hot pursuit, and Beaufort plunged after them, bellowing for Walter to stop. Amelia immediately followed, whether in the hope of actually helping or just for the fun of it.

Alice grabbed maybe-S.B.'s arm. "You *are* S.B., aren't you?"

"Get off me," he snapped, shaking her free. Miriam could see the inspector now, sprinting across the graveyard, and Rose jogging along behind her. Jasmine was ahead of them, chasing her silly little dog, who was running as fast as her tiny legs could carry her straight for Mortimer. He'd gone a barely-camouflaged green and looked faintly ill.

Maybe-S.B. started down the stairs. "I'm out of here."

Alice reached out for him again. "You wait right here, young man."

The young man in question, who Miriam guessed was probably in his early fifties, shoved Alice away from him, not hard, but with enough force to make her stumble and fall back onto the steps with a very un-Alice-like gasp. "Don't *touch* me, you old—"

He never got to finish the sentence, which Miriam was quite happy about, because Mortimer gave a roar that seemed to startle the dragon as much as it did them. Before maybe-S.B. could do anything more than spin around, his mouth open to shout and a horrified look on his face, Mortimer had sunk his teeth firmly into the man's leg.

"Mortimer, *no!*" Alice hissed.

Miriam silently applauded the dragon as the man fell backward with a howl and slid down the steps. And suddenly she realised that the detective inspector was almost upon them, and the vicar's murderer was most likely lying right at her feet.

"Mortimer, *let go!*" she shout-whispered, and flung herself on top of maybe-S.B., wishing she'd taken one of those self-defence classes they had at the hall sometimes. Although this might be stretching the definition of self-defence a little tiny bit. The man gave a grunt of protest and tried to kick her off, but Miriam was both entirely happy with her comfortable proportions and not afraid to use them. She trapped his legs with hers, and while he was still wriggling Alice dropped neatly down next to her and jammed a grocery bag over his head, then did something fancy with her legs to immobilise his arms.

"Nice," Miriam said, and Alice grinned at her, a single lock of dislodged grey hair falling in her face.

"Well done yourself, Miriam."

Miriam had a moment to feel quite proud of herself, then the DI's voice shattered it.

"Everybody stop right now or so help me I'll arrest every single one of you!"

Miriam wondered if you really did have to wear orange in prison, or if that was just on TV. She didn't like orange. It clashed with her aura.

୬ፙ

AND THEN THINGS went from bad to worse. DI Adams had just hung her phone up (Alice had listened intently to the DI's side of the conversation), when Angelus came rushing back to Rose with his tail between his legs. Walter was in close pursuit, drool flying from his jaws and splattering the detective inspector's trousers as he lurched into her and sent her sprawling to the ground. Miriam wasn't at all sure if Walter had actually seen her and was just being ornery, or if he was so short-sighted that he'd entirely missed a human between him and his intended snack. But it did at least slow the old dragon down enough that Beaufort was able to pounce on him in a tackle not unlike Miriam's own, with the exception that he trapped Walter's mouth shut with one heavy paw. Amelia wasn't far behind, and she grabbed the old dragon's tail before he could knock anyone else flying. Primrose was in hysterics, and after biting the inspector she only got more excited, prancing around the dragons so anyone with half a brain could work out *something* was there.

"I'm going to eat the damn thing myself," Amelia growled, and Mortimer shushed her. He'd gone a peculiar shade of yellow after biting maybe-S.B., and couldn't seem to come out of it.

"What was that?" the detective inspector demanded. She got up, ignoring Alice's offer of help, her hand dripping blood onto the grass. Walter's nostrils were flaring.

"Nothing, Detective Inspector Adams," Alice said. "Shall we go inside and get your hand seen to?"

The inspector glared at her. "No one's going anywhere. Me included."

"This is totally unfair," maybe-S.B. complained. "These women *attacked* me!"

"Well, what were you doing in the church?" Miriam demanded, feeling quite emboldened after her unexpectedly effective capture. "You were *snooping!*"

"What were *you* doing in the church?" the inspector countered, pointing at Miriam with her uninjured hand. Miriam made an uncertain little noise. The detective inspector had been much less intimidating when she was on the ground.

"We were replacing the flowers," Alice said. "The old ones are still in the kitchen, if you'd like to check."

"And why were you doing that?"

The four members of the Toot Hansell Women's Institute stared at DI Adams as if she'd asked why they ate breakfast.

"Because it's what we do," Alice said patiently.

"Well. You shouldn't be," DI Adams said, then looked uncomfortable when the women continued to stare at her. After a moment she added, "I mean, there's still an investigation going on."

"Not in the church," Alice pointed out.

"Well, maybe there should be."

"There should be *now*," maybe-S.B. said. "But I'm busy. I won't press charges." He brushed his hands off and nodded at the women. "I'll be off." There was a growl from somewhere near his knees, and he looked alarmed. "What was that?"

"What was what?" Miriam asked innocently, giving Mortimer a pointed look.

"It might be my stomach," Alice said, patting her belly. "I didn't have much for lunch."

"You're not going anywhere," DI Adams said to maybe-S.B. "I want to know what you were doing in the church."

"I'm an aficionado of English village churches," he said, and Miriam snorted.

"Primrose? Primrose, come to Mummy," Jasmine called. Primrose ignored her entirely. She was trying to latch onto Amelia's tail while the young dragon flicked it about in an effort to keep it safely out of reach. Walter was making dangerous rumbling sounds, and Beaufort was whispering urgently in his ear.

"Mrs—" DI Adams pointed at Rose, and blinked a couple of times, her forehead furrowed with distress.

"Howard," Rose supplied.

"Yes. Mrs Howard—"

"Professor, actually."

The inspector took a deep breath. Miriam could actually see her trying to keep her temper. She was having a lot of trouble looking at Rose and Angelus, because there was a pile-up of dragons in the way. Her eyes were watering. "Of course. Professor Howard—"

"Rose is fine, though."

For a moment it looked as though the inspector was going to start shouting again, then she said, very quietly, "Professor Howard, please take your dog and go home. I may come by later to ask you some questions."

"Oh, that would be nice. I made fairy cakes just this morning."

DI Adams blinked firmly, and a forced smile appeared on her face. "Very good."

"Well, bye, then," Rose said, giving a general wave that took in the women, the dragons, and the unknown man. She pottered off, Angelus crowding so close to her side that he kept pushing her into grave markers.

DI Adams turned her strained smile on Jasmine. Miriam was starting to worry about the inspector. A tic had appeared under one eye, presumably from the effort of not seeing dragons. "Mrs Shaw. Please take your dog and go home also."

"Um. Yes." Jasmine made an ineffectual grab for Primrose, who danced away, her barks cracking at the edges and becoming almost silent. That was a relief, at least, Miriam thought. "I'll – it just may take me a moment."

"I *will* eat her," Amelia mumbled, and DI Adams glared at Jasmine.

"What was that, Mrs Shaw?"

"Nothing," Jasmine said, her voice far too high. "I'll catch her."

"I think we should go inside and have a cup of tea and get you patched up, Inspector," Alice said. "You and Mr ...?" She trailed off expectantly, and maybe-S.B. scowled at her.

DI Adams looked at her still-bleeding hand and sighed. "Alright. You have everything in the church?"

"Oh, yes. We keep the kitchen very well equipped."

"Of course you do." She nodded at the man on the steps, who was looking longingly across the churchyard. "Inside."

"What? But—"

"*Inside.*" She started toward the steps, stopped, and patted her pockets. "I don't – ugh. Can anyone see my phone?"

Everyone looked at the ground, but there was no phone in sight.

"I need my phone." The detective inspector sounded almost bewildered, and Miriam didn't really blame her. It was an unpleasant enough situation when you could see dragons. She hurried down the steps.

"Where did you have it?"

"I must have dropped it when the dog knocked me over," DI Adams said. She was running her boot through the grass, still not looking at the dragons, and Amelia twitched her tail out of the way just before the inspector stumbled on it. Primrose pounced on it, and Amelia gave a muffled squeak of outrage.

DI Adams straightened up, frowning. "What was that?"

"Primrose," Jasmine said, her face pink, and she hauled the dog away. "She, um, burped."

Amelia looked even more outraged, and Beaufort jerked his head toward the nearest gravestone. Miriam followed his gaze, and saw the phone lying just by Walter's outstretched paw.

"There it is, Inspector!" she exclaimed, then cringed as Beaufort glared at her.

"Oh, thank God," the inspector said, sounding almost like a normal person. With no sign of seeing him, she stepped over Beaufort's tail and picked up the phone, her fingers almost brushing Walter's claws. "That'd be all I need, a missing phone." She straightened up, stepped over the High Lord's tail again, and headed into the church, ushering a protesting maybe-S.B. ahead of her.

Miriam, her hands pressed to her chest, lingered just long enough to see Jasmine hurry away with Primrose, still mumbling apologies to Amelia.

"That was close," Miriam whispered to Mortimer.

He nodded. He'd gone back to that unhealthy yellow colour. "You best go inside. Lord Walter is going to be *so* unhappy."

Judging by the violent purple and green flashes on the old dragon's hide, Miriam rather thought he might be right. She hurried inside and went to put the kettle on.

§&

IN THE KITCHEN, Alice cleaned the inspector's hand with warm water and peroxide, then bandaged it neatly. "You'll probably want to go to a doctor," she said. "Never can tell with dog bites."

"Great. Is there one in the village?"

"No. One tried, but he had to move. Not enough clients."

The DI gave that puzzled blink again, then said, "Okay. Wonderful." She pointed at the man, who was grumbling to himself in the corner. "Name and contact details, then you can go."

"*What?*" Miriam said, before she could stop herself. "He was lurking around the church!"

"I wasn't *lurking*," the man snapped.

"You were in the supply cupboard!"

"You were in the supply cupboard?" DI Adams said. She had her reclaimed phone out in front of her. There was something that looked a lot like dragon drool on the screen.

"I was looking for the stairs to the steeple. I heard the, um, ladies come in, and was just going to slip out again without troubling them."

"Why not just ask us?" Alice asked, rinsing the bowl she'd used to clean the inspector's hand.

"I didn't want to disturb you. And sometimes people get funny about strangers wandering around their church." He put extra emphasis on "funny", leaving no one in any doubt that he thought they were all a bit funny, and not in a *ha-ha* way.

DI Adams shook her head. "Name and contact details."

"But—" Miriam began.

"Ms Ellis, you have been found *lurking* around the actual crime scene as well as this church. I wouldn't suggest you start telling me to arrest someone who looks less suspicious than you do."

Miriam wilted under the inspector's glare.

"Name," DI Adams said again.

The man sighed. "Stuart Browning," he said grudgingly, and Miriam and Alice exchanged glances.

"Phone."

He gave it, and the DI wiped her mobile on her trousers, then rang him. His pocket suddenly started blaring, *If you liked it, then you should have put a ring on it, if you liked it, then you should have put a ring on it,* and he hauled the phone out with a sigh, silencing it. DI Adams raised one eyebrow just slightly.

"Kids," Stuart Browning explained. "Can't be bothered changing it. They just go and change it to something even more embarrassing."

"Fine," DI Adams said. "Off you go."

"But—" Miriam started again, and Alice kicked her.

"Yes?" the DI said, and Miriam remembered she shouldn't know anything about S.B. Blood rushed to her cheeks, and for a moment the whole room got a little spotty around the edges, and she found herself thinking about orange jumpsuits again.

"You should let Alice take a look at your leg," she said to Stuart finally. "She's very good at first aid."

"I'm not letting either of you two near my leg," he said. "*You* sat on me, and *she* put a bag on my head. You'll probably put salt in it or something." He limped out, slamming the kitchen door as he went, and the DI took a sip of tea, but not quickly enough to hide a small smile.

"So?" Alice said. "What now?"

"Do you have anything to add to your story of being here to do flowers?"

Alice pointed at the old flowers, folded into a plastic bag on the counter. "No."

"And your W.I. friends? Here purely by chance, were they?"

"They often dog-walk together."

"Really?" The DI's raised eyebrow was back.

"Of course. The dogs get on very well."

The inspector shook her head. "Fine. Any idea either who was shouting for Walter outside, or who Walter is?"

"None at all."

"Fantastic." DI Adams took another mouthful of tea. "Then I shall be taking both of you home. And as I can't seem to trust either of you to stay away from crime scenes and out of trouble, I will be having you watched."

"You're putting us under *house arrest?*" Miriam squeaked. That was terribly close to actual arrest.

"Nothing formal," the DI said. "Not yet, at any rate."

Miriam looked at the remains of her tea and wondered what the black market in prison was like for herbal teas and infusions, and whether chia seeds were considered contraband. She also thought that if Alice and the DI hadn't both been the sort of people who frowned on public crying, she'd start right now. As it was, she'd wait until she got home.

13

ALICE

Alice bent down to look at PC Ben Shaw, his long legs tucked in underneath the steering wheel of his car. It was a baby blue Smart car, and she wondered how, exactly, he expected to give chase to anything in it.

"Hello, Ms Martin," he said, giving her an apologetic smile.

She patted the roof of the car. "Cutbacks?"

His cheeks were normally on the red side, and now they looked positively painful. "We couldn't really spare the patrol car, so I said I'd use mine. But then mine's in the garage, so I had to use Jasmine's. The inspector was spitting when I told her."

"I expect she was," Alice said, and offered him a bowl with a napkin neatly draped over it. "I only had salad planned for tonight, so it's not very exciting, I'm afraid. But it does have hazelnuts and blue cheese, and raspberry vinaigrette."

"Oh. Um—" His cheeks were so red now that Alice found herself wondering if they'd spontaneously combust. She knew it wasn't a scientifically documented phenomenon, but, well. She'd never seen anyone go that colour before. "The detective inspector says we're not to accept any food from any of you."

Alice raised her eyebrows. "As I assume she means the W.I., she does realise that your wife is one of us?"

"Yes. Well. She's not very impressed that I'm the one here, but everyone else was rota'd on in town. There wasn't any choice. And I did tell her that Jasmine couldn't have done it, on account of her terrible cooking."

"Well." Alice straightened up, neither entirely surprised nor entirely unhurt. The inspector was right to be cautious, but it irked her that she was still carrying around the weight of Harvey's disappearance after all these years. She was quite certain that the only other person being watched would be Miriam, and that was probably only because they kept being discovered together. She sighed. "Very well. You do have some dinner, though?"

"Oh, yes. I stopped at the bakery. They still had some sausage rolls and a cheese pasty left."

Alice gave him a severe look. "You'll shorten your life, eating that stuff."

"Not as much as eating Jas' cooking."

She smiled at him, aware that he was trying to make her feel better, and took the spare salad back through the little gate in her wooden fence and let herself inside. She put the bowl in the fridge for lunch the next day and leaned against the sink, looking out the window at the quiet green garden and its neatly mowed lawn. The house felt very still and full of anxious silence, and she could feel that horrible claustrophobia pressing down on her again, as if the police officer outside was only one of many, leaning over her too closely to allow her to breathe.

She pushed herself off the sink, took the shed key from its place on the key rack, and marched outside. There was still plenty of daylight. She'd do some pruning. Her rosebushes could do with a little tidying.

HER MOBILE RANG while she was frowning at a rosebush, trying to decide if she needed to take a little more off the left-hand side to make it symmetrical. She pulled her gardening gloves off and fished the horrible thing out of her pocket. She tried not to carry it on her, but she was expecting a few calls. Jasmine had already rung, apologising over and over for not stopping the detective inspector at the church, although, as Alice had pointed out, their plans had not taken into account the belligerent tendencies of Lord Walter. Then Priya had called and said that, so far, they hadn't turned up any suspicious male bakers. She'd been slightly cagey about it, and just kept saying that everything was fine and they'd keep looking, but her voice was higher that it usually was. Alice wondered what that might mean, but in the end she rather doubted that BestBakerBoy was their murderer. No one could get *that* upset over a village fete. Now she hit answer on the phone.

"Gert," she said, checking to make sure Ben was in his car. He was, sitting on the passenger's side with his legs out on the pavement. She picked up a handful of cuttings and strolled toward the back garden.

"Alice," Gert said. "How's house arrest going?"

"News travels fast."

"Of course," Gert said. "Any news on that end?"

"We met S.B. at the church."

"Ooh, was that who it was? Rose told me that Miriam tackled someone who looked like George Clooney."

Alice chuckled. "Rose needs a new prescription."

"I thought as much," Gert said, sounding disappointed. "Anyway, that's good, because I turned up nothing on S.B."

"Violet?"

"No luck there, either. Sue – that's my sister-in-law's niece's sister-in-law, in the council?"

"Yes," Alice said, wondering if she should go and make a cup of tea. This could be a long story if Gert insisted on listing all her relatives.

"She checked the marriage records, but the vicar's never been married. No siblings listed, or naughty little vicar babies. I've got her looking for cousins and so on, but nothing so far."

"Well, that's a shame." Alice tried to keep her voice neutral, but her stomach felt tight and hollow. That brought them back to the W.I. in general, and her and Miriam in particular. Miriam with the belladonna, her with the vanished husband. She hadn't missed the way the inspector looked at them after the phone call in the churchyard.

"It is." Gert was quiet for a moment, then said, more cheerily, "Shall I pop by with a bottle? We can play some cards?"

"Best not," Alice said. "But thank you anyway. I'm sure we'll come up with a new plan." She hung up and put the phone away, examining the long shadows of the garden and rubbing her thumb over the palm of her other hand restlessly. Then she sighed, put her gloves back on and returned to the rosebush, attacking it quite ruthlessly.

THE GARDENING MADE her feel better. The tidy execution of weeds that dared to invade her carefully laid flowerbeds, the judicious removal of overeager shoots and old blooms beginning to fade. There was always something terribly satisfying about bringing order to chaos, to corralling the out-of-control growth and shaping it into something beautiful and *suitable*. She'd never expect nature to follow such strict guidelines, of course. She was more than fond of the wild fells that rose up around Toot Hansell, of the beautiful disorganisation of heather and rock screes and tangled copses of skinny trees. That was as it should be. In her garden, however, a different set of rules applied.

The shadows were deep and rich by the time she dropped the garden rubbish in the compost bin, put her shears and trowel away in the shed, and let herself back into the house. She stood for a moment on the threshold of the dim kitchen, listening to the evening cries of the birds behind her, her back still warm with the last of the sun and a pleasant little sweat salty on her lips. She'd have a bath, she decided. It wasn't really a summer thing to do, but it'd be good for her after the garden. Stop her stiffening up too much.

She had one shoe off and was reaching down to remove the other when she stopped, a frown drawing tight lines at the corners of her mouth. In the centre of the kitchen was a rug. It was a big Turkish style thing, given to creams and pale blues that broke up the warmth of the polished wood floor and reflected the cream cabinets. She was very fond of it, and as it was far enough from the counter, the only mishap to befall it so far had been Miriam spilling red wine on it. There was still a pale grey shadow two thirds of the way from the left edge that made the younger woman go pink every time she saw it. But otherwise it was softly worn and perfectly clean.

Except for a few blades of grass, stark against the pale, as if someone had trodden across it on their way to the hall. And she didn't wear shoes inside.

For a moment, she considered going to get Ben. He *was* just outside, and while he was presumably there to make sure she didn't go off murdering anyone, rather than the other way around, she didn't think he'd object to coming and taking a look for intruders. Especially as she could think of no other reason that she would have an intruder than the fact that she'd been poking around in a murder investigation. She frowned at the grass. If there *was* an intruder. Might she have brought the grass in on her trousers earlier? Might she be mistaking her own unease for that sense of *wrongness*, of things being not quite right?

She took a deep, slow breath, steadying herself, then slipped her other shoe off and locked the door behind her. Unlike the rest of the population of Toot Hansell, she did lock her doors when she was out and when she went to bed. Although not when she was in the garden. She padded barefoot across the kitchen, her feet soundless on the heavy wooden flooring, and checked the door to the cellar. It had a tendency to slip its latch and swing open, so she'd put a pretty, old-fashioned bolt on the outside of it not long after she moved in. It was still shut, and she nodded sharply to herself. Clear.

She eased the corner cupboard open, and selected her least favourite frying pan, a flimsy thing with a cheery pattern of daffodils around it that had been a prize at the fete a few years ago. She wasn't quite sure why she'd kept it, but it could make itself useful now. She wasn't about to waste her good pans on some good-for-nothing's head. And it was plenty heavy enough to make a dent. She shouldered her weapon, and advanced slowly into the hall. Alice Martin, Chair of the Toot Hansell Women's Institute, was not the sort of person to call a police officer in on shadows and nerves. She wasn't going to have *that* said about her.

THE HALL BATHROOM WAS CLEAR. So too was the cupboard under the stairs. She moved quietly, methodically, aware that the sound of doors opening and closing would be giving her location away, but equally aware that leaving a hiding place unchecked was inviting disaster. The living room, with its big bay windows that looked over her garden (her wonderfully neat garden, a small part of her mind noted approvingly) was empty, and she could see Ben playing with his phone in the Smart car, not even glancing at the house. The living room had double doors that opened onto a small dining room. It used to have a door through from the kitchen, too, but she had blocked it off.

She rarely entertained, and she certainly never had dinner parties, so the dining room had become her library. Three of the four walls were lined with bookshelves that reached to the ceiling, and a small set of wheeled stairs roved around the room. There was an old wooden coffee table with a scarred top, and a couple of comfortable chairs with soft red upholstery. There was a window seat with soft cushions, and a chaise longue lived in here too. In winter it was a small, cosy space of different worlds and different times, while the snow fell soft beyond the windows and a fire grumbled in the grate. Alice loved her library, and now she glared at the double doors with something like reproach. They were closed. They were almost never closed.

She opened one door slowly, standing well to the side and ready to jump back. It was dark inside, the curtains on the window drawn, and she cursed herself for not noticing that when she was in the garden. She hoped she wasn't slipping.

No one jumped out, but a voice said, "Come in, Ms Martin. And shut the door. I don't want PC Clown Car out there to see us."

Alice considered her options. She thought she recognised the voice, and she didn't feel particularly afraid of its owner, but at the same time, he *was* in her house. She really should go and get Ben.

"Please, Ms Martin. I didn't want to sneak in like this, but as it appears you've already attracted quite a bit of attention I didn't have much choice. I don't really want the police in my business."

"And why do you want to talk to me?" Alice asked, still not moving. Her eyes were adjusting to the dark of the room beyond, and she could see a figure reclining comfortably in her chaise longue. Her *chaise longue*. The one she'd ordered all the way from London. She pursed her lips in disapproval.

"Because I have a feeling that you're going to be pointing the police at me. And I would really rather that didn't happen. I only want the same thing as you. I want to know who killed Norman."

Alice stepped into the room and pulled the door to behind her. There was a soft *click*, and the reading lamp went on, illuminating Stuart Browning looking very much at home on her plush red and gold chaise longue, with his feet up among the cushions.

"Please take your shoes off," she said. "I don't wear shoes in the house. And certainly not when I put my feet on the furniture."

Stuart looking startled, and maybe slightly deflated that she seemed less worried by his presence and more concerned with his footwear, then nodded and stood up. "Have a seat, Ms Martin."

"No thanks." She was still holding the frying pan at attention.

He sighed. "Look, I know you must have found the emails, to call me S.B. I think you've got the wrong end of the stick."

"What does it matter what I think? The inspector will have those emails, too."

He shook his head. "I know for a fact that Norm was super-careful about his personal email. He'd only have had his work account on his phone or computer. His private one he used just on one tablet, and that's the email I always contacted him on. So if *you* found it, *she* didn't. She'll be looking at an email address with nothing on it but junk mail and church stuff."

Alice thought about it for a moment, then said, "And? You were at the church. She's going to look into you."

"She's going to look into Stuart Browning, antiques dealer and legitimate businessman. Which I am."

"But not all you are." Alice lowered the pan. It was starting to make her shoulder ache, and she'd rather lost the element of surprise. "Who else are you?"

"Call me a childhood friend." He grinned, the expression lupine in the soft light of the reading lamp.

"A before-prison friend?"

He chuckled. "You *have* done your homework."

"I know people."

"I don't doubt it."

"So, if you're now a legitimate businessman, why don't you want the inspector looking at you?"

He tapped a thumb against his tooth and looked longingly at the chaise longue. "If you're not going to sit, can I? My leg's killing me."

"Just keep your feet off my furniture."

He grumbled but sat down in the middle of the big seat, his leg stuck straight out in front of him and his foot on the floor. "It *hurts*. It should be elevated, I'm sure of it."

"You shouldn't push old ladies if you don't want to face the consequences."

He looked at the pan pointedly. "I'm glad you at least left the 'harmless' bit out." He didn't ask what had bitten him, which was one less concern, at least. Alice wasn't at all sure how convinced he'd be if she told him the massive teeth marks had come from Primrose. Just a good thing Mortimer hadn't bitten him that hard.

Aloud, she said, "So. You don't want me to tell the inspector about the emails."

"Well, obviously you'd be incriminating yourself anyway, because you must have stolen his tablet."

Alice made a noncommittal noise. She'd preferred him earlier, squalling about his leg.

He grinned again. "But yes, I'd rather avoid drawing any undue attention. Some of my business dealings are not *exactly* pure as the driven snow. I mean, I got out of the drugs and all that about the same time Norm did. More money to be made in arts and antiquities, for an enterprising fellow."

"Why were you sending all those emails to the vicar, then?" She'd never called him by his first name before, and she wasn't about to start now. "They were rather aggressive."

He sighed. "They weren't. It's just how I talk to old friends. I liked Norm. We were close when we were kids, and he did good. When he started the whole man-of-the-cloth thing, he helped a lot of people. Kind of a shame he didn't stay around home to do it, you know?"

He sounded genuinely sorry, and Alice moved a couple of books off one of the chairs and sat down. "Why didn't he?"

"Too many memories, I think. He did some pretty bad things. I mean, I was no boy scout, but the things Norm would do for the right price ..." He shook his head. "Too much for him to face."

"So he wouldn't talk to you?"

"It took me about ten years to track him down the first time. And I didn't do it to ask him to work with me, or anything like that. I just wanted to make sure he made out okay. And when I saw what he was doing – well. You know. Getting kids off the streets. Letting them sleep in the church, giving them somewhere safe to go. I just wanted to tell him I was impressed, you know?"

"But he didn't want anyone from his old life back." Alice was leaning forward in her chair, the pan held across her knees, and something had slipped in her precise, nondescript accent. There were softer edges there.

"I turned up in Manchester once I found him, and he slammed the door in my face. But then I sent him a phone with email already set up, everything untraceable. We talked. We even met a couple of times. He was so afraid that I'd give him away somehow, that even being in contact with me would make someone look more closely at his past. I tried to explain he'd paid for what he did, and that everything he'd done since was more than anyone could ask of him, but he didn't believe it. I don't think he felt he deserved to be forgiven."

Alice nodded. "And then he moved."

"Yeah. He up and left. Sent me the phone back. But I found out where he'd gone, and figured good on him, you know? Nice quiet place. Maybe he felt he'd finally earned it."

"Those emails were new, though. You were asking to meet."

"Yeah, once I tracked him down I sent him the tablet. Told him he deserved at least something that wasn't just for work. He sent me a note – an actual note – to say thanks, then that was it. No emails, and the old email address just bounced back."

"But he gave you the new one."

His mouth twitched. "Not exactly. But it's not hard to find the email for vicar@toothansell.com. It's right on your cute little website."

Alice gave him a severe look. "It's a very professional website."

"It has lambs and daffodils on it."

"What did you expect, skulls and crossbones?"

He laughed and went to put his leg up on the chaise longue again, then caught her glare and just shifted his weight with a sigh. "Anyhow, I found the email, and he gave me his new personal one, I suppose to keep anyone else from stumbling across me. There are a few of us from the old days who have gone legit, or near enough, and we wanted to meet up. Bit of a reunion. We're getting on, you know? I thought Norm might be up for it, but I wasn't going to push it." He shrugged, ran his hands back over his hair, and sighed. "And then I hear – *this*. I came up to have a sniff around, see if it was maybe someone from back then who caught up with him."

"It was a poisoned cupcake," Alice said.

"Yeah?" He gave a short, unhappy laugh. "Well. That kind of rules that theory out, then."

"I think so," she said thoughtfully, and got up. In a gap on the bookshelves there was a bottle of Scotch whisky and two glasses. They were cheap, the sort of glasses that look like you could drop them on a stone floor and they wouldn't even chip, and they were old and scratched, and utterly out of character with the rest of the house. They were also the only ones Alice ever used to drink whisky. She'd never needed both before, but now she poured a little in each and handed one to the man in her chaise longue before taking a sip of her own. "Do you know someone called Violet?" she asked.

He swirled the whisky, sniffing the fumes, and nodded appreciatively. "This deserves a better glass."

"You'll have no glass if you're complaining."

"No, no. Just saying." He sipped his drink, then said, "I think Norm had a woman of that name hanging around back in the day. Bit wild, as I remember. I can ask around."

"Do that," Alice said.

Stuart took another sip, watching her over the rim of the glass. "What bit me?" he asked finally, his eyes sharp and dark.

Alice smiled at him, a sweet old lady smile. "Best not to ask," she said.

AFTER HE WAS GONE, slipped out the back door and over the fence, she checked the locks and ran the bath she'd promised herself. She sat on the side as it filled, checking the temperature with one hand, watching the bubbles rise and build and the steam smear itself across the mirror. Funny how the past always seemed to catch up. So often you thought you could just pick and choose what you carried with you, but it never worked that way. It all came along, in one form or another, and bled around the corners of your life until you laid it to rest or made peace with it. And maybe that was okay. Maybe that was how it was meant to be. We're the sum of *all* our lives in the end, the good and the bad and the terribly, unbearably ugly. It's all in what we do with it.

14

MORTIMER

As soon as the church door closed after Miriam, Beaufort released Walter, who let loose with a stream of cursing that wilted the nearby daffodils. Beaufort put up with it until the old dragon stopped for breath, then pointed toward the far side of the graveyard, where the wall gave only onto the stream and the wild land beyond.

"Home," he said.

Walter glared at him mutinously, and Beaufort stared back without expression. After a moment the old dragon gathered his legs under him and broke into a lumbering run, his ragged wings flaring to catch the air. He was still swearing as he gained height with great, ungraceful wing beats, and Mortimer caught the occasional "damn dog", and "stupid humans", as well as less palatable remarks regarding the parentage of everyone present. Beaufort stayed close to Walter all the way back to the caverns, not responding to his monologue, although he did send a warning little belch of flame at the old dragon's toes when he started to veer toward a field full of sheep.

They climbed steadily past the tangle of woodland that crowded up next to the stream, over the green of the grazing pastures and on into the high browns and greys of the fells, stitched with crumbling stone walls and studded with abandoned shepherd's huts and cairns and little grottoes filled with mysterious life. They dropped lower as they reached the deep lake that lay below the dragons' stony peak, the still waters dark and reflective and pocked with reeds. Walter dropped to the ground among the boulders that crowded the shore closest to the cliffs and spat angry purple fire at Beaufort.

"You fool," the old dragon snarled. "Hanging about with your human pets, acting like the last centuries haven't even happened, eating cake and drinking tea and forgetting the rest of us!"

Mortimer expected Beaufort to react furiously, given the way he'd ordered Walter out of the churchyard, but the High Lord just sighed, settling onto a boulder and folding his big wings along his back. The sun flushed his scales in their natural colours of emerald and gold, and he'd have looked entirely majestic if his shoulders hadn't sagged so much.

"I'm sorry, Walter," he said. "I know you don't agree with the idea of reconnecting with humans."

"It's stupid! It's dangerous! You *know* what happens!"

"No, I know what *happened*. Times change. People change."

"Humans don't. Stupid little animals."

Beaufort growled, a soft rumble at the back of his throat, and Mortimer exchanged an alarmed glance with Amelia. Contrary to popular myth, dragons were more inclined to settle problems with discussion rather than fighting, but some things just can't be talked out. And he'd never heard the big dragon growl before.

Walter grunted, unimpressed. "You're the High Lord, Beaufort. Do what you want. But you need to realise that some of us remember being hunted. Being slaughtered. Being blamed for everything from bad crops to the damn pox. They're superstitious things, humans. They don't like what they don't understand."

"I remember, too," Beaufort said. "But there's a difference between honouring memories and not moving on, Walter."

"They killed us for our *scales*. Our *teeth*. To prove their stupid valour. Why do you think it'll be any different this time?"

"You keep saying 'they', as if it's all the same people. As if everyone thinks the same. *They* weren't everyone, even back then. You know that, else we'd all have been extinct. The people of this tiny old village pretended they never saw us. They lied to the knights. To everyone. They protected us, even when we sometimes stole their sheep in the winters. They called us *their* dragons, and told stories about this hill and lake being haunted, to make sure no one would come up here. So if you want to talk about *they*, you need to remember that as well."

Walter shook his heavy head. "I still think you're asking for trouble. Not everyone's behind this public relations game of yours, Beaufort. Someone will challenge you."

"If they do, they do," Beaufort said calmly. "But I think we've hidden long enough."

"Damn tea parties and bauble sales. What sort of dragons does that make us?"

"Modern ones."

"It'll all end in disaster. You've got the bloody human police involved now. It's going to get to the council one of these days. You're drawing attention to us!"

"You're the one who chased the dog!" Mortimer blurted, unable to just keep watching Beaufort taking the grumpy old monster's tirade with barely a protest. "*You're* the one who made a mess of the whole thing!"

Walter bared his teeth at the younger dragon. "Watch your tone, cub. Poncey little dragon, with all your fancy *artwork*." He spat the last word like it was something rotten he'd bitten into.

"Hey!" Amelia snapped. "He's the reason you've got a nice warm barbecue to sleep on, rather than nothing but rocks! He even got it *for* you, you nasty old wyrm!"

Walter drew himself up to his full height, which would have been impressive if he hadn't still looked like his skin was four sizes too big for him. "I won't be spoken to like this! In my day I had *respect—*"

"That's enough, all of you," Beaufort said. "Walter, thank you for your help. I appreciate your concerns."

"*He's* a concern," Amelia mumbled, and Mortimer kicked her. "Ow!"

"You're wrong," Walter said to Beaufort. "Humans don't change. You'll see."

"Unless you intend to challenge me yourself, Walter, I think that'll do," Beaufort said. His voice was mild, but Walter sagged back down to his bent old dragon size.

"*I* don't, no. But you keep up this path, and someone will. Not everyone wants a High Lord who spends all his time mucking about with humans."

"I'm entirely aware that we have factions among us who would prefer we went back to the days of night raids and burning villages. However, as long as I'm High Lord, it will indeed be tea parties and baubles. Are we clear?"

Walter opened his mouth, no doubt to say something horribly unpleasant, and Beaufort snapped his wings wide, the sun lighting the delicate tracery of veins within them. The slump disappeared from his shoulders, and his neck arched as he glared down at the old dragon, the gold of his spines stark against the rocks.

"*Are we clear?*" he repeated, and the words were a rumble deep in his chest, which was darkening to a rich bruised purple colour. Mortimer took a step back and trod on Amelia's paw. She squeaked and pushed him off. Walter appeared to be trying to think up an appropriate retort, but settled for muttering some-thing about what Beaufort could do with his baubles, and lurched into the air, passing so low over Mortimer and Amelia that he almost knocked them into the lake. By the time they sat up he was already vanishing into the entrance of his own small cavern, the grey of his scales blending into the rocks above.

Beaufort, already fading back to his usual greens and golds, sat down and scratched his chin. "Well. That went about as well as could be expected, don't you think?"

{🐾}

MORTIMER CAME BACK DOWN to the lake as it got dark. The water had taken on the colours of the sunset sky above it, a delicate pale grey shot through with apricot and gold. There were clouds sneaking around the horizon, hinting at rain to come, but for now the air was cool and clear and full of the sounds of night creatures emerging. He landed among the boulders and padded through the smooth rocks until he found the High Lord, stretched out on his belly on the sun-warmed stone, his gold eyes half-closed and his front paws folded under his chin.

"Um, sir?" Mortimer said. Sometimes he still didn't know how to address Beaufort. There were days when the old dragon felt like an over-enthusiastic child, racing from one idea to the next and throwing himself into each with wild abandon and little thought for the consequences. On others … Well, on others he was the High Lord. Older than anyone could exactly say, with a scar on his shoulder from a knight's lance and claw marks on his belly from a cowardly challenger who had set upon him while he slept. There were more battle scars than the old dragon could remember how he'd come by, so he made up stories to thrill the hatchlings, stories of krakens and trolls and giants.

He'd outlived the cause of every twisted ridge of scar tissue. He'd watched villages become towns, towns become cities, cities spread and grow and sprawl. He'd seen cart tracks become roads that burrowed across the land, watched humans take to the air and the sea and beyond. He'd watched his own kind and others fade and shrink and even die out, while the humans rose, and rose, and rose.

Sometimes it exhausted Mortimer to even think about the passage of all those long years, to imagine waking morning after morning, to look out on sunset after sunset, to deal with squabbling dragons, and trade disagreements with dwarfs, and arguments with dryads over wood, over and over and over. Sometimes he couldn't understand how the old dragon kept going. And sometimes he understood perfectly why Beaufort treasured scones with cream and jam, and the perfect joy of a good cup of tea.

"Hello, lad," Beaufort said, not moving from his spot.

"Ah, hello. Um, have you eaten?"

"I've been thinking."

Well, that didn't sound good. "Have you?" he said, trying not to sound too anxious. Many things came of the High Lord's thinking, but in Mortimer's opinion they were mostly chaotic and rather alarming things, such as wearing dog costumes to sneak into the Toot Hansell Christmas market.

"Yes. Maybe we need to involve everyone more."

"Oh. In what, exactly?"

"Well, I know you have Amelia and now young Gilbert helping with the baubles and so on, but maybe we could get some more dragons interested. Kind of a community effort."

Mortimer had visions of Walter glowering as he tried to shape one of the delicate baubles that bloomed into floating flowers when they were lit, and shuddered. "It takes a, um, certain touch."

"*Hmm.* Yes, I see what you mean. I couldn't do it. Not enough patience." Beaufort sat up and eyed the younger dragon thoughtfully. "We must consider these things, though, Mortimer. Walter was right when he said that what humans don't understand, they dislike. Or worse. But dragons are no different."

"Um. Yes?"

"Yes." Beaufort stretched his wings out. "We've kept our friendship with the W.I. far too quiet on our side as well as the human side. It'll do everyone good to meet the ladies and understand they're really very lovely people, and not at all likely to want to kill us for our scales, claws or hearts."

Mortimer thought it was a surprisingly sensible suggestion, and said so (leaving out the surprising bit).

"Wonderful. Let's think about the best way to do it, after all this murder unpleasantness is over. Now, shall we go and see how Alice and Miriam got on with the inspector?" Beaufort was already on his feet, pulling himself skyward with heavy beats of his wings, setting the wildflowers nodding in alarm. Mortimer scrambled to catch up as the old dragon went circling over the lake, low enough to drag his toes in the water and kick up spray that glittered in the fading light.

"I had another thought, too," Beaufort called as he banked toward the village.

"Oh?" Mortimer asked, falling into easy flight next to him and, for once, feeling quite comfortable with the High Lord having thoughts.

"The vicar used to work with these at-risk youth types. I'm not sure I understand exactly what they're at risk from, but we should partner them with some of our more bored young dragons. Our lads and lasses could protect them from whatever's after them, and it'd be a sure cure for boredom. Perfect, eh?"

Mortimer recovered just before he ploughed into a scrubby bush and winged hurriedly after Beaufort, head swimming with visions of delinquent dragons and small humans with big grudges. Perfect. Perfect like the efficiency of Viking pillaging.

🐉

WITH THE DARK pressing down around the village, turning it into a postcard of glowing windows nestled under the stars, they flew all the way to Miriam's. Against that moonless sky, they could have been bats or night birds, barely seen and rarely imagined, and they landed in her shadowed garden entirely unseen.

The lights were out downstairs, but one of the upstairs windows was propped open, the room beyond lit with soft warm light.

"Miriam!" Beaufort called, not at all quietly, and Mortimer shushed him. "What?" Beaufort asked.

"What if the police are around?"

"Why would they be around?"

"Because things were a little weird at the church."

"Nonsense. That man was *much* more suspicious than Miriam. He positively reeked of wrongdoing." Beaufort looked back at the window. "*Mir*-iam!"

Mortimer was puzzling how to explain to Beaufort that the inspector may not have taken the man's scent into account when conducting her investigation, when Miriam appeared at the window.

"*Shh!*" she hissed, then vanished again.

The dragons looked at each other, suddenly worried, and a moment later they caught the faint sound of the gate latch opening. Beaufort slipped into the shadows of the apple tree, and Mortimer tried to conceal himself under a large rose bush without losing too many scales to the thorns.

The light came on in the kitchen and Miriam flung the door wide. "Are you there?" she whispered.

Mortimer watched the detective inspector come around the corner of the house, walking on the grass next to the path so that her footsteps were silent to anyone but the dragons and the night creatures, who paused their busy snuffling to wait out the threat. She stopped in the shadows, and he saw a frown dimple her face as

Miriam, in a large purple top printed with "My Sister Went to Cancun & All I Got Was This Lousy T-Shirt", and a rather violently green-and-orange sarong, leaned out into the garden and called a little more loudly, "Are you *there?*"

The inspector examined the garden, and Mortimer willed himself to *be* the rose bush as her eyes passed over him. She frowned, pinched the bridge of her nose, looked again, then shook her head.

Don't say our names, he willed Miriam. *Don't!*

As if she'd heard him, she straightened up, reached inside, and stepped into the garden holding a saucer of milk with little torn chunks of bread around the edges. "Are you there?" she asked again. "Come on, little pixies, we need our guardians at the moment." She stood barefoot on the grass looking up at the stars, while Mortimer reflected that she was more likely to attract hedgehogs than pixies with milk, but that hedgehogs were generally more useful and definitely more friendly than pixies, so that was alright. Miriam sighed, set the bowl down among the dandelions under the faded blue bench that sat beneath the kitchen window, and went back inside. A moment later the lock turned, and the light went out.

The inspector stayed where she was for a little longer, then snorted to herself and went silently back around the house. Mortimer listened to the gate click closed behind her, then scuttled down the path that led to the stream. Beaufort was already ahead of him.

THEY DIDN'T TALK on the way to Alice's house, and this time they checked the front first. There was a very small car parked outside her gate, and they could see a police officer leaning against it, looking tired. They watched him pace the length of her fence a few times, then sit back in the front seat with his legs on the pavement. He opened a packet of biscuits, turned the radio on, and settled himself to pecking at his phone. The dragons ran from their shelter in the woodland next to Alice's garden, scrambled over her fence, and scooted around the back of the house. They hunkered under the outside table for a moment, waiting, but there was no shout, no sound of footsteps. Just the whisper of the radio. The officer seemed to be listening to an audiobook about how to improve one's career prospects through positive thinking, which seemed to Mortimer to be the sort of thing Beaufort would be very enthusiastic about.

When they were sure they hadn't been noticed, Beaufort whispered to Mortimer, "Just nip up to the window, lad, and see what's happening, will you?"

Mortimer looked at the ivy-clad wall and sighed. "Can't you? What if I mess up the stone? She'll shout at me."

"She won't shout at you. And, really, how can you expect a dragon of my age to be climbing houses?"

Mortimer gave the High Lord a disbelieving look, and Beaufort grinned at him.

"Well – well, I expect mince pies. And I don't care if they're only for Christmas."

"Once all this is over, I will personally ask Miriam to make you all the mince pies you can eat."

Mortimer gave him a final glare, mollified somewhat by the promise of non-seasonal mince pies, and ran across to the house. He scampered up the side of the little lean-to annex that housed the boot rack and coats and rain hats and carrier bags and other such things, then scaled the wall beyond, hoping he wasn't causing too much damage. A moment later he lifted his nose level with the windowsill and whispered, "Alice?"

She put her book down and looked at him over her reading

glasses. "Mortimer. Do you often sneak into women's bedrooms unannounced?"

He thought about it. "First time."

"Keep it that way." They looked at each other, then she gestured at him impatiently. "Well, come in. I'm fairly sure a dragon hanging half out my window may be more noticeable than not."

Mortimer wriggled over the sill and found himself sitting on a small but rather comfortable window seat. "This is nice."

Alice put her bookmark in, smiled at him, and said, "Yes, I rather think so myself. Now, I don't want to go down to the kitchen to put the kettle on, as I'd rather Ben Shaw didn't report to the detective that I was up and about in the middle of the night. But I did bring some biscuits up, just in case." She took a tin from the bedside table and offered it to him. Mortimer jumped from the seat and took it eagerly, and she said, "I guess you're looking for an update?"

"Yes, please," Mortimer said around a chocolate Hobnob. He knew the women of the W.I. could sometimes be peculiar about packet biscuits, but he never understood it himself. They were rather nice.

Alice updated him, in quick, precise sentences, and sent him back to Beaufort with the biscuit tin.

જ

BEAUFORT EXAMINED the biscuits and selected a custard cream. "Violet, then," he said.

"Yes." They had retreated to the edge of the graveyard, made uneasy by the presence of the police but unwilling to go home. There was no watch on the vicarage tonight. DI Adams obviously felt she'd isolated the most likely suspects.

Beaufort nodded. "I do believe it's time for some more direct action, Mortimer."

The younger dragon sighed. "I'm breaking in again, aren't I?"

"Only if you're willing to."

Mortimer thought about Miriam, pretending to feed pixies in her nightclothes, and Alice wielding frying pans as she confronted not-very-legitimate businessmen in her reading room. "Yes," he said. "As much as I need to."

"Well done," Beaufort said, and stashed the biscuit tin behind the headstone of Gerald Jones, who had died in 1753 and whose final words were "It's only a graze".

"Where are you going?" Mortimer asked, running after Beaufort as he started toward the vicarage.

Beaufort gave him that charming, yellow-toothed smile. "I'm not letting you have *all* the fun."

Mortimer wasn't sure whether to feel reassured or alarmed.

15
DI ADAMS

It was getting light, the stars fading, the sky paling from indigo to a deep and promising blue-grey. Dawn was on the way. Finally. DI Adams stretched and yawned, rolling her neck to work out the cricks. The sun was still nothing more than that gentle lightening of the sky, which meant it probably wasn't much after 4:30am. Still a good couple of hours before James came to relieve her.

He'd not been exactly keen when she'd called him and told him to make the drive up from Leeds. DCI Temple had been even less keen when she told him why she needed James up here, and Skipton had made a right bloody fuss over her using even one of their officers. You'd think they'd all forgotten it was actually a murder investigation. DCI Temple had even gone so far as to suggest – not saying anything outright, just to *suggest* – that perhaps the whole thing was an accident, and that DI Adams had her big city hat on and was looking for trouble where there was nothing there.

She sighed. But it hadn't been like there were any other weird or wonderful ingredients in the cake. If there had been other herbs, maybe she could have believed that someone had put the belladonna in by accident, but her most likely suspect in that case would be PC Ben Shaw's wife. She struck DI Adams as the sort of person who'd make just that sort of mistake, but common knowledge seemed to be that she couldn't cook well enough to create a cupcake anyone would eat.

Which left the one woman who'd been snooping around the vicarage *and* the church, and who had the damn bush growing in her garden. It was hard to believe Ms Ditzy Hippie was the murderer, and the motive of a few disagreements about paganism versus Christianity seemed a bit shaky, but well. Eliminate all other possibilities and all that. Maybe Miriam Ellis had been the one to make the mistake. It didn't seem that improbable, what with all the midnight wanderings and plates for pixies. But there remained the question of where the other cupcakes had gone, as so far no one else had dropped dead. Not that she was aware of, anyway.

She rubbed her eyes and yawned. After the debacle at the church she'd gone back into the village centre, such as it was, to stock up on whatever sort of stale energy drink the dusty shop had on hand, but judging by how she felt now they'd been as out of date as the sandwiches. And there had been another Toot Hansell weirdness. She'd gone into the little bakery with its tiny but surprisingly well-stocked deli section looking for something decent for the stake-out (although it was unlikely to be as decent as the food she'd had delivered to her earlier in the day. But it was best to be safe where elegant murderers were concerned). There had been no one behind the counter, and after waiting for a moment or so she shouted, "Anyone here?" It probably wasn't the done thing in the village, but there was a decent-looking coffee machine behind the counter, and she was going to have to help herself at this rate.

A skinny man with very little hair and an immaculate apron

peered around the corner of the kitchen door at her, and whispered, "Are they gone?"

"Are who gone?"

"The ladies."

Oh, God, not the ladies again. "Which ladies?"

"The W.I."

Of course. "Why are you hiding from the W.I.?"

"They're making me very nervous." He came out cautiously, rubbing his hands on his apron.

DI Adams thought that he wasn't the only one they had that effect on. "Why are they making you nervous, exactly?"

"They keep *watching* me."

"Watching you?"

"Yes – look! There's one now!" He ducked down behind the counter, and DI Adams turned to watch a large woman with very curly, very dyed hair stroll casually past the plate-glass window, glancing inside with apparent disinterest. She matched the face to a name from the hall. Hart, Carlotta. She turned back and peered over the counter.

"She's gone."

The man straightened up warily. "Another one'll go past any minute. You watch."

They watched, and after a couple of minutes DI Adams said, "Can you make me a long black coffee while we're waiting? Three shots, splash of milk?"

"Well, I suppose. You keep an eye on them, though, alright?"

"Shall do." She leaned against the counter, and a moment later Teresa sauntered past, still in her pink Lycra. The inspector decided not to say anything. She'd never get a coffee at this rate.

The coffee machine growled and spat promisingly, and eventually the man turned around and waved the takeaway cup in the direction of the counter, peering past DI Adams and not looking at what he was doing. She grabbed the cup before he could drop it, and decided that the stale-looking biscuits she'd bought at the shop earlier would have to do. She didn't fancy asking him to do anything that involved knives.

"I'll go talk to them," she said, pulling out her wallet.

"*Would* you? I'd really appreciate it. I'm sure they're scaring away customers."

DI Adams thought that he might be doing that quite well himself, considering he looked like he hadn't had a decent meal in about six years and kept scuttling about the place in panic, but she just said, "It's no problem."

"Thank you! Thank you so much!" For a moment she was afraid he was going to hug her over the counter, but he just piled a variety of wrapped slices and a banana off a display and pushed them at her. "No charge! No charge at all! Just please, please make them stop!"

"Um, sure. I'll do that." She wondered about asking for a bag, then decided he might have a small breakdown over a demand of that level. So she stacked the food in her arms as well as she could, and walked out of the shop straight into a petite woman in a pretty, multicoloured dress. The woman stumbled backward with a yelp, and DI Adams grabbed her before she could fall, dropping the food and the coffee as she did so.

"Sorry! Sorry, God – are you okay?"

The woman looked up at her with wide eyes, then nodded firmly. "Yes, thank you, DI Adams."

Kaur, Priya. More bloody W.I. The DI looked at the coffee splashed across the cobbles and sighed. "Are you and the other ladies stalking the baker, by any chance?"

"Of course not," Priya said, her eyes even wider. "Why on earth would we do that?"

"The baker says he keeps seeing you walking past."

"Well, a few of us were planning to meet in there. Probably no one wanted to be the first to arrive." Priya smiled and tapped her nose with a manicured finger. "One mustn't appear too eager."

"No?"

"No." Priya peered around the inspector's shoulder. "Look, there they are now!" She waved, and DI Adams turned to see Teresa, Carlotta, and Pearl all waiting at the corner of the square. They waved back enthusiastically, and the inspector sighed again.

"Right. Well." She wanted to say *behave yourselves*, but that would be like telling her mum and aunts to behave. It seemed like a bad idea. "Enjoy your coffee, then."

"Thank you." Priya started toward the shop, then turned back. "Can we get you something, Detective Inspector?"

"No! No, thank you." She gave the four women a smile, then stooped to pick up her empty cup and the food. She might be coffee-less, but there was no chance she was going back in to face the baker. She didn't want to imagine what sort of state he'd be in with the W.I. actually on the premises.

¾

GOD, she wanted that coffee now. Or sleep, preferably. Her vision had gone back to normal after the churchyard, no more blurry edges or that weird sense of her eyes sliding away from, well, whatever, but the whole incident had left her with a horrible headache, which the sleepless night hadn't helped.

Then there was that thing late last night, when she'd gone to see what Miriam was up to. She could have sworn she'd heard *other* voices in the garden before she got there, but she hadn't seen anyone except Miriam with her pixie food. One of the voices, though, had sounded like the commanding one that had shouted for Walter in the graveyard. She'd never seen him, either. She *should* have seen him, but maybe he'd hidden behind a gravestone or something. She had been kind of busy being knocked over by the dog. She thought. There had been something off about the timing, the way the dog ran past and *then* she fell, but her mind kept sliding away from it, the way her eyes had from the church steps. And Miriam's garden earlier in the day. *And the bridge. The bridge in London. Your eyes wanted to slide then, too. And your mind.*

"Shut up," she said to the car, and rubbed her eyes. There was no point thinking about it. About *that*. She'd been overworked, under-rested, running on caffeine and adrenaline. She'd got the kids back. It didn't matter that there had been all that confusion over who (*what*, her mind suggested unhelpfully) had taken them in the first place. She was in a better place now, anyway. She'd taken time off. Done some work on herself and her stress management techniques. Had the MRIs, just to be sure. She was fine. And Leeds was far less stressful. *Not so many bridges, either*, her mind added.

"That is entirely enough of that," she told herself firmly, and opened the car door. Air would help. She hadn't had enough sleep, was all. And it was the deathly quiet of this place, no distractions. Her mind was just up to unpleasant tricks, seeing connections where there were none. Nothing else to it.

The early morning air was cool against her skin, smelling somehow newly minted, as if the trees had brewed it up just for her. No hint of exhaust smoke, no stench of stale beer or chippie grease or just the packed mass of humanity that makes up a city. The greens of Miriam's garden, and those of her neighbours, were slowly emerging from the washed-out colours of the night, and the one streetlight at the end of the lane went off, leaving the sleeping houses tranquil. It was a place untouched, rolled back in time to when there were wild places still, and the world felt unworn and *possible*.

DI Adams breathed deep, and thought that there might actually be something to this country air thing. She swung her legs out of the car, thinking that a bit of a walk and a stretch in the thin light of the new day seemed both decadent and sensible, and put her foot on something that *squidged*. She closed her eyes, said something rude about country living, and looked down, expecting to see a cow pat under her boot.

It wasn't a cow pat.

It was a rabbit.

It was a very dead, very cooked rabbit. Its skin was still on, but the fur was singed away, and its lips had been baked back from its teeth in a horribly cheerful rictus. She stared at its eyeless sockets and contracted limbs, then stepped past it and got slowly out of the car. The rabbit was lying on a neat collection of several large green leaves, as if being artfully presented at one of those trendy eateries that always seem to disdain plates. And there were some flowers next to it, some sort of wildflowers maybe? God knew what they were exactly, she wasn't a botanist. She looked at the house, but there was no face at the window, no spying rabbit-roasting woman. She nudged the tiny corpse with her toe and said something anatomically incorrect about what the donor of this meal could do. Then she snapped a couple of pictures on her phone and got back into the car. Sod the countryside.

DI ADAMS WAITED until she felt that it was a reasonable sort of hour for country folk to be up. They got up early, didn't they? Wasn't that one of those country living things? James had messaged to say that he was on the way, but he wouldn't be here for another hour or so, and she quite frankly didn't fancy waiting any longer. Every time she looked out the door the bloody rabbit was staring back at her sightlessly, and it was downright unnerving.

She got out of the car again, picked the rabbit up gingerly by one charred paw, and marched to the house. She didn't bother going around to the back door, just walked straight through the gate and up the path to the front, then looked for a doorbell. There didn't seem to be one, which was just typical. She banged on the door with her free hand, her *it's the police so open up if you know what's good for you* knock. There was no response, and she hit the door again, harder this time, using the side of her fist, and she was mid-knock when it opened, revealing a wide-eyed Miriam who jumped back with a squeak.

The inspector dropped her fist hurriedly, and Miriam stared at her, wiping her hands anxiously on a tea towel.

"Um, good morning, Inspector?" she offered. She was dressed, after a fashion. She still had that terrible sarong on, but the souvenir Cancun T-shirt had been swapped for one of those long-sleeved, scoop-necked things that you always saw in stores that sold incense and crystals.

DI Adams thrust the rabbit at her. "What is this?" she demanded. "What *is* this?"

"It's, well, it's a rabbit?" Miriam said, looking bewildered. She was still wiping her hands like Lady Macbeth.

"I can *see* it's a rabbit, you—" The inspector stopped and took a deep breath. She wasn't going to shout. Shouting meant things were getting out of control again, and they weren't. *They weren't.* Anyway, she was already starting to doubt the woman had anything to do with the rabbit. She looked too confused to be faking. "I can see it's a rabbit, Ms Ellis. Why was it outside my car door?"

"Outside your car door?" Miriam repeated blankly.

"Yes. It was outside my car door. With flowers. I stood on it. On the rabbit." It was surprisingly difficult to keep her voice level. "Why? Why was there a rabbit and flowers outside my car door? And how? How did it get there? I didn't see anyone, and I've been watching *all night.*" She sounded plaintive to her own ears, and swallowed hard. This was no good. She needed caffeine.

"Oh dear," Miriam said, wiping her hands on the cloth with a little more enthusiasm. "Oh, oh dear."

"Oh *dear?* That's all you can say?"

"Yes. I mean, no. Oh dear."

"What? Oh dear *what?*"

"I, well – oh dear."

"Ms Ellis! Do *not* say oh dear again!" DI Adams jabbed the rabbit toward Miriam as she spoke, with rather more violence than she had intended, and the well-cooked body tore free, leaving her holding the leg. Both women looked down as the carcass landed on the hessian doormat with a meaty thud. There was a moment's silence, then the inspector said wearily, "Oh, bollocks."

"Come in," Miriam said. "I'll make you a cuppa."

"What about the rabbit?"

"Bring it in. No point wasting it."

She turned away, and the inspector followed her through the house and into the quiet warm of the kitchen, gingerly cradling the dead rabbit.

"It's a village custom."

"Dead rabbits."

"Yes. A mark of respect. It means that we accept you. Like a welcome present."

"A dead, burned rabbit left outside my car door is considered a welcome present."

"Country customs." Miriam gave the inspector a little smile, but DI Adams didn't return it. She didn't feel like smiling. A dead rabbit was a mark of respect? A *welcome present?* What sort of back-woods horror show was this?

"What happens if you really like someone?" she demanded. "A dead cow by the back door?"

Miriam gave a little hiccough of laughter and glanced at the oven. DI Adams followed her gaze, and her stomach rumbled. She knew it was a risk, eating or drinking anything, particularly as Miriam was about as close as she had to a suspect, but she'd gratefully taken the tea the woman had made. And whatever she was baking smelled amazing, all spices and rich brown sugar sweetness. She rubbed her forehead and wondered if things might start making more sense if she had something to eat. The rabbit lay on the draining board, staring blindly at the ceiling, and answering that question pretty firmly in the negative.

"Ms Ellis. Miriam. I need you to tell me what's really going on here." DI Adams leaned over the kitchen table, confidential, woman-to-woman. It wasn't an approach she was particularly familiar with or good at, but desperate needs and all that. "I'm not a bad person. I'm not trying to persecute anyone or get innocent people in trouble. I'm just trying to get to the bottom of what's going on. But you need to be honest with me. So let's start with how the rabbit got there. Because I know it wasn't you. I never saw you leave the house."

Miriam sighed. "I told you. I think a friend of mine must have left it there."

"So what's this friend called?"

"Walter."

DI Adams frowned. Miriam had barely hesitated over the name, but she looked distinctly uncomfortable, and she was playing with the tea towel again. "Walter? Was he at the church?"

"Yes. I mean, no! No, I didn't mean Walter. I meant – I meant Melvin."

"Melvin."

"Yes. Melvin. Melvin, um, Melvin Walters. That's who I meant."

The inspector sighed and took a sip of tea. It was good tea, strong and lightly sugared. Not poisoned, as far as she could tell. "Miriam, you're not helping yourself."

Miriam had been avoiding looking at her, staring at her hands instead. Now she risked a little glance up. "I'm sorry. I really don't know who left the rabbit. But I do have a feeling that it might have been a friend of mine."

"So tell me his name."

"I can't."

"Why not?" DI Adams could feel a tic starting just below her eye. Jesus. She hadn't even had that in London.

"He's a very private individual."

DI Adams wondered briefly if banging her own head against the table would help matters. "So why would a very private individual leave a dead rabbit outside my car?" *And when?* she wanted to scream. *How did I not see him?*

"He's, um, very eccentric. And traditional. He absolutely would have meant it as a welcome gift. And in case you got hungry, you know. He's always very concerned that everyone has enough to eat. I think he's seen some shortages before."

Great. So her mysterious rabbit donor was old enough to have lived through rationing, and he'd still been able to sneak up on her. That was just fantastic. "He couldn't have left a packet of biscuits?"

Miriam appeared to think about it. "Not really, no."

"Okay." The inspector rubbed her face, feeling tiredness collected in the corners of her eyes like dust. "Tell me about Walter, then. From the graveyard."

"I can't."

"Is he a very private individual too?"

"I don't really know him," Miriam said, and this time she looked like she was telling the truth, although her cheeks were still very pink.

"What about the belladonna?"

"What about it?" She sounded nervous.

"Why do you have it in your garden?"

"It's a native plant. I try to encourage as many traditional plants as I can." There was a tremor in Miriam's voice, and she pushed her hands into her lap, not looking up from her tea.

"It's a highly poisonous traditional plant."

"Yes, but, but I'm, but I—" Miriam stopped, and the inspector watched in astonishment as her face went from over-rouged to pancake-white. *"Oh-my-God-you're-going-to-arrest-me-the-vicar-was-poisoned-and-it-was-belladonna-ohmygodohmygodohmy—"*

The inspector clapped her hands together in front of Miriam's nose, hard, and the older woman jerked back with a gasp. "Calm down, Ms – Miriam. I didn't say that."

"But it was! It was, wasn't it? Oh, God, and now you think *I* did it! I'm going to go to prison, and there'll be no local produce, and I'll have to wear orange, and someone will make me join a gang, and—"

DI Adams got up and searched through the cupboards until she found a bottle of rather ancient-looking Cointreau behind the vinegar in the pantry. She splashed a generous measure into the bottom of a glass, reflecting that if Miriam *were* the murderer, she was an exceptionally good actor. She put the glass in Miriam's hand and helped her lift it to her lips, which finally interrupted the breathless monologue regarding what horrors jail was going to hold for her. Miriam took an enormous gulp, and promptly descended into a coughing fit, spraying DI Adams with sticky alcohol.

"Fantastic," the inspector said with a sigh, and went to find a cloth.

BY THE TIME she'd cleaned herself off, Miriam had calmed down enough to finish the glass. "More?" DI Adams suggested.

Miriam grimaced. "No, thanks. It's horrible stuff."

"Does the trick, though."

"I guess." She took a deep breath. "Are you going to arrest me?"

DI Adams shook her head. "No, I'm not going to arrest you. But something's still off about your story. You definitely know more than you're telling me, and that doesn't make me very happy." She tried to give Miriam a meaningful glare, but the woman was sponging Cointreau off her top and missed it. "Are you sure you don't want to tell me about Walter? Or your mysterious friend, since he's apparently so harmless?"

"I can't," Miriam said apologetically. "I really would help if I could. You're very nice."

DI Adams tried to remember the last time she'd been described as "nice", and thought it was probably back when she still wore pigtails and purple bobble hair ties, if at all. "How about how you knew the vicar was poisoned, then?"

"Oh, small village." Miriam waved a little vaguely, and DI Adams sighed. Probably PC Ben Shaw telling his wife. It was how these things tended to work.

"And the W.I. stalking shopkeepers?"

"What?" Miriam's hair was bushed out around her face and her eyes were red-rimmed from coughing and tears, and there was no mistaking the confusion in her voice. DI Adams had an idea that she didn't look an awful lot better herself.

"Never mind. You really need to think about your friends, Miriam. You're putting yourself in a bad position, and if they are innocent, well, you'd only be helping them in the long run if you told me the whole story." The inspector waited for Miriam to respond, but when all she got was that same wobbly smile she finished her tea and got up, putting the mug in the sink. "Thanks for the tea."

"That's okay. Are you sure you don't want some breakfast?"

DI Adams glanced at the rabbit, cold and rigid on the draining board, and shuddered. "No thanks," she said. "I seem to have lost my appetite."

She was halfway to the door when her phone rang. She answered it with an apologetic smile to Miriam. "Yeah?"

"DI Adams? Ma'am? Ah, it's PC Ben Shaw. There's a Situation at Alice – Ms Martin's house."

She could hear the capital "S" in his voice. He sounded like he was trembling with excitement. "What sort of situation?"

"You'd best come over, ma'am. I think the murderer's been here."

"On my way." She hung up and shoved the phone back in her pocket, then shook a finger at Miriam. "*Stay here.*"

"Is Alice okay?"

"I'm sure she is."

"Am I under house arrest?"

"No, but your cake's burning." The DI headed for her car as Miriam gave a yelp of alarm and ran back to the kitchen. She spun the car around with a snarl of loose gravel and headed for the road to Alice's, checking her rear-view mirror as she went. Yep. Miriam was running across her garden, no doubt heading for some secret local footpath, her coat half on and her hair wild. DI Adams hoped she'd remembered to turn the oven off. And that the secret footpath would take longer than the road. She gunned the engine and took the corner with a squeal of tyres.

16
MIRIAM

Miriam couldn't remember the last time she'd actually run anywhere. She was fairly certain she wasn't really built for jogging, and when she did exercise she much preferred swimming. She'd been quite good at it in school. But it wasn't helping her much here, unfortunately. She slowed to a walk, readjusted her sarong and pressed a hand against the stitch in her side, trying to slow her breathing. The Cointreau had made her head a little swimmy, but she kept going, and decided that if she did have to go to prison, she'd become one of those prisoners who did weights all the time and got all muscly. Although that probably still wouldn't help with running. Which made sense. The jailers would hardly want to encourage prisoners to become good at running.

The sunlight had crept down from the fells while the inspector had been talking to her in the kitchen, and now it washed across the valley, drowning the village in soft, clear light. There were heavy clouds slouching on the horizon, and it felt like it would rain before the day was out, but for now the sun was strong and bright, and rendered the landscape in luminous shades of green. The beck sparkled next to the path in the light filtering through the trees, and the smell of damp earth and wild garlic crushed under her bare feet rose around her. She wished she could stop, just for a moment, to watch the world wake up and the day come in. But the stitch was gone, so she broke into a clumsy jog again, thinking that she should have stopped to put on her flip-flops on the way out the door. She'd already stubbed her toe twice.

❧

A SKINNY, faintly-trodden trail branched off from the main footpath that ran through the woodland and meandered its way to a small gate at the back of Alice's property. Miriam hurried along the trail, trying not to lose her sarong to some of the more over-friendly shrubs and long grass along the way. She didn't pause when she got to the little wooden fence, just let herself through, and only looked up when she stopped to pull the sarong back down over her knees. It had been impossible to run with it all the way down to her ankles. The detective inspector was standing by the back door, watching her with a certain amount of unsurprised exasperation, while Alice stood next to her with her arms crossed and Ben hovered at the corner of the house looking like a new boy at school who can't remember where his classes are.

"Hello, Miriam," Alice said.

"Um. Hello." Miriam hesitated where she was for a moment, suddenly aware that she hadn't brushed her hair yet, and that she wasn't exactly sure what she was doing here. Alice certainly didn't look in need of moral support. Her hair was neatly brushed, and her pale blue blouse was printed with darting swallows, and it looked crisp and freshly pressed over a pair of flattering three-quarter trousers. She gave Miriam a smile that suggested she'd been expecting her for morning tea, rather than being in the middle of a Situation. "Is everything alright?" Miriam asked. "What happened?"

"I had a visitor," Alice said. Miriam thought she could hear a barely detectable tremor in her voice, something that would go unnoticed to anyone who hadn't shared a hundred cups of tea and slices of lemon drizzle cake and glasses of dark red wine with her. She wondered if the older woman's arms were crossed because she was cold, or to hide a shake in her hands. She straightened her back and marched across the lawn, feeling suddenly steadier. *Stronger.* Maybe there wasn't much she could do, but she could be here. Sometimes that was all that was needed.

{a}

"I DID TELL you to stay home," DI Adams said, sounding tired.

"You said I wasn't under house arrest," Miriam replied, putting her shoulders back and crossing her arms in an unconscious imitation of Alice.

"This is a crime scene. Why are you two *always* in my crime scenes?" That tic had started up under the inspector's eye again, and she put her fingertips on it with a sigh.

"Maybe I should make some tea," Alice said. "Everyone's very tired." She didn't look very tired, though. She looked like she'd just got back from some four-day spa weekend. Miriam looked down at herself and realised there was flour all over her shirt, drifting onto her folded arms. At least her top was white. She dusted herself off surreptitiously.

"No tea," DI Adams said. "You two stay right there where I can see you. PC Shaw?"

"Yes, ma'am?" Ben looked so alarmed that Miriam felt sorry for him.

"Can you please try to ensure that no one else comes charging into the crime scene?"

He flushed. "Yes, ma'am."

The inspector turned back to the women and waved an

admonitory finger at them. "*Stay.*" She went to the back door, taking her phone out, and Miriam tried to see what she was looking at. There was a sheet of paper held to the door by something she couldn't quite make out. It was difficult to see against the dark wood, but it looked – well, it *looked* like – she gave a little, horrified gasp.

"Is that a *knife?*"

"Yes," Alice said, and this time she did sound tired. Miriam looked at her more closely, seeing a dusting of make-up covering the shadows under her eyes, and unfamiliar lines around her mouth. "Quite a big one. A kitchen knife, if I'm not mistaken, Inspector?"

"*Shh,*" the inspector said, not turning around.

"It looks like a kitchen knife of some sort," Alice said to Miriam. "And a note."

"A *note?* What does it say?"

"To stop digging around the vicar's murder," Alice said, and rubbed her eyes.

"I did say *shh,*" the DI said, turning around finally.

"Who sent it?" Miriam asked, one hand pressed to her chest. "Is it a threat?"

"Well, the knife would indicate so," the inspector said, and Miriam felt her ears go pink. "Although quite a sensible message, really. Not that you two seem very good at listening to sensible messages." She pointed at Alice. "And you heard nothing?"

"Nothing."

"Your bedroom is where?"

Alice pointed to a window resting open above them, to the left of the lean-to roof.

"And everything was locked?"

"Everything on the ground floor, yes. Upstairs, my window was open, as you see."

"No other signs that someone tried to break in?"

"None at all."

The inspector watched Alice for a long time, as if deciding whether to believe her or not, then wandered a little closer to the wall, staring up at the open window.

"Do you think it was Stuart Browning?" Miriam whispered to Alice.

"No," Alice whispered back.

"Why not? Amelia said he stank. And he was very rude."

"I'll explain later," Alice said, then smiled as the inspector turned around.

"What are these scratches?" the DI asked, pointing at several sets of parallel lines scoring the stone among the ivy. Some of the leafy strands were disturbed, pulled loose of the wall. Alice and Miriam looked at each other, then went to stand next to the inspector. Miriam swallowed a sigh. They were very *dragonish* scratches.

"I'm sure I don't know, Detective Inspector," Alice said. "An owl, perhaps?"

"An *owl?*"

"Yes. Maybe it was chasing mice in the ivy."

DI Adams looked at Miriam. "They do that?"

Miriam shrugged. "I don't know. I'm not much of a twitcher."

The inspector turned to Alice, her expression carefully blank.

"Bird-watcher," Alice explained. "Ornithologist of sorts, I suppose."

The inspector nodded slowly and followed the path of the scratches up to Alice's window. "Mice inside, are there?"

"It does happen," Alice said with a sigh. "The perils of life in the country."

Miriam personally thought that mice wouldn't dare take up residence inside Alice's house, and maybe the DI shared such reservations, because she took some photos of the scratches, then said, "Mind if I go in and take a look from inside?"

"Be my guest," Alice said pleasantly.

DI Adams pulled on a pair of latex gloves as she walked to the door, and paused on the threshold to glare at the two women. "Don't touch *anything*. Got it?"

"Got it," Alice said, and Miriam nodded firmly, trying her best to look trustworthy. The inspector looked unconvinced, but she vanished inside, and Miriam rushed to take a closer look at the note. It was printed in black font on plain white paper.

"*Get ur noze out of the vicars biz!!*" she read aloud. "*Or els itll be bad for u!!!*"

"Very imaginative," Alice said. "And it's in that funny font Rosemary likes so much, and keeps wanting to use for the newsletter."

"Comic Sans," Miriam said, making a face and peering at the knife more closely. "This is fancy." It had a smooth, deeply polished wooden handle with loops of some bronze-coloured metal securing it, and the long, fine blade had Japanese characters stamped into it.

"*Hmm.*" Alice came to stand next to her, peering over her shoulder. "You're quite right. I hadn't looked that closely. How odd to waste a good knife on something like this."

Miriam gave her an alarmed look and was about to ask if she was sure she was feeling alright, because Alice never missed *anything*, when the inspector shouted from the window above them, "Hey! I said don't touch anything!"

"We're *not*," Miriam said indignantly.

"Well, move away, anyway." The inspector frowned at them both until they retreated from the door, then she vanished back into the room.

"How can you be sure it wasn't Stuart Browning?" Miriam asked Alice, keeping her voice low in case the DI was still lurking beyond the window.

"I had a lot of visitors last night."

Miriam listened as Alice described the night before in quick, precise sentences, her voice low and emotionless. She found herself wanting to put her arms around the taller woman and tell her it was all somehow going to be alright, but Alice wasn't the sort of person who invited hugs. She didn't even look like she *needed* a hug, but no one could really be *that* calm after finding a stranger in their house, could they? She'd have been scared enough if Stuart Browning had knocked on her door, let alone turned up in her reading room. "Are you *sure* you're okay?" she whispered.

Alice shrugged. "I've had worse nights."

Miriam tried to imagine that and couldn't. "So Beaufort and Mortimer are trying to find out something about this Violet person?"

"I believe so. I suggested they try the vicarage again, since the police seem rather occupied with the two of us."

Miriam shivered. She didn't like the idea of the police being *occupied* with them. "So what do we—" she fell quiet as the DI let herself out of the house and looked at the two women with an expression that said she knew exactly what they'd been talking about. Miriam hoped not. She didn't fancy explaining dragons to the detective inspector.

"There's a tech team on the way here to dust for prints and see what other evidence we can pick up," she said. "Do you need anything from inside, Ms Martin?"

Alice raised her eyebrows. "I take it we're not to stay."

"You can if you want, but we may be some time, and you won't be able to go inside while they're working."

"You need the whole house?"

"We can't be sure it hasn't been broken into, Ms Martin. We'd like to check everything, the garden included. You don't *have* to let us, of course, but this has become a crime scene. And a warrant is ... very formal."

"You're welcome to look wherever you want, Detective Inspector," Alice said. "I'd just like my handbag."

"Of course. I can have PC Shaw take you to the village hall and keep you company while we search."

Alice gave a very small smile. "I'd rather go to Miriam's."

"Yes, you must," Miriam said firmly. "We'll have breakfast."

The DI looked like she wasn't exactly enthused by the idea, and Alice added, "Unless you're arresting one of us, Inspector, I believe we're free to do this."

The DI sighed, and shrugged. "PC Shaw will accompany you. You're not under arrest, but I'd rather know what you two are up to. Neither of you has been exactly cooperative so far."

Alice opened her arms with a smile. "You have my whole house. What more do you want?"

The inspector looked unconvinced, but she started inside to get Alice's bag. At the threshold she paused and looked back. "Ms Martin, do you know anything about a local custom involving rabbits?"

"Rabbits, Detective Inspector?"

"Yes. Dead rabbits, left outside my car door."

"Rabbits!" Miriam said, nodding. "You know, Alice."

"I do?"

"Yes, tell me about rabbits, Ms Martin," DI Adams said, leaning in the doorway.

"Rabbits," Miriam said, still nodding, and grabbed Alice's arm. "The ones that—"

"Ms Ellis, please let Ms Martin answer."

Miriam managed to stop nodding, although her head still felt very wobbly and she could feel a fake smile stretching the corners of her lips. She squeezed Alice's arm hard enough to make the other woman wince.

Alice looked from Miriam's death-grip to the inspector, and back at Miriam, and for a moment the world seemed far too light and airy. Miriam wondered if she was going to faint with the sheer stress of it. Then Alice patted her hand and smiled.

"Oh," she said. "*Rabbits.* Of course. You must have caught someone's eye."

DI Adams frowned. "Ms Ellis said it was a sign of respect."

Miriam opened her mouth to say that it was the same sort of thing, but her tongue was sticky, and all that came out was "*Hunh.*"

"A very *specific* sign of respect," Alice said, ignoring her. "No one would go to all that trouble for just a little pleasantry. I do believe you have an admirer."

The inspector glared at her and said, "Pleasantry? It was a *dead rabbit.*"

"Very tasty with potatoes," Alice said.

DI Adams looked like she had something more to say on the matter, but finally she just turned and went inside. Miriam could just hear her mumbling, "Fantastic."

THERE WAS a little confusion over how they were going to get to Miriam's, because Ben's Smart car was too small to fit them all in, and DI Adams said she didn't want Alice to take her own car. She also didn't want anyone to take *her* car and didn't want to leave the house to take them, so Miriam and Alice ended up walking back to Miriam's on the road, with Ben Shaw creeping along behind them in the tiny car.

Miriam opened the front gate, and she and Alice waited while Ben unfolded himself from behind the wheel with a groan.

"You poor thing," Miriam said. "You must be exhausted."

He nodded heavily. "Graham's coming out from Skipton to relieve me."

"That's good." She led them around the back, to the kitchen door she'd left wide open in her sprint to Alice's. "Let's get you a bite to eat at least."

Ben looked dubious, then said, "Well, as long as you don't tell the DI." He deposited himself in a chair at the kitchen table while Alice put the kettle on and Miriam fussed with her apple cake. It hadn't burned too badly, but the coconut flour did make it dry out terrible easily. Never mind. Enough cream and no one would notice.

They couldn't talk very freely with Ben at the table, which was no doubt exactly as the inspector intended, and as tired as he was, he steadfastly refused to discuss the investigation.

"I don't know much, anyway," he said, taking an enormous bite of scrambled eggs on toast. "The DI kind of keeps everything to herself."

"But that person at the church, the Stuart Browning fellow ...?" Miriam asked. She still wasn't convinced that he could have had nothing to do with it. No one who just turned up *inside* someone's house unannounced like that could be up to any good.

"Some antiques dealer." Ben finished his eggs and helped himself to a slice of cake. "This is amazing, Miriam. Thanks."

"My pleasure," she said, and wondered where the dragons were. They wouldn't come rushing up to the door, not after last night, but she just hoped they weren't getting themselves into any more trouble. They were all in enough of that as it was.

BEN WAS REPLACED RATHER QUICKLY, not by Graham, but by the tall skinny detective constable called James, who had been helping DI Adams at the village hall on the first day of this whole horrible thing. Miriam couldn't believe that it had only been a couple of days. It felt like an awful lot longer. It was still so terrible to think of the vicar, alone in his silent, worn rooms, treating himself to a cup of tea and a little cupcake. Small joys turned against him. She sighed, loudly, and both Alice and James looked at her in surprise. He had his phone and a slice of cake in front of him, and she was reading something on her e-reader. It was an oddly domesticated scene.

"Are you quite alright, Miriam?" Alice asked.

"Yes," she said, looking at the crossword she'd been trying to do in the local paper, although mostly she'd been doodling on the ads. "No. The poor vicar. It's just all so, so *horrible*." A tear blobbed onto the newsprint, and she wiped at her eyes hurriedly. This was no good, crying in front of Alice *and* a strange police officer. This was no good at all.

James cleared his throat loudly and said, "Shall I put the kettle on?"

"What a good idea." Alice moved her chair next to Miriam's and patted her back with surprising compassion. "Poor you. We haven't even had time to grieve, have we?"

"No," Miriam managed, trying not to sound too blubbery. "And I saw him. I *found* him! And I just, I'm just so *sad* for him, all alone in that big old place, and all he wanted was some cake and tea—" She was definitely blubbering now, there was no getting around it. Partly for the vicar, partly from tiredness, partly for the horrible fact that there was a police officer in her kitchen, a *detective*-type police officer, and that meant she might still be going to jail, and all because she had belladonna growing in her garden. She hadn't even *done* anything! Well, apart from aiding and abetting dragons in a housebreaking, and withholding evidence. She broke into fresh sobs, and Alice handed her a tissue. She took it with shaking hands, hoping that her cellmate would be half as nice to her.

"There we go," Alice said, still rubbing her back. "You have a good cry, Miriam. It'll all be fine. You'll see."

Miriam wondered momentarily whether Alice was quite right, and kept crying, just stopping to sniffle a thank you to James when he put a mug of tea down in front of her. He retreated to the door and stood there looking pointedly out at the garden.

The DI knocked on the back door just as Miriam's sobs were

dying down to hiccoughs, and she burst into a fresh wail as James let the inspector in.

"I didn't do *anything!* I *didn't!* I know I have belladonna in the garden, but I *didn't!*" Or at least that was what she tried to say. Judging by the confused looks on everyone's faces, it was mostly just a bray of snuffly sound.

"Is she alright?" the inspector asked.

"Just a little stressed and tired," Alice said. "As are we all. Apparently she believes you're going to arrest her for growing belladonna."

DI Adams sighed, and nodded. Miriam froze, her sobs stuck in her throat. Then she sniffled and wiped her nose. "I'll come quietly," she said, straightening her back. She might go crying, but she could have *some* pride. "Can someone water my garden?"

DI Adams gave her an amused look and shook her head. "Not you, Miriam." She looked at Alice. "Alice Martin, I'm arresting you on suspicion of murder."

Miriam gave a horrified little gasp, but Alice just nodded as if she'd expected nothing less and got up. "Very well," she said. "Let's get this over with."

MORTIMER

T he night was still as Mortimer followed Beaufort through the graveyard, the vicarage cool and quiet, and there was no one to be seen on the paths or at the church, which loomed silvered and graceful in the faint light of the stars. Dragons see well in the night, their prismed eyes collecting and reflecting the smallest drift of light, but even to Mortimer it felt dark under the trees, and the vicarage seemed foreboding where it crouched before them.

It took them a little while to find a way in. The windows all seemed to be shut and latched, the doors firmly locked. Finally, on the third circuit of the building, Mortimer spotted a tiny gap on a small sash window with frosted glass, where it hadn't been pulled all the way down to the sill. It didn't prove easy to open, though. He tried standing on Beaufort's broad back and hooking his claws into the gap, struggling to push it up, but it wouldn't budge. Beaufort got impatient and insisted he should have a go, so Mortimer reluctantly crouched in the garden for the High Lord to use him as a step ladder.

The old dragon's weight just about made Mortimer's legs

buckle, and by the time they were finished there were deep Mortimer-sized dragon footprints in the soft earth among the geraniums, and he had a new twinge in his front left shoulder to add to his collection from falling down the stairs. But, to be fair, the High Lord did manage to muscle the window open with a screech of swollen wood and sticky paint.

But it was too tight for Beaufort to fit through, with his broad shoulders and wide expanse of wings. He shoved his nose into the gap and looked around, then grunted and jumped off Mortimer's back, tearing divots out of the lawn as he landed.

"In you go, lad. Then pop round the back and let me in the kitchen door."

Mortimer, shaking dirt off his snout after having it shoved rather unceremoniously into the flower bed when Beaufort jumped clear of him, said, "Should we both go in? Shouldn't one of us stay outside and keep watch?" He was thinking he'd quite like to be the lookout, given the choice. The air drifting from the window smelt stale and sad, and even with no cars waiting out front, and no one else in evidence, the place felt *watched*.

"There's no one around, and no one likely to be. Two sets of eyes are better than one. We can cover more ground."

Mortimer sighed. He was right, of course. That was the problem with Beaufort. He was quite often right. Mortimer crouched back on his hindquarters and jumped, hooking his front paws over the windowsill. He wriggled his shoulders through, folding his wings as tight as he could against his back, and feeling the rough skin of his spines scraping on the window above him as he peered into the shadowy room.

"How's it looking, lad?" Beaufort called from behind him.

"It's a toilet, Beaufort. A *toilet*." Mortimer eyed the bowl below him unhappily.

"Oh, you'll be fine. In you go!" Beaufort gave the young dragon's tail a slap that was probably meant to be encouraging, but it startled Mortimer so much that he squawked and kicked the wall wildly with his back legs, straining against the window frame with his front paws. For one horrible moment he thought he was going to be stuck like that partly dressed yellow bear humans liked so much, half in and half out, then he forced the rounder part of his midriff through, the longest of his spines slid under the window with an audible snap, and he was plunging head-first toward the toilet bowl.

He yelped, threw his front paws out to catch himself, and planted them on the seat as if he were about to do a handstand. His body and tail slid through the window after him in a rush of uncontrollable momentum, and he flipped over with an alarmed squeak and landed on his back on the floor, just in time to be hit on the nose with his own tail. *"Ow."*

"Everything alright in there?" Beaufort called from outside, and Mortimer wriggled around in the tiny space between the toilet and the door until he could sit up. He supposed that since nothing was broken, things were as near alright as they seemed to get at the moment, so he climbed onto the toilet seat and peered out the window at Beaufort.

"I hit my nose."

"Oh dear." Beaufort looked at him critically. "You haven't lost any scales that I can see."

Mortimer patted his snout, *humph*'d, and went to let the old dragon in.

THE HOUSE HAD the feel of somewhere long unused, shut up and left years before, the air stale and the thin starlight that came through the windows draining everything of colour and life. Mortimer shivered, wishing they'd waited until the morning to go investigating. Maybe they were more likely to be seen, but this place felt awash with ghosts.

"What are we looking for, exactly?" he whispered to Beaufort as the old dragon sniffed around the kitchen.

"A way to find Violet Hammond. An address book, perhaps?"

"From what Miriam said, he didn't *want* to find her."

"That's not to say he always felt that way." Beaufort opened the pantry cupboard and snuffled inside.

"He's hardly going to keep an address book in with the beans."

"No, but he might keep some – ah, yes." Beaufort held a box up and peered at it in the dark. "Apple pies? Mr Kipling's apple pies. I don't know who Mr Kipling is, but they look rather nice."

"Beaufort! It's a crime scene!"

"They'll only go to waste." Beaufort tucked the box under one front leg and headed for the hall. "We need to keep our energy up, lad. This may take some time."

Mortimer sighed and pattered after the High Lord, wondering if it was really stealing when the owner of the pies was, unfortunately, deceased.

THEY WERE in the kitchen when the sun came up, chasing ghosts away and turning the dim, dusty corners of the house into bright, still-dusty corners. Mortimer's belly had won out over any moral objections, and he and Beaufort were sitting on the floor, sharing a can of condensed milk and a loaf of sliced white bread.

"I just don't understand it," Beaufort said, licking condensed milk off one claw. "The man has an entire room full of mannequins, old hiking gear, and bags of tinsel. How are there *no* personal papers?"

"Everyone keeps those sort things in the Cloud nowadays,"

Mortimer said, pouring a generous dollop of sticky sweetened milk onto a slice of bread.

"The cloud? What cloud? Clouds are just water particles. How can you keep an address book in a cloud?"

"Um." Mortimer crammed the bread into his mouth to give himself time to think. He'd heard Miriam talk about it, but he didn't really know what it was. Beaufort always thought he knew all these things. "It's not that kind of cloud," he managed around the bread, hoping the old dragon didn't ask any more.

Beaufort huffed. "Used to be, humans just knew where their friends lived. Third hut past the lake, and so on. Then they built roads and made addresses, and suddenly it was number 3, Butcher's Row. Then it was writing letters and sending them to different countries, and you had to know all these details, like states and counties and numbers and so forth. Now it's not even written down, and no one knows where anyone is." He punctured another tin of condensed milk with one heavy claw. "Everyone's just names on the internet thingy."

"True," Mortimer said. "But people chat to each other from all over the world because of it. I mean, just think – we haven't even heard from the Loch Ness cousins since I got my back teeth in. If we used internet we'd be able to *see* each other."

Beaufort *hmm*'d, pouring the sweetened milk carefully onto a piece of bread. "I suppose. But it doesn't help us an awful lot right now, does it? What we need is a good old-fashioned street address."

Mortimer accepted the messy sandwich Beaufort offered him and took a thoughtful bite. They did indeed need a good old-fashioned street address. Miriam had looked, but the vicar hadn't had Twitter *or* Facebook on his tablet, which, as far as Mortimer understood things, was unusual. Although it made sense, given what Stuart Browning had said about him being so scared of his past catching up with him. So the vicar himself was old-fashioned.

His only online contact had been his email address, which just identified him as the vicar of Toot Hansell. Mortimer was willing to bet that there were no photos of him on the church website, and that even if some popped up elsewhere, he didn't look much like he had when he was younger. However, Violet had known how to find him. She'd found – or been given – both his email *and* his actual address, just like Stuart. What if she'd been sending him not just emails but actual mail? What If ...

Mortimer got up suddenly and hurried into the living room.

"Lad? Where're you going?"

Mortimer heard the soft percussion of the High Lord's claws on the carpet as the big dragon followed him into the musty stillness of the living room. It still smelt faintly of cake and death, but Mortimer ignored that. He was looking at the birthday cards arranged on the mantelpiece.

"They were friends," he said aloud. "Maybe more than friends, before he was a vicar. So she'd send a birthday card." He stood on his hind legs to carefully lift the cards off the shelf and check the insides. Most were from the Women's Institute, or churchgoers, but one, with a slightly garish teddy bear on the front, said *Here's to the old times* in it, and was signed 'V' in flowery, curving script. He held it out to Beaufort, who took it and sniffed deeply.

"It's been too long," he said. "All I can smell is this room."

"The scent won't help us anyway." Mortimer patted a wicker basket that sat next to the hearth, full of magazines and junk mail circulars. "But this might. Humans need help starting fires. Miriam puts *all* her paper rubbish in her box by the fireplace."

Beaufort looked from the basket to the younger dragon, and gave him that enormous, snaggle-toothed grin. "The envelope."

"With a return address, if we're lucky." Mortimer sat down and began shuffling through the papers, the remnants of the condensed milk on his claws making the pages stick to them. But he didn't pause to clean them off. His heart was pounding. They were going to catch the killer.

☙

THE ENVELOPE WAS ALMOST at the bottom of the pile, and Mortimer was starting to doubt that the vicar had kept it. But there it was, a pale mauve colour with that same swirling script spelling out the vicar's name in the centre, the return address for a V. Hammond on the top left corner. They stared at it together, then Beaufort patted Mortimer on the shoulder hard enough to make him stagger.

"You did it, lad! You found her!"

Mortimer gave a lopsided, self-deprecating little shrug, partly because the shoulder Beaufort had just patted didn't want to move. "That's if she is the murderer. Seems a bit strange, to be sending him cards one week, murdering him the next."

Beaufort peered at the postmark. "That's last month. Plenty of time for a human to change their opinion of someone. And maybe she was even lulling him into a false sense of security so she could get close to him."

"Maybe." Mortimer put the cards back, then followed Beaufort into the kitchen. The floor was a mess of crumbs and condensed milk droplets, and one of them had sat in an apple pie, smearing it across the linoleum. A squirrel had appeared from somewhere and was sitting on its haunches eating a piece of apple in the centre of the debris. It chattered at them threateningly. "Oh dear."

"Indeed," Beaufort said. "It must have come in through the window."

"I mean the mess! We need to clean it up."

"We don't have time, lad. We have a murderer to catch."

"We can't just leave it! Someone's going to come in, and—" Mortimer broke off as the faint, unmistakable sound of a key in the kitchen door shattered the stillness. They spun around at the same moment, colliding with each other, then scrambled to squeeze under the table, Mortimer trying desperately to get his wildly cycling colours under control. He shut his eyes, as if that would help, then opened them again to see a set of large human legs in luminous yellow trainers standing on the floor just in front of him. He could have reached out a claw to touch them, and had to fight a sudden urge to do exactly that.

"What on *earth* ...?" A woman's voice said, sounding confused. "Who did this?"

The squirrel, which had retreated to shelter under the overhang of the cabinets, rushed out to snatch another piece of apple, chittered loudly, then darted back again. The woman shrieked.

"Oh, you *filthy* creature!" The legs vanished, then rushed back, and Mortimer caught sight of the head of a broom as it swung at the squirrel and missed. The animal was rushing wildly about the kitchen as if it wanted to escape but couldn't work out how, and he silently willed it to run out into the hall, to lead the woman away before she got to wondering who had opened the cans that were sitting on top of the bread bag in the middle of the floor.

The squirrel gave a squall of alarm as the broom came whistling toward it again, then shot under the table and took shelter behind Beaufort's wing. The High Lord jumped, bumping the table, and the woman gave another shriek.

"Who's there? *Who's there?*"

Beaufort and Mortimer exchanged alarmed glances, and the younger dragon wondered how sensitive the cleaning lady might be. She wasn't a W.I. member and likely wasn't expecting dragons, so who knew what she might decide she saw when she bent down to peer under the table. She was expecting to see *something*, but there was no telling what it would be. Maybe a whole platoon of rabid, can-opening squirrels. Maybe two giant, toothy squirrels. Maybe she'd just pass out. You could never predict what way people would go. He tried a reassuring smile on for size as the woman crouched down, her knees coming into view. Then her hands, clutching the broom that was extended straight toward them. Any moment now. Any moment.

"Janet?" Miriam's voice came from the door, and Mortimer let out his breath in a gust of relief that charred the edge of the table-cloth. Janet screamed and straightened up, and the broom vanished as she spun around. Mortimer guessed she was probably brandishing it at Miriam. "Sorry! I didn't mean to startle you."

"Miriam! Miriam, oh my God, I think someone's in here!"

"What? Why?"

"Look at the mess!" The end of the broom reappeared, waving at the filthy floor. "And there was a squirrel!"

"A squirrel?"

"Yes! It ran under the table!"

"Um, I don't think the squirrel opened those cans."

"I *know!* That's why something else has to be in here!"

There was a pause, then Miriam said, "Let's go check the rest of the house and make sure they're not in there somewhere."

"But the table—"

"That was the squirrel. You said so yourself." Miriam's feet appeared, clad in a pair of pink clogs, and led the way into the hall.

The dragons waited to make sure they were gone, then shot out the door, closely followed by the squirrel, still clutching its piece of apple.

THE DRAGONS WERE LYING on the far side of Miriam's very old, very green Volkswagen Beetle when she came back out of the vicarage. She frowned down at them both, then opened the driver's door. "Get in."

They scrambled in, Mortimer hurrying Beaufort along when

he stopped to examine the gear stick. There was a momentary confusion of legs and tails and wings, then they were both wedged in the back seat, peering at her eagerly.

"We've got Violet's address!" Mortimer exclaimed, waving the envelope at her.

"Oh? Is that why you stopped to have a celebration in a dead man's house?" she demanded, cranking the engine rather harder than was necessary.

The dragons exchanged glances. "We were going to clean up," Mortimer offered.

"Oh? Well, that makes *everything* better." Miriam released the handbrake and promptly stalled the car. "*Dammit!*"

"Miriam, we've been searching most of the night and all morning," Beaufort said gently. "We didn't forget about you. Alice told us we needed to focus on finding this Violet person."

Miriam gave a large, dramatic snuffle, and started the car again. This time she pulled away smoothly, but only drove until the vicarage was out of sight before she pulled off the narrow lane into a space in front of a farm gate.

"Miriam?" Beaufort put a heavy paw on her shoulder, rather more gently than he had on Mortimer's earlier.

"What's the address?" she asked, pulling out her phone.

Mortimer read it off, but she was struggling to type it in, and kept missing letters and swearing. Finally she just dropped the phone and covered her face with both hands.

"What is it?" Mortimer asked quietly. "Where's Alice?"

"She's been arrested," Miriam managed, and Mortimer couldn't contain a horrified gasp. "There wasn't even time for the crime scene people to get here. Detective Inspector Adams found the rest of the cupcakes in Alice's compost bin and took her away. The inspector said – she said that the knife in her door didn't have any prints on it, and anyone could have done it, including Alice. They *arrested* her, Mortimer. They're taking her to jail. Even if we find

Violet, how do we know she had anything to do with the murder? How do we prove it if she did? They've got all the evidence they need. I'm just a silly old woman with bad hair, and you two aren't even meant to *exist*. What are we supposed to *do?*"

And she burst into tears, resting her head against the steering wheel and sobbing hard enough to shake the little car, while outside the sun shone on regardless, and sheep watched them from the field with golden-eyed indifference.

18
ALICE

Alice sat in the passenger seat of DI Adams' car with her handbag held firmly on her lap, knees and feet together, staring directly ahead through the windscreen. James, the detective constable, had offered to drive her to Leeds, but DI Adams had said she'd do it, and when James had opened the back door of the car the inspector had shaken her head and pointed to the front.

"I don't think she's going to overpower me and force me off the road, James," she'd said.

"One can't be too careful," Alice had observed, and everyone had looked at her in astonishment. It had stopped Miriam crying, if nothing else.

But the inspector had insisted, and now here they were, purring along the skinny roads tucked between sturdy dry-stone walls, the car's GPS reciting instructions now and then in a strange fake English accent, and the radio on low. Alice hoped Miriam would hold herself together. She'd been very upset, poor thing, first at the ridiculous notion that she might go to jail herself, then even more upset, if that was possible, when the inspector had started reading Alice her rights. And now it all rested with her, and the dragons. It wasn't an entirely reassuring thought.

"I'm going to grab a coffee," DI Adams said, as they pulled into a garage with two pumps and a cow looking over the wall at them with bland interest. "Would you like anything?"

"No, thank you," Alice said, not looking at the inspector.

"We've got a good hour before we get there, and that's if the traffic's okay. So probably more. Food? Bathroom?"

"No, thank you," Alice repeated.

The inspector sighed, tapping the wheel with her fingers as if she wanted to say something else, then got out of the car. Alice waited until the door shut behind her to take a deep, shuddering breath, trying not to let her shoulders shake or her posture change. She wondered if she should have just told the inspector about the tablet. But that was admitting withholding evidence, and would implicate Miriam, as well as raising questions about where and how they had got it. No, she had to just let the situation play out. They couldn't really charge her. She didn't think, at least.

So she just had to be calm. The longer she kept the inspector away from Toot Hansell, the longer Miriam and the dragons had to find the real culprit, if they could. But even if they couldn't, they'd find something to point the investigation away from the W.I., and, more importantly, the inspector away from the vicinity of dragons. It was far too clear that the DI realised that there was *something* out of the ordinary in Toot Hansell, even if she couldn't tell what. And Alice had no intentions of allowing her to get interested enough to start asking questions some of the W.I. might not be able to answer without lying. Especially as an awful lot of people just didn't seem to know the importance of being able to tell a good, believable lie when necessary.

§

THE INSPECTOR DROPPED two bottles of water and a packet of Hobnobs into the console between the seats, and handed Alice a takeaway cup of tea.

"I know you said you didn't want anything," she said, putting her own cup into the holder. "But you might change your mind. And there's no point getting tired and hungry over all this."

"Over all this?" Alice said, amused. "You've arrested me for murder, Detective Inspector."

"Yes. You're my best suspect."

"But?" There was reservation in the inspector's tone, a chink in the weight that was crushing Alice to silence.

"But it still doesn't add up for me. Right now, I have to take you in. The cupcakes were in your compost, and there were no fingerprints on the knife, no signs of a break-in or an intruder, or any evidence anyone had been there but you."

"So whoever put the knife there put the cupcakes in my compost bin. They didn't need to break in. They'd know I'd call you over the knife, and that you'd search everything."

"It's a possibility I'm entertaining, Ms Martin, but you *were* at the crime scene the night after the murder. You had easy access to belladonna. The vicar was afraid of you. The dean has confirmed that."

Alice snorted, a very unladylike sound. But such ridiculousness called for snorting. "There's a difference between being afraid someone will be sharp with you and being afraid someone will kill you. And honestly, if you arrested every woman a man was afraid of, you wouldn't have time for much else."

"I know that. My superior, however, wants some results."

"So you're arresting me just to keep him happy?"

"Not exactly, Ms Martin. I do have enough to charge you. It would likely get thrown out, but it's enough to start with. Until you or Ms Ellis give me some real answers, at least."

"I can't believe you think I'd be so silly as to call you to the house if I knew the cupcakes were in my compost."

"That *does* seem rather out of character," DI Adams admitted. "But panic makes people do strange things."

"Do I look panicked to you, Detective Inspector?" Alice asked.

DI Adams examined her. "Well, no."

"You're wasting your time on this when you could be searching for the real killer."

"Convince me of that, then."

Alice sipped the watery tea and looked through the window at the green fields rolling away from the car, clouds chasing their own shadows out across the fells. "It's going to rain this afternoon," she said.

THE TRAFFIC WAS AWFUL, but then, Alice had never been near Leeds when the traffic wasn't awful. It was the curse of cities, she supposed. That, and the way the buildings and people pressed around her, making her feel small and ineffectual. She'd never liked them.

DI Adams inched the car forward, stopped, and sighed. "Guess you never have this problem in Toot Hansell."

"No. Getting stuck behind a tractor is a problem sometimes. And sheep."

"Sounds smelly."

"Better than exhaust fumes."

DI Adams grunted in amusement and took a Hobnob. "We should be there in about fifteen minutes, though."

"That's good."

"Is it? Everything's on record once we get inside."

"In my experience, DI Adams, everything is always on record when it comes to police and journalists."

The inspector glanced at her sideways. She looked tired, Alice thought. Dark marks under her eyes, the hair that had been so fiercely pulled back on the first day escaping in springs and ringlets. But shadows or not, those eyes were sharp.

"And you have had experience with that before," the DI said.

"As you know. I rather imagine it's one of the reasons you've used to justify arresting me."

"A prior murder charge does make you rather a person of interest."

"A *dropped* murder charge."

"And a still-missing husband."

Alice sighed, and resisted the urge to rub her temples. No one needed to know that she had barely slept last night, either. "Which is irrelevant to the current problem."

"It's precedent."

"You're clutching at straws."

DI Adams chuckled. "No. On paper, there are plenty of reasons to pull you in. I could even make things stick long enough to hold you well past forty-eight hours. Reasonable suspicion and all that. If I wanted to."

Alice finally put her handbag in the footwell, and turned her most severe look on the inspector. "What exactly are you suggesting?"

The inspector gave her that amused glance again, as if the severe look held no threat for her at all. Alice felt a twinge of admiration. The detective inspector was proving to be most interesting.

"I'm suggesting you talk to me, Ms Martin. As two people, not as a detective and a civilian. I'm suggesting you tell me everything you know about what's going on in Toot Hansell, because a lot of things just aren't adding up."

Alice looked back through the windscreen. "I'm not sure that will help you the way you think it will, Inspector."

"Well, maybe you should let me decide that."

Alice pressed her hands against her knees, refusing to allow herself to fiddle with the hem of her blouse, or to pluck at her trouser legs. Calm. She could make this work. Give the inspector enough to keep her away from the dragons, and her out of the suffocating claustrophobia of a police station. Aloud, she said, "You may call me Alice. And I would like a decent cup of tea, not this takeaway rubbish."

DI Adams grinned. "I know just the place."

THE PLACE WAS a small tea shop with pink tables and blue chairs set on the pavement outside, yellow gingham cushions clashing quite wildly with everything else. There were cacti in bright metal pots on the table, and a chalkboard menu hung on the door. It was terribly appealing, but no one sat at the little tables. The clouds had crawled in with the afternoon, and a gusty little wind snatched fretfully at Alice's hair as the DI opened the door. Inside was crowded with plants, and people chatted in the depths of soft chairs and sofas. It smelt of coffee and toasting tea cakes, and the young woman at the counter had pink hair that matched the outdoor tables.

The DI pointed to a small table flanked with two big chairs in the corner. "That'll do us. Tea?"

"Yes, please." Alice went to sit down obediently, noting with approval that the table was wiped clean, there was no dust on the windowsill, and the sugar bowl had a dedicated spoon sitting in it. Small things mattered. Everyone always forgot that. She watched the inspector laugh at something the young woman said, then turn back to Alice, still smiling. Yes, she was interesting. But interesting didn't mean she should be told everything, and certainly not when it came to dragons. Interesting meant Alice would have to be very careful indeed, and try to avoid lying where possible. She had a feeling that the inspector might have a very good nose for lying.

"Tea's on its way," DI Adams said, sitting down in the chair opposite Alice with a sigh and a stretch.

"Wonderful," Alice said.

"So." The inspector leaned forward, her hands between her knees and her dark eyes fixed on Alice's. "Tell me. I don't actually think you murdered the vicar at all, but you need to convince me, or I'll hand you over to my DCI anyway."

Alice frowned at her. "But what on earth did you arrest me for? You gave Miriam such a fright!"

"But not you?"

"Of course, me too. But you saw Miriam. She was beside herself!"

"Do you think she might do something rash?"

Alice opened her mouth to reply that something rash was always a possibility with Miriam, then frowned. "You did it to see what she'd do. You don't think *she*—"

"No. For a while I wondered if it was a joint effort, given the belladonna, but the motive's not there, and she's—" She made a wavy little movement with her hands that Alice felt did actually describe Miriam quite well. "You might be capable, but you'd have such a perfect alibi it makes my head hurt to think of it."

Alice raised her eyebrows slightly. "I'll take that as a compliment."

"*Hmm*. Maybe. Anyway, the two of you together are impossible. I needed you out of the way and her pressured to do something. Hopefully something that'll point to the actual murderer, since I think you know more about that than you're saying."

"That's – well, that's just not very sporting," Alice said, and leaned back as the young woman with the pink hair arrived with a tray.

"Tea?" she said, smiling at Alice.

"Yes, thank you." It came in an old-fashioned tea pot with a mismatched cup and saucer, a proper tea strainer in its own little dish, and a chunky china jug of milk. "Oh, this looks very nice."

"Thanks," the woman said, placing an enormous mug of frothy coffee in front of DI Adams. "There you go. Back from the coffee-less wilderness." She patted the inspector's shoulder and wandered off again, pausing to wipe an already-clean table.

"You must be quite a regular," Alice observed, pouring a little milk into the cup.

"Best coffee in town, and it's right next to the station. I think I pay their wages with my caffeine habit." DI Adams stirred her coffee vigorously enough to slop it over the sides of the mug and onto the saucer. "Damn."

Alice *tsk*'d and passed her the napkin from under the teapot. "Well, that's a good start."

The inspector wiped off her mug, then took a sip, closing her eyes with an expression of pure pleasure. "Oh, I've missed that."

"We do have coffee in Toot Hansell, you know."

"Not like this. Now. Back to you and Miriam."

"If you insist. I was saying you're very unsporting." Although she couldn't help feeling a grudging admiration for the inspector. *Of course* Miriam would rush off to hunt down Violet. *Of course* she'd keep searching for anything that would point to anyone other than Alice, and she'd never even think to watch for someone trailing her. "Who's watching her?"

"James. Apparently she's already made a stop at the vicarage, and now is off toward Manchester."

"Is she, now?" Alice stirred the tea (loose leaf, this really was quite a wonderful spot), and placed the little sieve over her cup before pouring.

"We're assuming she went to track down someone from the vicar's past. If she is actually on the path of the murderer, you should be happy we're following her. It could be dangerous."

Not with dragons, Alice thought, and smiled slightly. "I see your point."

"So tell us who she's looking for, and we can take this out of your hands. I'm assuming you have the vicar's tablet."

Alice managed to contain a jump of surprise, raising one eyebrow instead. "Why would you think that?"

"We found a charger that didn't fit anything. Stood to reason it was for a tablet, and that he kept all his personal emails on it, because there were none anywhere else. The vicarage computer had nothing that wasn't strictly work-related, and his phone looked like the first Nokia I ever owned. And it seems to me that even a vicar would have a *few* personal emails. So, why did you take it?"

"It – well, it seemed like a good idea at the time," she admitted. "We did think his emails would be on his phone and his laptop as well. We didn't mean to keep anything from you, but it was a bit awkward to put back."

The DI looked like she might be rolling her eyes if that wasn't terribly unprofessional. "You don't say. How did you get it in the first place? Did you break into the vicarage?"

"No," Alice said honestly.

"What about the scratch marks on your wall. They were at the vicarage too. What's that all about?"

"Um." She took a sip of tea. "Yes. I don't know about the scratches."

"Honesty, Alice. Honesty is what's going to stop me from hauling you into the station and putting you in a cell for a night or so. I don't even need to charge you for that. Although I could throw in a charge of possessing stolen property and obstructing an investigation, just to spice things up."

Alice tried not to think about the stink of the cells, the cold metal of the seatless toilet, the way the solid walls had pressed in around her, windowless and featureless and full of the promise of days and nights passed in a crush of fear and boredom and terrible, empty loneliness. "I can't tell you much about the scratches, inspector." That was honest, at least.

"Why do I feel you mean *won't?*"

"They're nothing to do with the murder."

"They're to do with how you got the tablet."

"But that's irrelevant."

DI Adams leaned back with a sigh, frowning at Alice like a disappointed teacher. "Let's try this differently. What did you find on the tablet? Where is it, and where might Miriam be going?"

Alice thought about it for a moment. None of that suggested dragons. And it seemed the inspector was willing to look in other directions than the W.I., so maybe it was time to hand things over after all. "I feel a little silly," she said. "We rather thought you wouldn't look past the W.I., given the circumstances."

DI Adams sipped her coffee. "You really have quite a low opinion of law enforcement, Ms Martin."

"Alice," Alice said. "And that may change."

THE EXPLANATION of the possible suspects didn't take long. DI Adams was less convinced about Stuart's innocence than Alice was, especially when she learnt he'd been in Alice's house.

"You should have called PC Shaw," she told Alice, giving her that disappointed look again.

Alice gave a very small shrug. "I was confident he wouldn't hurt me."

"I'm less confident." She tapped her fingers on the arm of the chair, and Alice thought the inspector might have missed her meaning. "We'll need to pull him in."

"I think this Violet person should be looked into," Alice said.

"She will be. But by us, not you. Now, if I take you back, will you give me the tablet? Or do I actually have to lock you up to make you cooperate?"

Alice inclined her head, acknowledging defeat. "I'll give you the tablet."

"And you'll stop messing about in my investigation?"

"I will do my best."

DI Adams glared at her. She had quite a good severe look herself, Alice thought. Although she didn't have the practice Alice did.

"You *will* stay out of it, Alice. This is a murder investigation, not a bake sale."

"Understood, Inspector."

"I'll lock the both of you up, you and Miriam. I'll charge you."

"That would be rather unnecessary. And Miriam's already worried because the jumpsuits won't be organic cotton."

The inspector emptied her mug, looking like she was trying not to laugh. "Just start behaving, alright? I don't *want* to fill our jails with meddlesome women of a certain age, so don't make me."

"Of course, Inspector."

"Right then. I'll take you back and tell James to intercept Miriam." DI Adams got up, and waved Alice away as she tried to pay. "I've got it." She shrugged her jacket back on as she went to the counter, and Alice smiled. She hadn't promised to stay out of it. She'd only said she understood.

THEY WERE through the traffic and back on the A59, the inspector sipping at another giant cup of takeaway coffee that the young woman had passed her before they left, and muttering about wanting to be past Harrogate before it got too bad. Alice could feel the tight bands easing from around her chest more and more the further they got from the city, feel the weight that had been trying to crush her shoulders lifting. Even the darkening afternoon felt lighter than the morning had on their way in. She took a surreptitious breath, filling her lungs, trying not to seem too relieved. It didn't do to give too much away.

"Oh, and Alice," DI Adams said, and Alice turned toward her with an amiable smile. "What's this?"

Alice looked at the item the inspector was holding out, glittering and alive with light even in the dull day, running with golds and greens and blues, full of the promise of magic and hidden, mythical things.

"I'm sure I don't know," she said, trying to hold onto the smile but feeling it becoming something stiff and fixed. "A guitar pick, perhaps?"

The dragon scale glittered at her, calling her every sort of liar in the world.

"Honesty, Alice," DI Adams said, and rolled the scale in her fingers. "That's our word of the day."

Alice folded her hands together in her lap and watched the road.

19

MIRIAM

"Someone's following us," Mortimer said. Beaufort had wriggled his way into the front seat, where he'd spent the first twenty minutes of the drive examining the cracked dashboard and asking what things did, leaving the younger dragon crouched on the back seat, peering anxiously out the windows.

"Why would anyone be following us?" Miriam asked, checking the rear-view mirror. Beaufort had bumped it at some point, so all she could see was Mortimer's tail. She adjusted it, but that didn't help. Now it just showed her Mortimer with his nose pressed to the tiny back window of the Beetle. "I can't see anything, Mortimer."

"It's a grey car. It's been behind us since we left Toot Hansell."

Which was almost an hour ago. Miriam didn't like to push her old car too much, and she absolutely refused to take it on the motorway. Too many trucks, too many people going far too fast, and just too many cars in general. Which meant it was going to take them well over two hours to get to the address Mortimer had found, and also meant that they were sticking firmly to quieter, less travelled roads. It *was* a bit strange that the car was still with them and hadn't overtaken them. Miriam would be the first to admit that she wasn't at any risk of speeding tickets.

"Are you sure it's the same one? There are a lot of grey cars about. And all these modern ones look the same."

"Of course I'm sure," Mortimer said indignantly. "I've been *watching* it."

"Oh dear," Miriam said, tightening her grip on the steering wheel. "Oh, I don't like this! What if it's the murderer?"

"We should confront him," Beaufort announced.

"No!" Miriam almost yelped the word.

"That does sound like a terrible idea," Mortimer agreed. "We should hide."

"Where are we going to hide a *car?*" Beaufort demanded.

"I don't know. Under a tree."

"Be sensible, lad. He's not approaching by air."

Miriam sighed and rolled her shoulders, trying to make herself relax her grip on the wheel a little. She didn't like driving all that much, and she certainly didn't like driving long distances. Driving long distances with two arguing dragons wasn't exactly top of her list of things to do on a bright spring day. Not that it was looking all that bright now, with those lurking clouds getting lower and more threatening at every moment.

"I'm pulling over," she announced.

"What?"

"But he'll catch us!"

"The murderer may be Violet," she pointed out, "and if it is her, then we may as well confront her now as drive all the way to Manchester." It'd also save some wear on both the car and Miriam's nerves.

"I'm not sure about this," Beaufort said, as Miriam put on the indicator and pulled into an abandoned, dilapidated garage. There was a large folding table piled with unwashed vegetables just outside the boarded-up door, and hand-lettered cardboard signs showed the prices.

"Neither am I," Miriam admitted. "But I'm going to go and buy some tomatoes, so you two keep an eye on that car, okay?"

"Okay," the dragons said, not sounding particularly okay with the plan at all. Neither was Miriam, if she was honest about it, but she couldn't think of what else to do.

She clambered out of the car and went to examine the vegetables. They weren't very healthy-looking, certainly not as good as the ones she got from her own garden. But now she was looking she felt too awkward to leave without buying anything, so she selected the least anaemic tomatoes and dropped a couple of pounds into the honesty box.

"Here she comes!" Mortimer hissed from the car, and Miriam managed not to look around as a grey car cruised past at the same sedate pace she'd been maintaining earlier. Her back twitched as it went by, as if she expected to be suddenly assaulted – by a carefully aimed kitchen knife, perhaps. A fancy one. She turned back to the road with her tomatoes and tried to read the license plate before the car was too far away, but she was too late. She should have kept her driving glasses on.

"Did you see?" she asked the dragons. "Was it her?"

"I couldn't tell," Beaufort said. "She had her hand up."

"It was kind of a big hand," Mortimer said. "I think. You know, for a female human."

Miriam tried to remember if the woman who had chased the vicar from the village hall had had unusually big hands, but she couldn't. She might not have noticed, though, considering she was more concerned with the fact that anyone was chasing the vicar at all.

"Well, they're gone, anyway. Maybe they weren't even following us." She put the tomatoes in a bag and popped them in the footwell of the back seat. "Don't stand on those, Mortimer."

He regarded them suspiciously. "We should have brought the biscuits."

☙

THE LITTLE GREEN Beetle purred steadily down the road, and Miriam felt quite proud of her, with her load of dragons. She wasn't used to either distances or passengers, so she was really running terribly well.

"Good girl," she said, and patted the steering wheel. Beaufort looked on with interest.

"You talk to the car?"

"Oh, yes. She's called Bessie."

"Does she talk back?"

"Well. No. She's a car."

"I see," Beaufort said thoughtfully. "Like we talk to trees, I guess. They don't talk back, only dryads do that. But we know they're listening all the same."

"Um. Yes. Like that." Miriam felt slightly vindicated for all the times she'd talked to her plants.

"She's back!" Mortimer yelped.

"What?" Miriam jammed the brakes on, sending Beaufort crashing into the dashboard, and Mortimer into the footwell. "Sorry!" She hit the accelerator again, and the dragons fell back into their seats.

"I say," Beaufort protested. "That was a bit rough."

"Sorry, sorry. Mortimer surprised me. She's back?"

"Yes! Same grey car."

"She must have waited in a side road or something for us to go past. Oh dear! Oh, this is no good at all!"

"Can't you go faster?" Beaufort suggested. "I'm sure these things go faster." He patted the dashboard encouragingly, raising a small cloud of dust.

Miriam nudged the speed up a tiny bit, clutching the wheel so tight her fingers hurt.

"Still there," Mortimer announced.

"Should I pull over again?"

"Not if it's the same car," Beaufort said. "We already tried that."

"But is it the same? What if it's another grey car? You know, the same kind?"

"I'm sure it's the same," Mortimer said.

Miriam took a deep, shaky breath. Tailed. She was being *tailed*. It was a horrible feeling, like knowing someone was peering through your curtains in the night. Or she thought she was being tailed. She had to be sure.

A brown and white sign showing a picnic table and toilets appeared ahead, and she put the indicator on. "I'm pulling over. We need to be certain it's the same car."

"Miriam, I'm not sure—" Beaufort began, but she was already slowing, and she shook her head.

"No. I'll go into the loos, and you watch the car. Make sure it's the same one. If it is, we'll detour, or turn around, or do something to lose her." She said it with more confidence than she felt. She had no idea how one was meant to shake a tail.

"I suppose." The High Lord sounded doubtful, but there was no time to discuss it further, because Miriam was already pulling into the parking. She could still see the road, but the toilets were further back than she'd have liked, more isolated. There was no going back now, though. There was only one way in or out, and she certainly didn't want to pull out again right in front of the murderer and give herself away.

She put the handbrake on and looked at the dragons, hoping she looked more confident than she felt. "Keep a good eye out, okay?" They both nodded vigorously, and she got out and headed into the old toilet block, smelling disinfectant and damp.

§

"MIRIAM! *MIRIAM!*" She was washing her hands when Mortimer called her from the doorway, and she jumped so badly that she almost came out of one of her clogs.

"*What?* What are you doing out of the car? What if someone sees you!" She hurried out to him, drying her hands on her skirt. "Where's the grey car? Did it go past?"

"It came in! It's on the other side of the toilets," he whispered, already scampering back to the car. "Hurry!"

Miriam ran after him, trying not to slip in her loose shoes and figuring that all this detecting really meant she should work on her fitness a little more. And rethink her footwear.

Mortimer piled into the car as Miriam jerked her door open and stared at the interior. "Where's Beaufort?"

"He's coming! Get in!"

Miriam swung herself into the seat, wondering what the old dragon was up to with a tight knot of misgiving in her stomach. "What's he doing?"

"Hang on, hang on – now! Start the car now!" Mortimer was almost bouncing with excitement, and Miriam turned the key as Beaufort came galloping around the corner with his wings tucked against his sides.

"What have you been doing?" Miriam demanded as the High Lord scrambled into the front seat.

"Go! Go on, drive!" He was flushed red with excitement, and shut the door on his own tail, yelped, and tried to reorganise himself. "Drive, drive!"

"Shut the door first! You'll fall out!"

"I won't, quick, go before he gets here!"

"Hurry *up!*" Mortimer wailed, leaning out of the back seat to try and help Beaufort in. The big dragon buffeted Miriam with one wing as he tried to get himself organised, and she squeaked, but got the car into first and headed toward the main road. Beaufort had his tail in, but one wing still out, and Mortimer was trying desperately to pull him into the car.

"Ow! Be careful, Mortimer!"

"Sorry, I'm sorry!" He dropped back into his seat and wriggled around to peer out the back window. "Oh, do hurry up!"

"Beaufort! Get in, we're almost at the road!"

"I'm trying!" One flailing dragon leg hit the gear stick, knocking it out of gear, and the car gave a juddering roar of alarm. Beaufort roared back, scorching the headlining.

"*Beaufort!*" Miriam slammed the brakes on, even though they were barely crawling along. "Get out and start again! This is *not* working."

"No, don't stop!" Mortimer shouted. "He's coming, he's coming!"

"Beaufort, now!"

The High Lord threw open the door, half-fell out onto the road, then launched himself back into the car, making sure to tuck his tail in tidily. He slammed the door and grinned at Miriam. "There we go!"

"Go!" Mortimer was shouting. "Oh, go, go, go!"

Miriam shoved the car into gear and floored the accelerator, pulling back onto the road with only the quickest glance to make sure it was clear. The little car laboured down the road, revving wildly and leaving a cloud of black smoke behind them, until Miriam recovered herself enough to start working her way up through the gears. Mortimer still had his head stuck in the back window, but she couldn't see anything in the wing mirrors.

"Is she there?" she demanded. "Is she still following us?"

"He," Beaufort said. "And it's unlikely."

"Why?" She gave him a suspicious look. "What did you do?"

"I may have tapped his tyre," Beaufort said, looking at his claws thoughtfully. "They're quite delicate things, you know."

Miriam glanced at his claws too, and thought that a lot of things might be a bit delicate when confronted with them, then looked back at the road. "He? Who was it?"

"I don't know," Beaufort said. "He did seem a little familiar, though."

RELUCTANTLY, Miriam decided that getting on the motorway was their best hope of staying ahead of their mysterious pursuer. He wouldn't expect it after all the time on the back roads, and hopefully they'd be most of the way to Violet's by the time he got the tyre changed. Beaufort was quite crestfallen when she explained that everyone carried spare tyres, but she assured him that it had bought them some time, at the very least.

She drove with her hands tight on the wheel and her chin stuck forward like a determined turtle, while the astonished dragons watched the trucks overtaking them.

"Miriam," Beaufort started.

"Shh!"

The dragons fell silent, and they continued like that until the phone announced brightly that their exit was coming up. Miriam navigated it with grim concentration, and found herself plunged into a wilderness of superstores, roundabouts and traffic lights that was no less intimidating than the motorway had been.

"Miriam?"

"Shh!"

Her shoulders didn't relax until they were following the phone's instructions through a maze of semi-detached houses, all very pale and new and bright, some with bright new cars sitting outside, and bright new curtains in the windows, and even bright new grass on the tiny lawns.

"This is interesting," Mortimer ventured, and Miriam nodded, then gave him a slightly apologetic smile in the rear-view mirror.

"Motorway driving is horrible," she offered by way of explanation.

"That was a lot of cars," he said, sounding awed. "A *lot*."

"So many," Beaufort said, his voice slow. "And you can barely breathe the air." He was very still, coiled into the small front seat, his chin resting on his paws as he looked at the identical houses marching past. "No room for anything."

Miriam looked at Mortimer, and he gave a little half-shrug, his eyebrow ridges pulled down anxiously. Miriam tried to imagine what the country used to look like, the endless forests and wild lands and rocky fells and clear lakes, and felt an echo of Beaufort's sadness, something deep and slow that dragged at her bones with the inevitability of it all.

"*You have arrived at your destination,*" the phone announced, and all three of them jumped. Miriam pulled the car to the kerb between a red BMW SUV and a light blue Audi, and they stared at the house. It didn't *look* like the lair of a murderer. There were pale pink curtains on the downstairs windows, and a birdbath in the middle of the front yard, and a child's mountain bike lying by the front door.

"I suppose we should go in," she said, suddenly not at all sure this was a good idea.

"Absolutely," Beaufort said, rousing himself. "Let's get Alice's name cleared once and for all!" He hooked the door handle with his claw and poured himself out onto the pavement.

"Should you come in?" Miriam asked. "I mean, what if someone sees you?"

"Well, we aren't letting you face her alone," the High Lord said indignantly as Mortimer climbed out after him.

Miriam thought about protesting, then decided that if one were to face down a murderer, one should do it accompanied by dragons, and got out. Her phone started to ring just as she closed the door, but she left it. It could wait.

§

MIRIAM RANG the bell with a dragon to either side of her, and they waited expectantly. No one answered.

"Maybe she's out?" Mortimer suggested.

"Or avoiding us," Beaufort said. "I'll check the back, make sure she doesn't try and run." He headed off around the house, and Mortimer and Miriam looked at each other.

"Try again?" the dragon suggested.

"May as well." Miriam rang the doorbell again, letting her finger linger on it for a while, and this time when she let go she heard footsteps on the stairs inside. She straightened her back and tried for a stern smile.

The door was jerked open by the woman she'd seen at the village hall, and Miriam swallowed a little gasp of astonishment. She hadn't really expected that they'd find her, but here she was, in skinny jeans and a floaty tank top, her thick hair piling down over her shoulders.

"Yeah?" she said, looking Miriam up and down.

"Um—"

"No. Not interested in your religion, or cult, or whatever." Violet started to shut the door, but Mortimer put his paw in the way, and she looked down, bewildered. "Are you – why won't this shut?" She swung the door back and forth a couple of times, but Mortimer kept his paw in place even though it looked rather painful to Miriam.

"It must be jammed," Miriam said politely. "Are you Violet?"

"Why?" She glared at Miriam. "What do you want?"

"I'm from Toot Hansell," she began, not quite sure how one went about getting someone to confess to murder. Violet's face tightened, and she renewed her efforts to slam the door, eliciting a grunt of protest from Mortimer. Not the best approach, then. "I just wanted to ask you a few questions about the vicar."

"What are you, police?" The slamming stopped, and Mortimer shook his paw, wincing.

"I'm, well. I'm an investigator," Miriam said, figuring that was close to the truth.

"Yeah? Show me some ID."

"I, well, I don't have any on me."

Violet snorted, and told Miriam to leave in fairly impolite terms, then slammed the door again. This time Mortimer braced his shoulder against it, and it hit hard enough to shudder. Violet peered at the floor in astonishment, but with no sign of having seen a dragon. "What the—" Even as she spoke, there was a crash from further back in the house, and she forgot the door, spinning around. "Who's there? Is there someone else here? You b—" She abandoned the door and sprinted back down the hall, shouting that she was calling the police.

Miriam and Mortimer looked at each other.

"Would a murderer call the police?" Miriam asked.

"Unlikely," Mortimer said. "Unless she's bluffing."

There was shriek from inside, then Beaufort came racing out the front door, looking alarmed.

"Beaufort? What did you do?" Miriam asked.

"I knocked over a vase. And maybe a small table. With fruit on it. Then she came in and stepped on my tail, and fell over when I ran."

"Oh dear," Miriam said, as Violet reappeared at the door. She was holding a pineapple, and had her phone clutched in the other hand. It was on speaker.

"I've got her here! She's right in front of me! But she must have an accomplice who went in the back while she was talking to me!"

"Please calm down, ma'am," the voice on the phone said. "We're dispatching a unit immediately. Do not pursue the suspect, but please describe her to me."

Violet brandished the pineapple at Miriam. "Some old hippie chick with grey hair and a tie-dyed dress."

Miriam looked offended.

"Please be more specific, ma'am."

"Hang on, I'll take a photo." Violet tried to juggle the phone and the pineapple, and the voice on the other end spoke up again.

"She's still there? She hasn't run away?"

"No, I told you – she's right in front of me!"

"Ma'am, are you *sure* she tried to rob you?"

"*Of course I am!*" Violet shrieked into the phone.

"We should go," Mortimer said.

Beaufort was watching Violet with the fascination of a biologist discovering a new species. "Why does she have a pineapple?" he asked.

"Yes, we should go," Miriam said. "She really has called the police. And murderers don't call the police, I don't think."

"Who are you talking to?" Violet demanded. "And who's a murderer? Are you a murderer?" She screamed, a full-throated yell that made Mortimer scuttle backward straight into the birdbath, and threw the pineapple at Miriam. Miriam ducked, and Beaufort caught the fruit, then dropped it hastily to the ground in case Violet thought it was floating in mid-air. She was *very* indisposed to see dragons. "Have you come here to murder me?"

"Of course not!" Miriam exclaimed, even more offended than before. "Do I *look* like a murderer?"

"Well, I don't know what murderers look like! And someone in your stupid village killed my brother!"

"It's not stupid—" Miriam started hotly, then stopped. "Your *brother*? The vicar was your brother?"

"Well, foster brother. Same thing."

"Excuse me?" the phone said. "What's this about murder?"

"It was Colonel Mustard in the drawing room with the candle-stick," Miriam blurted.

"It was *not!*" Violet snapped.

There was a sigh from the phone. "Very funny. Has anyone broken in or not?"

"No," Miriam said.

"Yes," Violet said, just as firmly.

"So do you need the police or not?"

"No, it's a misunderstanding. I'm leaving," Miriam said.

"You can't leave! You broke in!"

"How did I break in? I'm standing right here!"

"You're wasting police time," the phone voice said wearily. "Call me back if you make a decision." The line went dead.

Violet huffed and glared at the phone. "This is what I pay my taxes for?"

"Why were you chasing him?" Miriam asked. "The night he was murdered, at the hall. You were chasing him."

"I wanted him to come to my oldest's birthday," Violet said. "It's his eighteenth on the weekend. But Norm wouldn't. He said there'd be too many people from his past there, and he didn't want to deal with it." She sighed and rubbed the back of her neck. "We weren't super-close, you know? But he helped me out a lot, after he got clean. He helped a lot of people. I wanted him to feel he had family."

"I'm sorry," Miriam said, and the woman nodded.

"Sure. Just leave it, okay? I never want to hear about your horrible village again." She stepped back and closed the door, and Miriam caught a hint of relief on her face as it shut smoothly.

She turned back to the dragons. "I guess it wasn't her."

"It might be the man who was following us, then," Beaufort suggested. "He did smell familiar."

Miriam nodded wearily and trudged back to the car. "That doesn't help us get Alice out of jail."

20

DI ADAMS

"So you got a flat," DI Adams said, with less patience than she'd have liked. "It happens."

"I know," James said, his voice tinny over the Bluetooth in his car. "But this was weird. I pull into the car park behind her, and since she's in the toilet already, I take the car around the back, so she won't see me when she comes out. And I'm just sitting there, waiting to hear her start the car, when, *pssht!*"

"*Pssht?*"

"*Pssht.* The tyre goes. I mean, there was no one there, I'm not saying anyone did it, but there's a gash in it like someone stuck a knife in the damn thing."

DI Adams gave Alice a suspicious look, but she had armed herself with dusting cloths and polish and was heading into the hall to tackle the fingerprint dust residue left by the crime scene team. "You're sure there was no one else there?"

"I'm sure."

"And you don't think she saw you?"

"Not there, no. That was before you messaged to tell me to intercept her. And I didn't catch up to her again until I was pulling into the house they'd gone to. A Mrs Violet Hammond, it turned out."

"And?"

"And nothing. She waved a pineapple at me."

"Mrs Hammond?"

"No, Ms Ellis."

"A pineapple?"

"A—"

"Never mind. But she was leaving. You didn't get there in time to stop her talking to Mrs Hammond."

"No. And she must have shaken Mrs Hammond up quite a bit too, because she screamed at me when she opened the door. Wanted to know if I was conspiring with the crazy hippie and was I the one who had broken her fruit bowl."

"Her fruit bowl?" DI Adams sat down in one of Alice's kitchen chairs and leaned back to stare at the ceiling. "Is that where the pineapple came from?"

"I don't know. Maybe." He sounded doubtful. "Is that important, d'you think? I could go back and ask if she's missing a pineapple."

"I doubt it's relevant to the investigation at hand." DI Adams was tired. The conversation was making her tired. The whole *investigation* was making her tired, and DCI Temple had been on the phone twice on the drive back to Toot Hansell, asking her what she was playing at, and should he turn her desk into a ping-pong table since she had so little use for it, and was this the speed the police worked at down south, because it was unacceptable here.

And she still had to drive back to Leeds with the bloody tablet. Preferably before the world ended, judging by the weight of the clouds hanging about the place. Everything had the hot, humid feel of a thunderstorm on the way, something violent and packed with fury, and on the drive up she'd glimpsed the occasional stab of lightning in the clouds already. She wanted her bed, and a large bowl of something spicy and hot and probably terribly bad for her. She wanted to not be talking about the relevance of pineapples.

James had said something, and she'd missed it. "Sorry, what?"

"I said, Mrs Hammond was up here the night the vicar was murdered, so it's conceivable she brought the cupcake up with her and gave it to him. But she couldn't have brought the others up to plant them at Ms Martin's last night. She was in London, apparently. That's if we're sure that's when they were planted. And that they *were* planted."

"PC Shaw saw Ms Martin working in her garden last night, and she had a load of clippings. Even if she had been amateurish enough to dispose of the cakes in her own compost, she'd at least have covered them with yesterday's garden waste."

"Makes sense. I'll follow up on Mrs Hammond's alibi, and there's no guarantee she didn't have an accomplice, but it's not looking that likely."

"Thanks, James. Drive safe."

"Cheers."

DI Adams hung up, and stayed where she was, examining the slim, un-cobwebbed beams of the ceiling. The answer had to be in the tablet. It *had* to be.

"Alice?" she called.

"Yes, Detective Inspector?"

The inspector jumped. Alice was standing in the doorway, cloth in hand. She hadn't even heard the woman enter the room. Jesus, she *was* tired. "Has Miriam called you back yet?"

"Finally, yes. I was just coming to tell you. They – she's on her way back."

"Did she say anything about seeing DC Hamilton? James," she added, when Alice looked puzzled.

"She did. They passed each other as she was leaving Violet's, apparently."

"Uh-huh. Anything about a flat tyre?"

Alice raised her eyebrows, frowning slightly. "Not that she said to me, no."

It had been a stretch. DI Adams couldn't quite imagine Miriam, knife between her teeth, crawling around a public rest stop to stab a police officer's tyres. "Or a pineapple?"

Now Alice looked actively concerned. "Have you been sleeping, Inspector? You drink an awful lot of coffee. It can't be good for you."

"I like coffee. Coffee is how I get through the day without arresting everyone I meet." Not entirely an exaggeration. She'd tried to switch to alternating decaf and full-power once in her early days with the police, and had nearly punched her partner for chewing his gum too loudly. She worked best when caffeinated.

"Well, maybe I should put a pot on," Alice said. "Why don't you go into the living room and relax on the sofa for a moment? I'll bring it through."

"I don't need to relax. I need to get this tablet and get back to Leeds before the storm starts. Did Miriam tell you where it is?"

Alice sighed. "She did. Are you sure you won't have a cup of coffee to go?"

DI Adams hesitated, thinking of the skinny, winding roads and the trek back to Leeds. "Alright. Yes. I'll get my cup from the car. Then let's get to Miriam's and get this damn thing."

She hurried outside just as the first drops of rain started, fat and full of promise.

BY THE TIME they got to Miriam's house, Alice leading the way in her Prius, they had to run for the back door to avoid getting soaked. As it was, DI Adams was wearing big splats of rain all over her top and trousers by the time Alice found the spare key under the flowerpot and let them in. Alice, of course, had put on a pale blue rain jacket and pulled the hood up, so only the legs of her trousers above her wellies were damp. DI Adams had a feeling that the woman would be perfectly prepared for monsoons, or forest fires, or tornadoes, or tea with the Queen. It was annoying.

She plucked her shirt away from her chest, trying to dry it a little, and looked around the kitchen while Alice went to find the tablet in whatever hiding place Miriam had come up with. It was warm in here, the AGA purring to itself in the corner, the small panes of the thick-silled windows whispering as the rain splattered them. It was a cosy place to be, the sort of place you imagined sitting through long winters, while soup bubbled on the stove and the tarnished saucepans that hung from the heavy beams reflected the light of candles dully. There should be a cat, too.

"Does Miriam have a cat?" she asked Alice as she came back into the room with the tablet.

Alice handed the tablet over, looking at the inspector curiously. "No. She's allergic."

"That's a shame. This place looks like it'd suit a cat."

"I'm sure you're right." Alice gave her that concerned look again and handed her the tablet. "Are you certain you won't stay? It's going to be terrible driving conditions. And a long way back to Leeds."

"I'll be fine." She looked out at the dark sky as she said it, seeing the bushes shivering in the wind as it crawled about, stirring the garden with furious fingers. She *would* be fine, but the sooner she was off, the better. "Are you coming?"

"No. I'll wait for th— Miriam. I can catch her up on what we talked about, and make sure she knows she doesn't have to worry about being arrested."

"Why do you keep saying they?"

"Do I?"

"Yes." DI Adams watched her closely, looking for a tell. It was impossible. Alice looked just as she had all day. A little tired, maybe, but otherwise nothing more than mildly interested in the DI's questions. Not even the threat of the jail cell had seemed to move her much. Not for the first time, DI Adams wondered if she should be digging a little more deeply into Alice's past. The missing husband. The move to this tiny village and immersion in the tranquillity of village life after a career in the RAF, which had included active duty and flying helicopters. Not the sort of person you imagine giving their life over to bake sales and garden parties.

"I must be tired, Inspector."

"I imagine. A lot of excitement for a little village."

"It is indeed." Alice smiled, and handed the inspector a plastic bag. "For the tablet. Don't want it getting wet after all this fuss."

"Thanks." DI Adams tucked the tablet into the bag as she followed Alice to the front door. "Don't you get bored?"

"Of what?"

"Of *this*. Village life. Fetes and baking and gardening."

Alice opened the door, and DI Adams thought her smile was the first really genuine one she'd seen. "A quiet life can be a wonderful thing, Inspector."

DI Adams looked at the rain pummelling the path and already forming puddles on the lawn, and said, "But you were RAF. You were a wing commander. This hardly compares."

"You've obviously never dealt with the Women's Institute. Or judged a fete bake-off."

DI Adams snorted. "I'm sure they're thrilling."

"You've met the W.I. Do you think I'm joking?"

The inspector stared at Alice, still smiling that real, unfettered smile, then returned it with one of her own. "I see your point."

"Indeed. Drive safely."

And DI Adams, feeling thoroughly dismissed, ran for her car, protecting the tablet with both the bag and her body while the rain pelted through her hair and ran in streams down her face and the back of her neck.

੬ఎ

THE DRIVE to the main road was the sort of experience that DI Adams hoped not to repeat, and which reminded her why she didn't live in the country. The narrow roads were swept with sheets of rain that were being thrown about wildly by the wind, obscuring the twists and turns ahead, and dusk had already arrived with flagrant disregard for the fact that there should have still been a few hours of daylight left. With no streetlights it was all but impossible to see whether there was a straight or a curve coming up, an uphill or a downhill. Everything was lost in the rain and fading light.

She crept along, hunched over the wheel and muttering abuse at the 4x4s that roared past her in the opposite direction, throwing walls of water onto the windscreen. At one stage she had to nudge her way through a collection of alarmed, lost sheep, and at another there was a small river washing across the road. She drove through it with her toes curled, as if that'd help keep the tyres on the tarmac.

After what seemed like an inordinately long amount of time, to the point where DI Adams had taken to accusing the GPS of getting her lost, she came to a stop at a T-junction. Across the intersection were two road signs, reflective in her headlights. *Leeds 52 miles*, one said, pointing left. The other pointed in the opposite direction. *Skipton 11 miles*, it said.

She glared at them through the frantically working wipers, blurring and clearing with each sweep. Fifty-two miles to good coffee, a decent meal, her own desk – even though it would come with a bollocking from the DCI – and, if she ever made it there, her own bed. Okay, so the techs would already have gone home by the time she got there, but she could get a rush on things. Hand over the tablet and be done. Get a shower and a change of clothes. Just fifty-two miles. In a bloody ridiculous hurricane. As if to underline the point, the car shuddered in a howl of wind, and a branch went scudding across the road, pulled this way and that by competing gusts.

DI Adams groaned and put her indicator on, pulling out into the dark road.

"HOW CAN you call this a 24-hour police station?" she demanded of the PC on the desk. He smiled at her nervously.

"Um, because it is?"

"You, one person, PC"—she wiped rain out of her eyes and peered at his name badge—"PC McLeod, do not constitute a 24-hour police station."

"Well, it's not just me."

She looked around the empty office beyond the desk, then back at him, eyebrows raised.

"Everyone's out. The storm. We've got one car patrolling, keeping an eye on things in town, two out checking on villages near the river, another out helping with road diversion signs, and someone's cat's stuck on the roof and won't come in."

She glared at him, half-suspecting he was joking, seeing if the city cop would believe such a cliché. But he was still giving her that anxious smile, and looked mildly terrified, as if she might drag him out of his seat by his ear or something. She sighed.

"Isn't that more the fire brigade?"

"They're busy."

"Of course they are." She waved at the locked door to the offices. "Can I borrow an interview room?"

"Sure." He buzzed her in, relaxing visibly now that she'd

stopped her interrogation. Then she paused and turned back, and his shoulders bunched up around his ears.

"Anywhere I can get a takeaway and a decent cup of coffee, or does that all stop at 5pm as well?"

"I can call for delivery, if you want. Pizza or curry?"

She considered. Curry was nicer, but pizza was better cold, and she had a feeling she'd be here a while. "Pizza. Vegetarian, with some chillies on it." PC McLeod grabbed the phone as if she'd just entrusted him with the most important task of his career, and she added, "Coffee?"

"We've got some of those sachets back in the mess room. Those lovely frothy ones. Instant cappuccino, you know? They're really good."

DI Adams mentally hit her head against the wall, but managed to say, "Great. Can I get you one?"

"Ooh, please. Three sugars."

She nodded and headed for the mess room. Maybe she should try three sugars. It might make the lovely frothy coffee palatable.

DI ADAMS SLUMPED in her chair with one arm on the table, eyes sticky with weariness, chewing on a piece of tepid pizza that really needed a lot more chilies, and stared at the tablet and her yellow notepad. That was it. That was all she had. Everything else, every forensic report and interview and crime scene photo was in a file on her desk in Leeds. She could access the electronic ones, of course, from one of the computers here, but she liked paper. She liked laying things out, moving photos around, writing lists and crossing things off and adding new things, using Post-its for ideas and drawing doodles on the corners of files. It helped her to think, no matter that everyone from her DCI to the PCs thought it was old-fashioned. It worked for her.

She straightened up and poked idly at the personal email folder again. The vicar's secretiveness, his fear of being connected to his past, suggested some pretty bad people could still be looking for him. She should get some sleep, then go down to Manchester in the morning, interview Stuart Browning properly. Even if he hadn't had anything to do with it (and despite some misgivings she had an odd faith in Alice's hunch that he hadn't) he might be more willing to share some names with an inspector who could choose to look or not look into his business dealings as she saw fit.

Violet Hammond was covered, but most likely a dead end. The more DI Adams thought about it, the more it looked like it was going to be someone from the vicar's past. It had to be. Who else could have had a grudge against a village vicar like this? Especially one who, by all accounts, had been quite a good sort.

She put the tablet back down, stretched, and took a last mouthful of the dusty-tasting coffee, making a face. Jesus, people drank this stuff by choice. She pushed back from the desk, walked a small circle around the interview room. It all pointed to someone from his past, but it didn't *feel* right. Something was missing. Pretty strange choice of murder weapon, for a start. It had certainly thrown the Women's Institute straight into the role of most likely suspects, which was a nice bit of distraction.

She sat down again and leaned back in the chair, tapping her teeth with her pen. A lot of work to frame Alice. Risky, too, planting the cupcakes and leaving the knife with PC Shaw being right outside. Strange someone hadn't just come up from Liverpool or Manchester or wherever, offed the vicar using a more usual method, and scooted. All this effort to direct the investigation toward the W.I. As if the vicar wasn't the only target. As if – she grabbed her phone, flicking through the photos quickly, and pulled up the shot of the note on Alice's door. Unlocked the tablet again and ran down the email list until she found what she wanted. Stared from one to the other, a smile starting to curve the corners of her lips. Then she jumped up and ran to the front desk, startling a squeak from the officer when she banged on the door. He fumbled with the buzzer to let her in.

"DI Adams?" he asked, his eyes huge. "Are you okay?"

"I need a computer tech. Right now. Immediately."

"I, well, we do have one—"

"Get them."

"She doesn't usually—"

"I'll sign off on any overtime. This is a murder investigation, PC McLeod. *Get them.*"

She glared at him until he got off the phone and told her the tech was on the way. Then she went back to the mess room and made another cup of crappy coffee. She was going to need it.

21

MORTIMER

They met the grey car on the road as they drove away from Violet's, and the man in the driver's seat stared at them in astonishment as they went past. They stared back, and Miriam grabbed the pineapple off Beaufort, holding it up to try and hide her face.

"That was him!" Beaufort exclaimed. "That was the man who was following us!"

"He works with DI Adams," Miriam said, lowering the pineapple cautiously now that they were past the police officer's car. "That's where you've seen him before."

"He's police?"

"Yes. So now we've damaged a police car, too." Miriam had a horrible tremble in her voice. "Has he turned around? Is he following us?"

Mortimer peered anxiously out the back window. "No, he's stopped at Violet's."

"Oh no! Oh, she's going to tell him we broke in!"

"We didn't, though," Beaufort said.

"You kind of did," Mortimer pointed out, then gave a nervous grin when Beaufort looked at him.

"Nonsense. Look, there's nothing to worry about, Miriam. We haven't done anything wrong."

"Other than damaging police property. And interfering in an investigation. Oh, and probably something to do with withholding evidence, with the tablet. Or maybe that was stealing? Or both." She hiccoughed. "Oh *no!* And now I've got the hiccoughs." She *hicc*'d again.

Beaufort and Mortimer exchanged glances. The little green car was crawling along, and if the officer wanted to catch them he could just jog after them, really. Mortimer checked the back window again. The man was talking to Violet, who was waving wildly and pointing down the street.

"We should probably go a little quicker," he suggested. "And maybe get off this road?"

"*Shhh!* I'm concentrating. *Hic.*" But she did put the indicator on and guide them carefully around the corner. "*Hic.*"

"*Boo!*" Beaufort made the sound into a roar, the reverberations shaking the car, and Mortimer let out a surprised little belch of flame. Miriam screamed and swerved, narrowly avoiding a lamp post as she drove the car straight into the kerb, where it stalled.

"*Beaufort!* What are you *doing?*"

"I thought scares were good for hiccoughs?" he offered.

"You frightened the *life* out of me!" She had her hand pressed to her chest, and Mortimer hoped her heart was strong. It paid to have a strong heart if you were spending any length of time with Beaufort.

"But are your hiccoughs gone?"

"I—" She paused, waited. "Oh. I think they are." She rubbed her face with her hands, then started the car again and pulled carefully away from the kerb. "Honestly though, Beaufort, I— *hic.*" She glared at him. "*Don't do it again!*"

Beaufort looked faintly disappointed.

MORTIMER KEPT watch out the back window, wondering when the sirens would start. He was still worried about tasers. But there was no sign of the grey car, and while Beaufort's roar might not have scared the hiccoughs out of Miriam, it had at least shaken her out of the panicked contemplation of her possible jail term. She drove the old Beetle at what was quite a brisk pace for her, hiccoughing regularly, and pulled in at the next petrol station she saw. She made the dragons lie down on the floor to ensure no one saw them, filled the car up with a very un-Miriam-like efficiency, and only after she'd bought three large mugs of takeaway tea and an iced fruit cake did she finally check her phone.

"It's *Alice*," she said, horrified. "Oh, *no*, what if I was her only call from jail? That's what they do, isn't it? You only get one call? Oh no, and I didn't answer!" She stared at the phone, tea forgotten, and only moved when a car behind her beeped, wanting to get to the pumps. She scrabbled for the keys and pulled them into a parking spot in front of the garage. "What do I do?"

"Call her back?" Beaufort suggested.

"Well, yes, but she was arrested. She won't have her phone on her."

"Maybe DI Adams realised it was a mistake."

"She seemed very sure," Miriam said, but she hit the call button anyway, the dragons watching her expectantly. A moment later, her eyes grew round. "*Alice?*"

Beaufort grinned, and tore open the fruit cake.

IT WAS A VERY long drive to get back to Toot Hansell, and barely any less stressful than the drive to Violet's house had been. Between the storm and the dark and Miriam refusing to go on any motorways (even though Alice had told her to hurry), and getting lost three times before they even got out of Manchester, it seemed to take twice as long as the drive out. Miriam leaned over the wheel, staring at the road ahead with her jaw clenched, and the building wind shook the little car as if it had a grudge against it.

At least there wasn't much traffic to deal with once they were past Skipton and heading into the Dales, but the rain grew heavier and the night so dark and murky that they seemed to be travelling in a shaky bubble, barely illuminated by the Beetle's yellow head-lights. Walls flashed into existence and vanished again, tiny villages passed in a blur of barely seen, dimly lit windows. The rain worked its way in somewhere and dripped on Mortimer's neck, and a couple of times water splashed up through the floor, and still the old car battled its way on. At least they knew they weren't in imminent danger of being tasered, he thought. And Alice was no longer under arrest. That made things a lot better, but he'd certainly had quite enough of being in a car. The novelty had well and truly worn off.

They finally passed the sign that read Toot Hansell, barely visible through the rain, and Miriam let out an audible sigh of relief. From there it was only a matter of minutes until she pulled the car up outside her own gate. The lights were on inside, glowing warm and brave against the storm, and the three ran to the front door, splashing through puddles. Mortimer lifted his face to the rain, delighted to be out of the confines of the car, although he'd had to sneak the tomatoes out with him. At some point he appeared to have trodden in them, and he emptied the bag onto the road as they ran. Hopefully the rain would wash away the evidence, although he wasn't quite sure what he was going to do with the very wet and squidgy canvas bag.

Miriam was fiddling with her keys, trying to find the right one in the faint light filtering from the small glass panes of the door, when it swung open in front of them.

"There you are," Alice said, and waved them in. "I was getting worried."

"It's the storm," Miriam said, shaking her hair out and splattering Alice with second-hand raindrops. "It's just awful out there!"

Mortimer considered the pace of some of the other cars on the road, and thought that the storm might be taking a wee bit more blame than was strictly fair, but decided it was more diplomatic not to mention it. Alice was handing out towels, and he took one gratefully.

"Make sure you wipe your feet," she told them, then said to Miriam, "Go take a shower and put some warm clothes on. I've made a little bit of soup to keep us going."

"Alice, you're wonderful," Miriam said gratefully, and Mortimer wholeheartedly agreed. Beaufort was towelling his ears and didn't seem to hear anything.

She waved them away. "Don't be silly. Just come into the kitchen once you're all dry. Mortimer, *feet*," she added, as he started to trot eagerly after her, and he sat down to clean the mud from between his toes. Beaufort sat next to him. He was still holding the pineapple.

"I don't think we've been very much help, lad."

Mortimer made a noncommittal noise. Some things weren't really meant to be agreed with.

"Here we are, after all that, and still no murderer. What do we do now?"

"Maybe we leave it to the police?" Mortimer suggested. "I mean, they don't seem to be looking at the W.I. anymore, so maybe it'll be okay?"

Beaufort *humph'd*. "I'd rather we sorted it out ourselves, so we *knew* it was all okay."

Mortimer nodded. "Maybe sometimes human stuff is just human stuff, though. Maybe we have to leave it. I mean, we wouldn't want Alice and Miriam helping out with cavern disputes, say. Or hunting rotas."

Beaufort used the pineapple to scratch his chin. "But they *couldn't* help with those. Whereas we can with this. Or I thought we could."

Mortimer bundled his towel up with the tomato bag. "We tried. We really did. No one could say we didn't."

"I guess so." Beaufort sighed, and looked at the pineapple. "Do you think Alice would like a pineapple?"

"I don't see why not." Mortimer led the way into the kitchen, warm and safe and full of soft light and the scent of spices.

ঌ৶

THE SOUP WAS rich and heavy and smoky and sweet, and Alice had made an enormous pot that even the dragons couldn't quite finish, not with all the thick slices of soda bread smeared with butter as well. Full, they sprawled on the floor in front of the AGA with their oversized mugs of tea, and Mortimer thought that he'd quite happily curl himself into a ball right here and sleep until the sun came out again. The rain was loud against the windows, and the wind was snarling in the chimney, but in here was a cocoon of safety against the night. He tuned sleepily back into the conversation.

"Honestly, Beaufort," Miriam was saying, as she carved the pineapple into chunks. "What were you thinking, leaving a rabbit for the inspector? She thought it was some sort of threat."

"Threat?" Beaufort said indignantly. "It was an offering!"

"An *offering?*" Mortimer demanded. "You left the detective inspector, who doesn't know about us, an *offering?*"

"She seems very stressed. A nice rabbit always makes me feel less stressed."

"A nice, dead rabbit," Alice said, chuckling. "Oh, Miriam, I wish I'd seen her face!"

"You don't. She was *very* upset."

"And flowers," Beaufort added. "I left flowers. I *know* humans like flowers."

"Flowers ... are very dependent on context," Miriam said. "And the context of a dead rabbit is not one we're familiar with."

"Flowers," Mortimer repeated, covering his snout with one paw. "Well, that's not suspicious *at all.*"

"Considering the dead rabbit," Alice said, "The flowers are rather minor."

"I thought they were rather nice," Beaufort mumbled, but he'd gone an embarrassed shade of lilac. "I picked them very carefully."

Mortimer plucked at his tail. "Look at this. *Look* at how I'm shedding. And this is why. Dead rabbits and flowers and detective inspectors."

"Oh, it's done now," Miriam said. "Have some pineapple."

"*Stolen* pineapple," Mortimer pointed out, but he was reaching for a piece anyway when glass crashed in the living room, and the sound of the wind screaming was suddenly inside as well as out.

Miriam gave a little scream of her own and dropped the plate of pineapple. Beaufort was already running for the hall, scales flashing back to his usual fierce green and his lips drawn back from his teeth. Mortimer plunged after him, belly hot with fire, tasting smoke on his tongue.

"Don't singe anyone!" Alice shouted, her stocking feet slapping on the slate tiles as she ran after them.

The curtains in the living room billowed in the wind howling through the shattered glass of the window. It wasn't a big hole, but the rain was tunnelling through, and when Miriam flicked the light on they saw the sofa was already splattered with water spots. Mortimer's ears twitched at a sound from outside, and he spun back into the hall, Beaufort on his tail. They collided at the door, struggling to get it open and push their way through at the same time, and crashed out into the garden shoulder to shoulder. Mortimer snapped his wings out, growling at the night.

"No, lad! It's too windy!" Beaufort shouted, but it was too late – Mortimer yelped as the wind lifted him into the air and dumped him on his back in a rose bush. He struggled free, cursing, and tucked his wings in as he scrambled over the fence and ran down the lane, looking for lights, a noise, a scent, *anything.*

"Beaufort!" he called into the teeth of the wind, and a moment later the big dragon came loping down the lane from the other direction. "Did you see them?"

Beaufort shook his head, steam rising about him as the rain hit his furiously hot scales. "He was too quick. I heard the car, but I couldn't see anything. Not even lights."

Mortimer gave a strangled growl of frustration. He'd never tackled anything bigger than a rabbit in his life, not even a sheep, but right now he felt that if he found whoever had done this he'd tear the top off their car and pluck them out like a bonbon.

"Beaufort! Mortimer!" Alice and Miriam were out in the lane too, and the heat burning in Mortimer's chest was suddenly swamped with cold. Humans were so terribly *fragile.* What if the car was still out there, just waiting for them to venture out?

"They're gone!" he shouted. "Go back inside. We'll keep looking."

"Rubbish." Alice staggered forward against the wind. "*Everyone* inside. We're doing no good out here in this."

Mortimer gave Beaufort a pleading look.

"Come on, lad. Back inside. Let's see what we can figure out."

Mortimer followed him in, grumbling.

&

IN THE LIVING ROOM, Alice and Miriam managed to cover the hole in the window with bin bags and gaffer tape, the plastic chattering in the wind. There was glass on the floor and the sofa, and water stains spreading on both.

"What now?" Miriam asked. She looked pale, but there were bright, angry spots on her cheeks as she collected the biggest bits of glass.

"There's no scent out there," Beaufort said. "There's too much rain. I didn't even catch a whiff."

"I saw the taillights when we first came into the living room," Alice said. "They had too much of a head start for us to be able to do anything."

"What did they throw?" Mortimer asked. He was starting to feel a little better, and slightly ashamed of his sudden desire to peel cars open.

"Come on," Alice said. "Leave that, Miriam. Let's see what our mysterious vandal has sent us."

They surrounded the missile cautiously, as if it might suddenly uncurl and bite them. It was wrapped in a black bin bag that matched the one they'd used to repair the window quite nicely.

"I suppose we should leave it for the police to look at," Miriam said, not sounding very keen.

"We could," Alice agreed. "Or we could cut it open very carefully and see what's inside."

"And what do we say to the inspector?" Miriam asked.

"That the glass tore it on its way in," Alice said.

They looked at the bin bag-wrapped object for a little longer, and Mortimer shifted side to side anxiously. He'd never wanted to interfere in police business, but they'd already interfered quite a lot. It seemed silly to stop now, when they might actually be able to find out something useful.

"I'll get some gloves, so we don't get our fingerprints on it," Miriam announced. "And scissors."

Beaufort picked the object up in one scaly paw. "Dragons don't have fingerprints," he said, and slit the bag neatly with a claw. The other three leaned forward, and Mortimer couldn't hear anyone breathing. Scents drifted to him, a mix of dark metal and rust, and a whiff of ugly emotion, fear and fury topped with a nasty worm of yellow jealousy.

"*Ew*," he said.

"Indeed," Beaufort agreed. "Whoever sent this was not a very happy person at all."

"Do you recognise the smell?" Miriam asked. "Is it Stuart Browning? It is, isn't it?"

"No," Mortimer said, who'd had a taste of the man as well as a smell, much to his shame. "He was more ... level. Dangerous, but not in an uncontrolled way. Measured. This," he took a wary sniff, "this is all emotion. No thought at all. Very unpredictable."

"I agree," Beaufort said.

Miriam puffed her cheeks out. "So what now? We're still no closer to knowing who it is."

"Let's see what's in there," Alice said. "Do you mind, Beaufort?"

Beaufort made a distasteful little expression, but he peeled the bag away and exposed an old weight, like the ones Miriam had next to her scales in the kitchen. Hers were lovely brass, though, a mellow gold in the sun, and she still used them with the old-fashioned scales to weigh out ingredients. This one was big, maybe two pounds in weight, with more flaking rust than painted metal. There was a note fastened to it with a rubber band. Beaufort tugged the band off and laid the note on the floor so they could all read it.

I told u!!!

Back of or els!!

Dont call the polce or youll pay!!!!!

"Is that the same as the note on your door, Alice?" Miriam asked, her voice shaky.

"I rather think so," Alice said. "Horrible font, basic white paper, and an over affection for exclamation marks and bad grammar."

"Which still doesn't tell us *who*," Mortimer said, and plucked at his tail.

"Do stop doing that, Mortimer," Alice said. "You can't be shedding scales all about the place." She sounded odd, and he gave her a confused look, but put his tail down. It was looking rather patchy.

"Wasn't there someone else who liked exclamation marks?" Beaufort asked. "And bad grammar?"

They looked at him, the room suddenly still.

"The emails," Miriam said. "The baker person, the one that was complaining about the fete."

"And about you," Mortimer said. "About the W.I. winning everything."

"Oh, well done, Beaufort," Alice said. "You're quite right. The textspeak was just the same, too."

"But we don't know who sent it," Beaufort said. "We even said no one could be so upset over a village fete. They'd have to be quite unbalanced."

"Well, I think that's rather a given," Mortimer said.

"Baker," Miriam said. "That's a baking weight."

"Or a butcher," Alice pointed out. "Or a shopkeeper of any sort, really. Very traditional. And very un-cared-for, by the look of things. Besides, Priya was looking into bakers. She hasn't found anything yet."

Miriam waved impatiently, like she was trying to find the right word for something. "*Baker.* The weight. The email. The fete, the weight, the email. Hang on. *Fate.* It was spelt wrong. And the knife. *The knife.*"

"Miriam, would you like to sit down?" Beaufort suggested. "Rather stressful, all this."

She gave him another impatient wave and pressed one hand to her forehead. *"Knife.* Fancy knife. *Chef's* knife. And fete spelled fate."

"What's she doing?" Mortimer whispered to Alice.

"Some sort of free association, by the look of things," Alice whispered back, which cleared up precisely nothing as far as Mortimer was concerned.

He was just opening his mouth to suggest that a nice cup of tea might make them all feel better, when Miriam yelped, *"Got it!"* and ran out of the room.

They stared at each other, then Alice said, "Well. We should probably go after her."

22

ALICE

A lice led the dragons into the warmth of the kitchen. Miriam was at the table, leafing wildly through the local newspaper, the one that she'd been doing the crossword in this morning. Was that only this morning? Alice rested her hands on the table, feeling immeasurably weary.

"Miriam, dear," she said. "Would you like to share with us?"

"It's here. It's here, it's here, it's – *here*." She stabbed at the page triumphantly with one finger.

Alice twisted the paper toward her. "Local bunnies all loved up?" she read. "Well, let alone the fact that it's hardly news—"

"No! Under that! The ad!"

"Harrows, the oral experience of Kingston Womoor," Alice read this time. "Be wowed, be awed, have your understanding of food radically re-examined."

"But why on earth would anyone want to do that?" Beaufort asked. "Food is quite wonderful. Why would we want to re-examine it?"

"That's Harold's place," Alice said. "A few of us tried it when he first opened up, to show support for a new business. But it was awful. He does all these weird things such as serving food in the dark, and has no cutlery, or no plates, or you have to eat on the floor with your hands behind your back or something equally ridiculous."

"That's him," Miriam said. "That's him exactly. Harold Minnow."

Alice sniffed. "Well, if I'd known it was an oral experience rather than just lunch, I'd never have gone. Plus he was very rude when Gert asked if we could at least have a candle to find our plates with." She examined the ad again. "But why do you think it's him, Miriam?"

"*Fete*. He spelled it *F-A-T-E* in his email, just like BestBakerBoy."

"But he was quite friendly in that email," Beaufort said. "Why would he hurt the vicar?"

"And he sent those silly caviar-custard tarts to the meeting, not cupcakes," Alice said.

"What if that was a distraction?" Miriam asked. "An excuse to be here while he dropped the cupcakes at the vicarage? *Anyone* would assume we made them."

"It still doesn't explain why he'd want to hurt the vicar," Beaufort said.

"He was very upset," Alice said thoughtfully. "He came to the fete two years ago, when he'd just moved here, and I rather imagine he thought he'd show us little country folk up. He entered all these fancy things in the baking competition – beetroot ice sculptures, and some sort of abstract lemon tart, and a green tea scone with something strange."

"That's not strange enough?" Mortimer asked.

"I agree, lad. That's doing unnatural things to a scone, that is," Beaufort said, his eyebrow ridges drawn down.

"Dandelion cream," Alice said. "Green tea scones with dandelion cream."

"That was it!" Miriam was hopping from foot to foot. "And he was so angry when he didn't place. He called us all some very unpleasant names, and the vicar as well."

Alice *did* remember. He was an unctuous little man, full of superiority, dispensing wisdom and condescending compliments to the other entrants in the competition. Saying things like how *nice* their cakes were, how *quaint* and *traditional*, as if that were a bad thing. The Women's Institute was built on nice, traditional recipes. They weren't about reinventing the wheel. They were about doing what they did *well*. Perfectly, in fact.

"He rather missed the point of the whole fete, didn't he?"

"He did. And then his beetroot ice sculptures melted before they could even be judged, and the lemon tart was so abstract no one knew what it was meant to be."

"And didn't one of Gert's grandchildren have a piece, and it made her terribly tipsy?"

"Yes! And no one would touch the green tea scones."

"Except for Rose, who thought they were washing-up sponges."

Both women laughed, and the dragons looked at each other in bewilderment.

"Um, I see how he'd be upset," Mortimer said cautiously, "But upset enough to kill the vicar?"

Alice nodded. "It does seem extreme. But the vicar was one of the judges, and after Harold was so rude at the fete the vicar also wrote a rather pointed rebuke in the parish newsletter. He didn't use any names, of course, but everyone knew who he was referring to. I don't think anyone in the area has been to his restaurant since, and he was banned from last year's fete. I think the frustration may have got the better of him."

"And then there's the knife," Miriam said, and Alice frowned at her. "Don't you remember him flashing around with his knives at the fete? He was doing a knife skills demonstration and being all fancy about it. There was nothing any of us could use. And he kept talking about how expensive all his knives were."

"I don't remember the knives so much, but now you mention it, I do remember that he cut himself about two minutes in," Alice said. "How clever of you, Miriam!"

Miriam flushed. "Well, this kind of reminded me," she said, and pointed at the ad again. Alice peered closer, at the photo of a scowling man holding crossed knives under the restaurant – sorry, the *oral experience* – name. Then she picked her phone up from the table and pulled up the photo she'd taken before she'd called Ben to see the knife in the door. She tilted it so the dragons could see, and waited. It didn't take long.

"Let's go pay Mr Minnow a visit," Beaufort said, and Mortimer gave a most uncharacteristic and frankly alarming growl.

GETTING TWO DAMP, muddy dragons into the back seat of her car was not something Alice had foreseen having to do, but they didn't have time for Miriam's driving, even if Miriam had been up to it. She found an old picnic blanket with waterproof backing in the boot and spread it out on the seat. "In you get," she told the dragons. "Try not to stick your claws into anything. This car is still quite new."

The dragons climbed in obediently, and Alice looked at Miriam, standing awkwardly next to the car. "What are you doing?"

"I'm quite damp myself," Miriam shouted over the wind, as it collected handfuls of rain and flung it in their faces.

"Well, you're not getting any drier, are you?" Alice asked, struggling to get her door open.

"I guess." Miriam scrambled gratefully into the car, which was already steamed up with dragon breath, and Alice followed, tucking her legs in just before the door blew shut with a slam.

"Well, then," she said, and fired the engine up. The headlights were cut short by the rain, but they did light someone's bin blowing sideways across the road, and the bushes along the lane tossing wildly, like seaweed tumbled in the tide. "Let's go catch a murderer." And she accelerated into the night, both hands on the wheel and the windscreen wipers going full tilt.

There was something terribly exciting about it, Alice thought. The tremble of the car in the wind, the heart-in-mouth moment when it shimmied on the wet road, the sudden glimpse of debris rolling past ahead or to the side of them, the crunch of fallen twigs under the tyres. No one was talking, and she kept her eyes on the road, ghosting around the corners and playing through the gears. She knew these lanes, knew every twist and turn of them, but they were rendered strange and unfamiliar by the storm and the dark.

"Do you think we could go a little slower?" Miriam squeaked the second time the car aquaplaned around a corner.

"We could," Alice said, not slowing down. Mortimer had braced himself behind Alice's seat, face hidden in the corner. Only Beaufort seemed to be enjoying it as much as Alice, peering out between the two front seats with an enormous grin on his face.

"I don't suppose we could open the windows ...?" he suggested.

"No, Beaufort. It'd ruin the upholstery," Alice said, swerving around a branch on the road and making Miriam yelp in fright.

"Alright then," he said. "This is terribly exciting, isn't it?"

Mortimer muttered something to the seat, and Miriam closed her eyes.

HARROWS, the oral experience, was in an old pub, a two-storey, blank-faced thing squatting behind a gravel parking lot next to the road. There was a self-conscious looking fishpond and gazebo-type thing surrounded with potted topiary stuck in the middle of the parking lot, and no other buildings nearby. Kingston Womoor itself was another two miles down the road. The pub was probably a nice enough spot on a summer's day, but right now it looked like it could play the part of a haunted house quite well. Alice pulled into the parking lot and switched the engine off, leaving the lights shining on the front of the building. It was entirely unlit, not even a glimmer visible inside.

"Power cut?" Alice suggested.

"Mortimer and I can see perfectly fine in the dark," Beaufort said. "We'll go in and roust him."

Mortimer made an unenthusiastic noise. He looked faintly ill.

"We should have called the detective inspector before we left," Miriam said anxiously, poking at her phone. "I've got no reception at all."

Alice checked her own phone, but it was no different. "Ah, well. That's why we have dragons," she said, and Beaufort nodded firmly. "Let's go in."

"And do *what?*" Miriam asked. "Tell him to turn himself in, or the invisible dragons will get him? That's not a *plan*, Alice!"

"Well, it's not the *best* plan," she admitted. "But I do believe it'll work."

"Of course it will," Beaufort said. "Although Mortimer and I could also just go in, and you two ladies could stay here."

Alice glared at him. "We two ladies *could*, but we have no intention of doing so. Besides, what if he can't see you or hear you at all?"

"We can make him see us," Beaufort said, and grinned.

"Stop that. You'll do nothing of the sort unless there's no other choice," Alice said. "I almost got arrested a second time today because I told the detective inspector that a scale was a guitar pick. You're not taking any unnecessary risks."

"A scale?" Beaufort asked, and Mortimer went pink with alarm.

"Never mind for now. Just try and keep a low profile, alright?

Miriam and I will go, and tell him we know everything and that he has to turn himself in. You two can be backup."

"I really wish we could just wait for the police," Miriam said plaintively, and Mortimer nodded vigorously, one paw over his mouth.

Alice sighed. Unwilling conspirators were worse than no conspirators. "Do pull yourselves together, you two."

Miriam started to say something, and hiccoughed. She clapped both hands over her mouth and gave Alice an apologetic look.

"You see?" Beaufort said. "You can't take Miriam in. How can any criminal take her seriously when she's hiccoughing?"

Miriam *hicc*'d again.

Alice shook her head and sighed. "Wonderful. Fine. Beaufort and I will go in. You two watch to make sure he doesn't get away." And she got out of the car before anyone else could start arguing with her, then reached behind the seat and pulled out a cane. It was black wood, smooth and beautifully carved, and the handle was the silver head of a dragon.

"Oh, that's very stylish," Beaufort said, following her out of the car.

She smiled at him. "It's also very useful." She swung it a couple of times, enjoying the feel of it in her hands, then headed across the parking lot with her shadow stretched ahead of her in the headlights and the big dragon at her side, following his own enormous winged image. They didn't look back.

No one answered at the front door, which was dark-painted wood and had a gold plaque mounted on it, inscribed with Harold Minnow's name. The bell didn't seem to work without power, and even when Alice pounded on the door with the head of her walking stick, there was no movement inside.

"This whole place smells awful," Beaufort said.

"Really?" Alice sniffed. "I can't smell anything."

"Not that sort of smell. Despair. Anger. Jealousy. So much of it, it's seeping into the stone." Beaufort nodded at the ivy, fluttering desperately on the walls in the onslaught of wind and rain. "It's killing everything."

Alice peered upward, sheltering her eyes against the storm, and thought he was right. Even in the uncertain light, the ivy looked withered and brown, and the wind was having far too easy a job of tearing it away from the walls. "How awful," she said.

"For everyone," Beaufort agreed, and led the way around the building to the back door.

The screen door to the kitchen had come unlatched and was banging violently against the frame, a shrill and angry staccato of sound. Alice was fairly sure that if no one was coming to check on that, no one was coming to answer her knock, either. She tried the door, but it was locked. She looked at Beaufort.

"I suppose we have to drive to town and call the inspector," she said, somewhat reluctantly. Beaufort looked equally crestfallen, but nodded.

"I suppose it's better," he said. "He really does smell like a most unpleasant man."

Alice sighed, and shouldered her cane to walk back to the car. As they emerged around the side of the building, headlights appeared on the road, coming from the direction of Kingston Womoor. Whoever was driving had the beams on high, and he was going much too fast, faster even than Alice had been. Alice and Beaufort paused where they were, watching, and the dragon let out a low, wary growl.

The newcomer pulled into the pub car park almost without slowing, narrowly missing the stone wall that surrounded it and sending gravel spitting out from under the wheels as the SUV rocked alarmingly. The headlights flooded the front of the building in bright white light, and the car headed straight for them. Alice looked at Beaufort in alarm. There was no point trying to hide - the driver could hardly have missed them.

The SUV growled to a halt, sliding in the gravel, and Alice raised her arm to block the light. The engine stalled, and a man scrambled out of the driver's side.

"Hey!" he shouted, his words not quite slurred, but soft at the edges. "Hey, what're you doing here? You're *trespassing!*"

Alice took a step toward the car. "Harold Minnow?"

"*You!*" He wasn't much more than a rotund silhouette, but she thought she recognised the voice, even without the self-satisfied edge it had had the last time she'd heard it. "You – you *cow!* What are you doing here?"

"Did you think I'd be in jail, Mr Minnow?" Alice asked politely.

"I – you – what?" He was trying to sound blustery, but Beaufort had growled when he'd called her a cow, and even against the light she could see the man looking around, as if he'd heard the sound over the roaring of the storm.

"That was the plan, wasn't it? Pin it all on me, with your nasty little cupcakes?"

"You crazy old trout! What the hell are you talking about?"

Beaufort growled, more pointedly this time, and Harold spun in a wobbly circle, looking for the source of the sound.

"What is that? What? Have you got dogs out here?"

"No dogs." Alice adjusted her grip on the walking stick as he took a step toward her. "Why kill the vicar, Harold? He was a nice man. He was just doing his job."

"You have no idea what you're talking about. You're insane! Everyone knows it!"

"Really?" Alice pretended to give this some thought. "And you. What are you? Some little man with a gimmicky restaurant, who killed the vicar because …?"

"My restaurant's amazing!" he shouted, closing the distance

between them until he was only a pace or so in front of her. His face was puffy and red, heavy shadows under his eyes. Alice could smell alcohol and cigarette smoke even through the rain. "You just couldn't understand haute cuisine if it bit you on—" Beaufort's growl rose over the wind, and Harold broke off, gazing around wildly. "What is that? I can hear something!"

"Your guilty conscience, perhaps? We know you killed the vicar, Harold. Why did you do it?"

"I didn't kill the vicar! Stop *saying* that!" He glared at her with bloodshot eyes.

"I think you did," she said, shifting her weight. "I think you held him responsible, because he didn't award your pathetic, pretentious little desserts all the prizes at the fete, and because he was honest about what a rude and horrible man you are. I don't think you're used to being told the truth."

"Pretentious! As if! My food is a thousand times better than any of that crap you dish up at the fetes," he snarled. "You think you're so fancy, Chairwoman of the Toot Hansell Women's Institute, like that means *anything* in the real world! You're nothing but some washed-up, dried-out, bitter old crone – ow!" Because he'd reached out to grab her, and Alice had stepped neatly back and snapped the cane around in a warning little tap, straight to his shoulder. "You *cow*, that *hurt!*"

"It was meant to." She had the cane back up now, waiting. "We have the emails. The weight you threw through the window, which I believe will belong to a set in your dining room, or up in your guest rooms. We have your knife, which will match your set."

"So what are you going to do?" he asked, rubbing his shoulder. "Tell this fairy story to the police? Here you are, on my property. I'll charge you with trespassing, tell them it's not the first time. Say you stole all the stuff from me. Who do you think they'll believe? A successful businessman, or some demented old woman?"

Alice felt the rumble of Beaufort's growls next to her leg. "I think you'll confess," she said.

"Oh, really? And how do you intend to pull off that neat trick?"

"No trick," Alice said, and found herself smiling. He really was a horrible little man. If anyone ever deserved this, he did.

"Crazy old witch," he hissed, and grabbed for her cane. She brought it around in another of those quick little raps, catching him on the knuckles this time and making him cry out in pain. He shoved his fingers in his mouth like an overgrown schoolboy and glowered at her. "Where's the dog? I can hear a dog."

"No dog," Alice assured him, and this time he took her by surprise, lunging at her while she was still speaking. She jumped back, but he had hold of the cane, twisting it as he tried to wrestle it away from her, and she kicked him in the shins. He yelped but didn't let go. He jerked the cane and she staggered, slipping in the gravel.

"Stop it, Mr Minnow!" Her voice was sharp, but her arm was hurting and her heart was going too fast for comfort.

"Out here on your own, are you? So you're stupid as well as crazy." He'd stopped trying to pull the cane away from her now, and was using his weight to push her back, trying to force her to the ground. Her knees were buckling.

"Mr Minnow, you don't want to do this."

"I think lots of people have wanted to do this to you," he said with a very unpleasant grin, and as she saw his shoulders bunch, ready to shove her down, she dropped the cane and spun away sideways in a crouch, twisting out of his path as he staggered to one knee. He snarled and raised the cane to swing it at her. And stopped.

The growling reverberated off the walls and shivered the rain, low and furious and full of the promise of terrible things.

Harold Minnow squeaked and dropped the cane, and Alice picked it up and smiled, toothy as a dragon.

23

DI ADAMS

D I Adams would not have minded if she never had to drive
the bloody ridiculous stretch of road from Skipton to Toot
Hansell ever again. She hadn't even been able to recruit anyone
else to do the driving, or at least to keep her company. The storm
had been getting steadily worse, and the station was full of police
pulled in from off duty, gulping coffee and vending machine
snacks, and pouring out again into the night to check on
pensioners and monitor water levels and probably rescue more
bloody cats, for all she knew.

"I'm sorry, DI Adams," the commanding officer said, not
sounding very sorry at all. "The murdered vicar can wait till the
town is secure against flooding and storm damage. He's not going
anywhere, after all. You'd be very welcome to help us out, of
course. Then we might be able to spare someone to help you
sooner rather than later."

"I have two women out there who seem to have taken it as a
personal mission to muck up this investigation," DI Adams replied.
"And one of them may be a target for the murderer. Isn't there

anyone nearby you can at least send to check on them? What about PC Shaw? He *lives* there."

"It's all hands on deck tonight, and we need them all down here, not up that way," the officer said, sipping the bloody horrible frothy coffee with every evidence of enjoyment. "Besides, no one's going to be up to much tonight. I'm sure they'll be fine."

She groaned. "You don't know them. Are the roads still okay?"

"No telling. In this, you could have a tree down any moment, flooding, all sorts."

"Fantastic."

"Welcome to the Dales, Detective Inspector." He smiled at her. "And I hope it's not the Women's Institute you're dealing with on top of all that. Bloody nightmare, they are."

DI Adams dropped her head in her hands, and the commanding officer patted her shoulder as he left. "Never mind, Inspector. You'll get it all tidied up tomorrow, and then you can forget all about them."

That was about as likely as forgetting an infected tooth, DI Adams reflected as she coasted the car around a corner. At least the tech had been quick and efficient, even if she'd turned up in a purple unicorn onesie and had said a sum total of five words to the inspector, three of which had been "I'll text you," before she took the tablet and scuffed away. The writing style of the emails and the note matched exactly, and she had no doubt that the address the tech tracked down would give her the murderer. The promised text had dinged in already, with not just the IP address, but the closest likely location for the computer using it, which was some restaurant or gastropub in the middle of nowhere.

The only thing she was worried about now was that she hadn't been able to reach either Alice or Miriam on their home phones or their mobiles, which seemed like a very bad sign indeed. She wasn't all that worried that the murderer had come back, but she did have a horrible feeling that the women might just have come to the same conclusion as she had. And while no one in their right minds would be out voluntarily on a night like this, she had some strong reservations about the minds of those two.

The sign for Toot Hansell flashed past, and she slid into the village, skimming down the rain-flooded streets and barely pausing at the stop signs. No one in their right minds, she reminded herself.

ALICE'S HOUSE was dark and silent, and no one answered the DI's knock. She could just hear the phone ringing inside when she tried the landline. It didn't mean that Alice was out hunting down a murderer, of course. She might have stayed at Miriam's. It would make sense. Alice's own home had been breached by a suspect, and it might be that she'd like some company. Although, admittedly, DI Adams couldn't quite imagine it. She scrambled back into the car without shedding her jacket and took the corners too fast on the way to Miriam's.

Miriam's was lit, unlocked, and empty. When the inspector pushed the front door open, shouting for Miriam, there was mud smeared across the hall floor, more mess than you'd think the two women could create. Which looked like a good enough reason to let herself in. She called out again, and wiped her own feet, trying to keep to the edge of the hall and not smear any footprints that might be intact. And also not to look at them too closely, because they seemed ... odd. And she didn't have time for that right now. She peered into the living room, and caught the light silvering the broken glass on the carpet.

"Bollocks," she told the house, spying the taped-up window. "Oh, bollocks, bollocks, *bollocks*." There was a balled-up bin bag on the floor, holding a weight which looked like it would match the hole in the window rather neatly. There was a note next to it, and *that* matched the note from Alice's door, and the emails.

"Well, crap," DI Adams said to the empty house, and ran back to the car, ignoring the rain. Alice had been right. It appeared that village fetes and bake sales were very risky affairs indeed.

She drove dangerously fast, trusting to other people's good sense that she'd be the only one on the road. Stone walls flashed past, unlit cottages illuminated by flashes of lightning that rendered the world in stark blues and greys, and her mind kept drifting back to Miriam's hall, and the muddy floor. The oddness of the footprints. So *many* footprints, two sets of wellies and – and what? Dogs? Too big. Too *clawed*. But they'd been there. She was sure of it. She could see them in her mind, clear and unsmudged. In the dark and the rain and the savage sheets of lightning, they seemed to fit, somehow. London hadn't fit. Or maybe it had, but she just hadn't wanted it to. She wasn't sure, and it didn't matter anyway. That was then, and this was now, and some things just have to be left behind.

She accelerated through a straight, and the GPS chirped at her. One more left turn, and she'd be there. She set aside London, and footprints, and concentrated on finding the place through the storm.

DI ADAMS HAD ARRIVED on many different crime scenes. Some of them were tragic, and she tried not to revisit those too much. Some of them were accidental, such as the woman pulled over for a broken taillight, who had had two men wrapped in bin bags shoved in the boot. They'd proved to *both* be her husbands, and were also both still alive, which had made for an interesting trial. Then there were the out-and-out funny ones, although admittedly not so many of those since she moved into the investigative branch.

But there were still some.

The woman who used Tinder to select men whom she hand-cuffed to their beds and covered in chocolate syrup and popcorn before clearing out their homes. She always chose the ones who were … well, not very nice people. It had been almost a shame to arrest her. The little old lady dealing Viagra out of her sock drawer, contributing to some rather alarming cardiac incidents in all the rest homes in a fifty-mile radius. Plus the literal cat burglar, who had been trained to have an eye for shiny, dangly jewellery.

But none of these were quite as *unusual* as what she encountered when she pulled into the pub parking lot, and her high beams hit the little group in the middle of it.

At first, she couldn't make sense of what she was seeing. There was a man with his back to her, as if her arrival was utterly unimportant, his arms raised as if to fend off an attack, and Alice was standing watching him. Her feet were planted wide and her hands were folded over the head of a black cane which rested on the ground in front of her, the rain pouring off her sky-blue jacket, and she looked like Death's favourite aunt filling in while he took the day off. Miriam stood next to her, arms folded, regarding the man in a manner that said she was very, very disappointed, wearing a bright yellow rain poncho of the sort that comes in a bag, and which you can buy at the pound shop.

And all that was alright, in a confusing what-the-hell sort of way, except for the other two shapes, coming and going on the edge of her vision and making it hard to look at the strange tableau directly. They were low, and stocky, and she saw them more in the way the rain outlined them than she did by actually *seeing* them, and she thought they had wings. The *things* in London, the things under the bridge that took the kids, they hadn't had wings. They'd had teeth and claws and breath that stank, but they hadn't had wings. Which made this something else again.

"Ah, crap," DI Adams said again, and stepped out into the rain.

*

"*POLICE!*" she shouted into the snarl of the wind. Could she hear something else snarling? Maybe. It didn't matter. She had a job to do. "Harold Minnow, I'm arresting you—"

He bolted.

"Every time," the inspector muttered, and started to run after him. The wind roared – or something did – and Harold Minnow screamed, slipped on the loose surface, recovered himself, and broke into a stumbling sprint. "*Stop!*" she bellowed, and he did. Not from choice, though. It looked very much as though someone had tackled his legs, sweeping them out from under him and catapulting him face first into the gravel with a wail of horror.

DI Adams jogged to his prone form and leaned over him, frowning. He was whimpering, both hands over his head and his face firmly planted in the rough surface of the parking lot.

"Is he okay?" someone asked, from somewhere around the region of her waist. "He was going quite quickly."

She ignored the voice, and instead looked at Alice and Miriam as they came to join her. Miriam looked suitably worried, but Alice looked as if she was enjoying herself a little too much.

"Harold Minnow, I take it?" the inspector said to them.

"He's just how I remember him," Miriam announced.

Alice poked him with the toe of her welly. "Are you quite alright there, Mr Minnow? You seem to have had a funny turn."

He yelped, looked up, then gave a squall of terror and pushed his face back into the gravel.

Miriam looked at Alice. "I hope that's not because of us."

"What else would it be because of?" the inspector asked, still not looking at the shapes the rain was making.

Alice and Miriam glanced at each other, then Alice said, "I think he's quite drunk. He was talking about monsters before."

"I see." DI Adams tried to pull the man to his feet, but he scrabbled wildly at the ground, squeezing his eyes closed and squeaking incoherently about crazy women and wild animals and dogs dressed as alligators. She looked at the two women, watching with interest. "What did you do to him?"

"As has been noticed," Alice said gravely, "I do seem to intimidate people."

DI Adams made a noise that was halfway between a laugh and scoff, and said, "Mr Minnow, if you don't cooperate and get up right now, I'll have to make you. And no one wants that." She prodded his shoulder.

"Get off! Don't touch me, you—" There was growl from somewhere around where the waist-high voice had been, cutting him off before she could tell him that he probably didn't want to finish that thought. He whimpered into the gravel.

"Get up, Mr Minnow." She ignored the growl, even though she could feel it in her chest like the bass at a concert. One thing at a time.

He turned his face a little and opened one eye timidly. "Are you arresting me?"

"Yes."

"Are – are you going to take me away?"

"Yes."

"Will I be safe?"

"Just get up, Mr Minnow."

He squeezed his eyes closed again, rolled over and offered her his wrists. She stared from him, to the ladies of the Women's Institute, to the odd shapes in the rain, then cuffed him. The growling stopped.

"You need to go home," she said to Alice and Miriam, pulling the sorry-looking man to his feet. He opened his eyes warily.

"We'll do that right away," Alice said agreeably, and shook her cane at Harold. He shied away with a little wail. "Make sure you tell the truth, Mr Minnow."

"I will," he blubbered. "I will, I will, I swear I will! Just get me away from these, these—"

"Mr Minnow!" Miriam said, sounding horrified.

"—ladies," he finished, subdued.

"Go home. Behave," DI Adams said. "I'm not asking any questions, and I'm going to pretend I never saw you out here. I recommend you do the same."

Miriam nodded, and scuttled toward the car. Alice was a bit slower to follow, still eyeing Harold.

"He may talk some nonsense, Inspector," she said. "He really was rather tipsy when he arrived."

"Go *home*, Alice."

"I am." But she shook the cane at the whimpering man one more time before she left.

DI Adams shook her head and bundled him into her car, cuffing him to the seat and strapping him in. "We've got a bit of a ride ahead of us. You going to behave?"

"Yes," he whispered, watching Alice's car pull out of the parking lot. DI Adams caught a hint of something in the Prius' back seat, seen and not seen, and sighed. She closed the door on Harold and climbed into the driver's seat, rolling her shoulders as she started the engine and wondering just how sleep-deprived you had to be before you started seeing things. She met the man's eyes in the rear-view mirror. They were teary, and there was blood on his face where he'd slid on the gravel.

"Officer?" he said, his voice shaky.

Well, it was better than whatever he'd wanted to call her before.

"Yes?" Half-expecting he was going to ask to use the toilet before they left.

"Are the cells dragon-proof?"

DI Adams turned in her seat so she could look at him properly, taking in his shaking hands and trembling lower lip. Yes, he was still on the tipsy side. But mostly he was terrified.

"Huh," she said.

⁂

IT WAS ALMOST a week later when she drove back into Toot Hansell. She wasn't even sure she wanted to *be* back, but here she was. The sun was out, painting the gardens in riotous splashes of colour that bloomed bright against the stone walls of the houses and the rolling green of the surrounding trees and land. She looked at the village properly for the first time as she drove through, not as a crime scene, just as a pretty little place wound about with rivers and bridges, dominated by the church and the graveyard and the fells that rose beyond them.

Her route took her past Alice's house first, and the surgically neat gardens that butted up against the woodland. She went up the little path to knock on the door, but there was no answer. Birds were squabbling on the lawn, and butterflies danced in the shade of the trees. She glared at them suspiciously as she got back in the car.

She drove to Miriam's, and sat for a moment before she got out, thinking about the dead rabbit on its bed of leaves and flowers, and wondering about the actual meaning behind it. But there was only one way to get answers, so she walked through the little gate and circled the house, noting that that window was fixed, and that the grass was even longer than it had been last time.

She heard voices before she got to the back garden, but they fell silent as she approached.

"Hello?" she called, not wanting anyone to think she was trying to sneak up on them. "Miriam?"

"Is that the inspector?" Alice called, and now she could see them sat at the sun-bleached outside table, teacups in front of them, as well as some rather generously loaded plates of cakes.

"DI Adams!" Miriam said, getting up and knocking the table with her leg, hard enough to slosh tea everywhere. "Is everything alright?"

"Perfectly," the inspector said. "I just wanted to update you, really, since we had you under suspicion for so long."

"Of course! That's – that's – thank you?"

"Can I pour you some tea, Inspector?" Alice asked.

"That would be lovely."

"I'll just get you a cup, then." She got up, rather more gracefully than Miriam, and went inside to get it.

"Oh, do sit down!" Miriam exclaimed, waving the inspector toward a chair, and began fussing with the cakes. "Would you like some?"

"Please." DI Adams leaned forward. "What have you got?"

"Oh, well, Victoria sponge, obviously."

"Obviously."

"And scones. And mince pies."

"Mince pies? In spring?"

Miriam laughed nervously. "It's sort of a treat. For a friend."

"Oh, are you expecting company?"

"No. Well, I mean, yes, but – oh, here's Alice with your cup!"

DI Adams narrowly avoided the fallout of tea as Miriam jumped up again, and noted the two empty plates and the half-drunk soup mugs of tea on the ground. There was more, too, in the shadows where her eyes didn't want to go, but she left it for now. "Pixies?" she asked.

"Of course," Alice said, pouring her tea. "What sort of cake can I get you, Inspector?"

"Some Victoria sponge, please."

"Excellent choice," Alice said, and cut her a generous slice. "So, I trust everything has gone well with the case?"

DI Adams forked up a mouthful of cake before she answered. It was soft and moist and tasted of the summer that was lurking just around the corner. She gave a sigh of appreciation and took a sip of tea. "It was all a bit of mistake, really. Mr Minnow was not the successful businessman he wanted everyone to believe. He was miles in debt, his restaurant was getting only middling reviews, so none of the real foodies were bothering to come such a long way, and of course all the locals were boycotting him after the fete fiasco."

"I told you fetes are a cutthroat business," Alice said.

DI Adams smiled. "Evidently. Anyway, he was furious about it all, and felt he'd been very unfairly treated." She took another sip of tea, thinking that it wasn't a bad substitute for coffee, and decided it was best not to mention the exact language Harold had used to describe how the fete had gone, or the Women's Institute themselves. "It seems that he only meant for the vicar to get sick, and for everyone to think the W.I. had given him food poisoning, so that no one would want to come to the fete. He thought one leaf in a whole batch of icing wouldn't do any serious damage. Stupid scheme, really, as even if it had worked the way he wanted, it wouldn't have got him anywhere, but there we go. It was just a petty revenge thing. He didn't think the vicar would die. Quite sad, really."

"Tragic," Alice said, and Miriam murmured her agreement.

"Just lucky he confessed so willingly, else we'd still be looking at you ladies."

"Very lucky," the women agreed.

DI Adams took another bite of cake, savouring the sweetness against the richness of the cream and the tartness of the jam. "Lovely," she said. "My compliments to the baker."

"Thank you," Alice said, inclining her head slightly.

Miriam topped the inspector's cup up, and for a moment all was quiet. DI Adams could hear the beck burbling beyond the back gate, and the music of a bird she couldn't identify lost somewhere in the ramshackle depths of the garden, and somewhere in the distance a lawn mower.

"So," she said, and looked directly at that blurry spot in her vision, the one just beyond the plates and mugs on the floor. It was hard to make it resolve into anything, and in the end she let her gaze slide away just slightly, so she caught them on the corner of her vision, two ... well, two *dragons*, because what else could they be, with their spined backs and taloned paws and wings folded neatly along their sides, smoke drifting softly from their nostrils? Two dragons the colour of the grass around them, basking like cats in the late afternoon sun. "Tell me about dragons."

As she said it they came into perfect focus, as if her eyes had only been waiting for her brain to catch up. They stared at her with startled eyes, one set old cracked gold, the other warm young amber. The smaller dragon squeaked and dropped his mince pie into his tea, and the bigger one smiled, exposing ragged yellow teeth.

"Oh dear," Miriam said, then they looked at each other in silence, the women and the dragons, while all around them was the rumble of bees, and the warm scent of early summer sun on green earth, and the sense that there are many, many kinds of magic in the world, and that friendship may just be the best of them.

🐉

A BEAUFORT SCALES MYSTERY

THANK YOU

Thank you so much for taking the time to read *Baking Bad,* lovely person! I hope so much that you've enjoyed this first foray into the world of tea-drinking, crime-solving dragons.

And because more people need to know how important it is to be properly prepared for dragons (i.e. with copious amounts of cake, not weaponry), I'd appreciate it immensely if you could take the time to pop a quick review up on the website of your choice.

Reviews encourage others to step into the world of Toot Hansell, meaning the word of dragons spreads! Plus they make me terribly happy and provide writer fuel, so leading to more dragons.

And if you'd like to send me a copy of your review, chat about dragons and baked goods, or anything else, drop me a message at kim@kmwatt.com. I'd love to hear from you!

Until next time,

Read on!

PS - head over the page to find your next read plus a *free* recipe collection!

A FESTIVE TALE OF ABDUCTIONS, EXPLOSIONS, & STOLEN TURKEYS

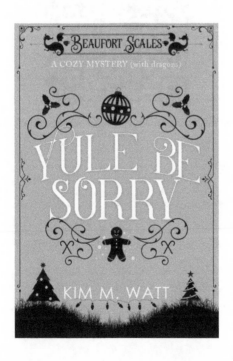

Deep in the Yorkshire Dales, someone's meddling in the affairs of dragons.

Which is already a terrible idea, but it also means that they're meddling in the affairs of the Toot Hansell Women's Institute.

And neither the dragons nor the redoubtable ladies of the W.I. are going to stand for that sort of thing. Providing they can evade kidnapping, police interference, some very volatile baubles, and the cat, of course ...

Grab Yule Be Sorry to catch up with the next instalment in the Beaufort Scales series today!

Scan above or go to books2read.com/YuleBeSorry to grab your copy

DRAGON-FRIENDLY RECIPES INCLUDED

Your free recipe collection awaits!

Lovely person, I hope you've survived the travails of a Toot

Hansell investigation without too many side effects, and now understand the full importance of being properly armed with cake and tea before commencing (investigations or reading, that is).

Now you can grab some dragon and W.I. approved recipes to ensure you're prepared for any other investigations that come your way!

Plus, if this is your first visit to Toot Hansell and my newsletter, I'm also going to send you some story collections - including one about how that whole barbecue thing started ...

Your free recipe collection is waiting - grab it now!

Happy baking!

Scan above or pop https://readerlinks.com/l/2369419/bbpbr in your browser to claim your recipes!

ABOUT THE AUTHOR

Hello lovely person. I'm Kim, and in addition to the Beaufort Scales stories I write other funny, magical books that offer a little escape from the serious stuff in the world and hopefully leave you a wee bit happier than you were when you started. Because happiness, like friendship, matters.

I write about baking-obsessed reapers setting up baby ghoul petting cafes, and ladies of a certain age joining the Apocalypse on their Vespas. I write about friendship, and loyalty, and lifting each other up, and the importance of tea and cake.

But mostly I write about how wonderful people (of all species) can really be.

If you'd like to find out the latest on new books in *The Beaufort Scales* series, as well as discover other books and series, giveaways, extra reading, and more, jump on over to www.kmwatt.com and check everything out there.

Read on!

a amazon.com/Kim-M-Watt/e/B07JMHRBMC
BB bookbub.com/authors/kim-m-watt
f facebook.com/KimMWatt
O instagram.com/kimmwatt
y twitter.com/kimmwatt

ACKNOWLEDGMENTS

To my lovely readers, including all you wonderful people who have been there right from the start, reading my short stories, pointing out my weird grammar habits, and giving me the most amazing feedback and (even more importantly) support, thank you. You're amazing.

To Lynda Dietz at Easy Reader Editing, thank you so much for being an amazing supporter, lovely friend, and truly excellent editor. It's scary handing a book baby over, but you made it both painless and fun (and any errors left over are probably mine from tweaking after the fact). Plus, who knew the amount of amusement that could be found in the strange capitalisation habits of corporations?

To all my wonderful writer friends, especially Anna, Alison, Audrey at the ATA, Debbie, Jon, and Jimmie, without whom my stories would be much less coherent and likely still living in a drawer somewhere. You're all amazing, and I'm so lucky to know you.

To Sylvie, Sophie, and my other non-writer friends, who indulged my increasingly eccentric and introverted tendencies, and have been known to feed me cake.

And last, but about a million miles from least, to Mick (the SO) and the Little Furry Muse (Layla). Because everything.

And, of course, to you, new reader who has just taken a gamble on a book about tea-drinking, mystery-solving dragons. You are entirely awesome.

ALSO BY KIM M. WATT

The Beaufort Scales Series (cozy mysteries with dragons)

"The addition of covert dragons to a cozy mystery is perfect...and the dragons are as quirky and entertaining as the rest of the slightly eccentric residents of Toot Hansell."

– Goodreads reviewer

The Gobbelino London, PI series

"This series is a wonderful combination of humor and suspense that won't let you stop until you've finished the book. Fair warning, don't plan on doing anything else until you're done ..."

- Goodreads reviewer

Short Story Collections

Oddly Enough: Tales of the Unordinary, Volume One

"The stories are quirky, charming, hilarious, and some are all of the above without a dud amongst the bunch ..."

- Goodreads reviewer

The Tales of Beaufort Scales

A collection of dragonish tales from the world of Toot Hansell, as a welcome gift for joining the newsletter! Just mind the abominable snow porcupine … (you can head to www.kmwatt.com to find a link to join)

The Cat Did It

Of course the cat did it. Sneaky, snarky, and up to no good - that's the cats in this feline collection which you can grab free via the newsletter (it'll automatically arrive on soft little cat feet in your inbox not long after the *Tales* do). Just remember - if the cat winks, always wink back …

CPSIA information can be obtained
at www.ICGtesting.com
Printed in the USA
BVHW081655110123
656095BV00004B/72